WHEN SHE GETS RILED

miriam
ALLENSON

Publishing History

Print edition published by MS Allenson & Associates
©2023

Cover design by getcovers.com
Formatting by Lisa Verge Higgins
Editing by Gemma Brocato and Paula Gardner
ISBN: 979-8-9887618-1-5

Books by Miriam Allenson

When She Gets Hot

When She Gets Smart

When She Gets Busy

When the Duke Finds His Heart

A Duke for Dessert

For the Love of the Dame

What people are saying about Miriam Allenson's Books

"Do you like to laugh? Then you should grab *WHEN SHE GETS HOT*, a hilarious romp starring the irrepressible Tootsie Goldberg. I rarely laugh out loud when I read, but Tootsie's fun quirkiness tickled my funny bone so hard, I snort-laughed. There's also a really hot cop that I drooled over. All the characters are so vivid that they leap off the page to perform their shenanigans. I highly recommend this fun mystery!"

—*Nancy Herkness, author of the Royal Caleva Series*

"When She Gets Hot is a rip-roaring, laugh-out-loud, escape from reality filled with Allenson's signature voice and wit. Tootsie is every Jewish woman's dream of strength and determination, and Steve—aka Black Windbreaker—is as yummy as my grandmother's brisket. You don't want to miss this book!"

—*Jennifer Wilck, author of A Reckless Heart and Home for the Challah Days.*

"Miriam Allenson's *WHEN SHE GETS HOT* is a delightful mix of stellar characters, fabulous shenanigans, and wonderful storytelling. I couldn't put it down. Get yourself a good beverage, pull up a seat, and get ready to do nothing but be taken for a fantastic ride! I look forward to more adventures with Tootsie!"

-Misty Simon, author of the Tallie Graver Mysteries.

"WHEN SHE GETS HOT is a fun, fast-paced read with delightful characters. Readers will love Tootsie."

-Tina Kashian, author of the best-selling Kebab Kitchen cozy mystery series.

"Who is wise? The one who learns from all people"

Sayings of the Fathers – Pirkei Avot 4:1

"Something will be offensive to someone in every book, so you've got to fight it"

Tootsie Goldberg, quoting Judy Blume

For all librarians who've bravely stood up against book-banning.

CHAPTER ONE

His shocking announcement came after an awesome first thing-in-the-morning reminder that sex could be good for a woman, meaning herself, Tootsie Goldberg, though she'd reached the half-century mark.

Mouth gaping open, she stared at her lover, standing across the room, coffee cup in hand, acting all innocent, as though he hadn't just dropped a bomb.

Tootsie snapped her mouth shut. "Seriously? You want to throw a birthday party for me? For my fifty-first birthday?"

"Yup." He hid a grin behind the rim of his mug.

She pointed to his cup. "What's in there? Some kind of crazy juice?"

He ambled over to sit down next to her at the kitchen table. He placed a kiss on her forehead just at her hairline. "Coffee."

"Then all I can think is you've lost your mind."

Stretching out his long legs, he folded his arms across his chest, and smiled. "Nope."

That smile of his...It almost but didn't quite touch his lips, but his dark eyes sparkled. He was enjoying himself too much.

It used to be that Tootsie hated cops...until she fell in love with this one. Though he was twelve years younger, and still looked and acted like a cop.

"Can't I convince you to forget about it?"

"Nuh-uh."

Though his name was Steve DiLorenzo, Tootsie called her lover man Black Windbreaker. It was because of what he wore...shirt, pants, boots, all black, and yeah, a black windbreaker. He'd been wearing all that the day she'd met him in January at the radio station where she'd worked for years. When the news broke that it had been sold and everyone had been fired, he was there, a cop working a side job in security to keep any unruly ex-employees from raising hell. It turned out that Tootsie herself was the hellraiser.

It didn't take long for her to change her mind about her Black Windbreaker. After the radio station situation was fixed, she didn't hesitate to invite him to live with her. That was definitely a good thing. Except on days like today.

Seriously, the man knew how to push her buttons.

"I don't want a birthday party. Besides, Thanksgiving is just around the corner. We've invited the immediate world, meaning your family, mine, and our friends. Won't that be party enough for you?"

"Nope."

She gave him a death glare.

His eyes didn't stop with the sparkling. "C'mon, Esther Ruth. You'll be the center of attention. You'll like that."

"You're calling me Esther Ruth?" Her Black Windbreaker was the only one she let call her by her birth names, which came from the Old Testament, neither of which she liked. "I'm rescinding permission for you to call me Esther Ruth."

This time the grin did lift his mouth. He took her hand, drew it to his beautiful, expressive lips, and placed a kiss on her palm. "You can't. It's too late."

She stewed. "I need to be protected."

Black Windbreaker was the protective type. He raised both eyebrows. "From your birthday? It's going to come whether you want it or not, and—"

Her hand flew up. "Don't say it." Recognizing that she was a year older was only one of the reasons why she didn't want a party and he couldn't protect her from that.

But he could kiss. Like now when he turned her hand over and began to kiss every freaking single one of her fingers. Did she hate that?

Uh, no. Still…

With a good, strong pull, Tootsie retrieved her hand from danger-of-the-wonderful-kind. "What makes you think I want to be the center of attention at a party featuring a birthday cake with a bonfire of candles on top of it? Why would I want to have my name written on a chocolate cake, the kind that I hope you know is the only kind I want, and I need to remind you that it better say Happy Birthday, Tootsie, not Happy Birthday, Esther Ruth."

Talk about sending mixed signals… Seriously, if it was going to happen, and she hoped it wouldn't, she still needed to know the cake would be right.

He retrieved her hand. "That was a lot there, babe. I'm not sure what it was. You mind telling me again, so I don't make a mistake with the cake?"

Sometimes she had to admit; she spoke in circles. Steve had been asking her for explanations of what she meant from the start, the day he'd come to her house with an arrest warrant because of her hellraising at the radio station.

The blizzard and the tree that had toppled over on top of his arrestmobile…car…parked in her driveway, meant instead of arresting her, he'd had to stay the night.

That was the night when she found out that a fifty-year-old woman could enjoy herself, thank you very much, in a quite specific situation, with a thirty-eight-year-old man.

Yowza.

She stood. "I'll be good with us going out for a nice dinner, just the two of us, and maybe a movie after."

He rose, too. "I understand you *thinking* you don't want a party, babe. As long as you understand that just wishing the day will pass with no one noticing doesn't mean your birthday won't come. It's coming."

She felt all itchy underneath her robe.

It wasn't like Steve wasn't speaking reality. Even in her mind, where her inner child had a wah-wah moment over the whole, *you're about to be a year older and what have you done with your life you should have and didn't*, Tootsie knew she wasn't acting like a rational human being.

Some people would question whether she'd ever acted rationally.

Black Windbreaker grabbed his black windbreaker. "How 'bout we talk about this another time?" he said, as he zipped the coat.

"That sounds like a good idea." Because wasn't that an awesome kick-the-can-down-the-road moment?

Tootsie took their dishes to the sink to rinse them and stow them in the dishwasher. "Now that we've dealt with that issue…" *Uh, no* "…I'm going to do what I need to do to get stuff done before I take my aunt Adele to lunch at that tapas place in Clifton."

Coming up behind her, her lover kissed her right in that special place where her neck met her shoulder.

One part of her wanted to tell him kisses weren't going to work with her right now, because she was ticked off that he'd brought up the birthday party idea. But oh Lord, his kisses made her world go around.

"Look at that," he said against her skin. "It took only a couple of weeks after your aunt buys the house next door, and you two are already best pals."

She snorted a laugh, which was hard, considering her knees were melting, courtesy of his kisses. "When Ben sold his house and went to live in that assisted living facility, who knew I'd get rid of one nonagenarian, and get another, and a relative, too?"

"Be fair, Toots. Adele just turned ninety, so she's a new nonagenarian," he murmured, his hands landing in places that would guarantee he would not be going to work soon.

"That's a distinction without a difference," she said, removing his hands from the point of danger. Maybe Steve could name his own hours...he could since he worked for himself. But she had hellraising business to attend to, a phone call to make, and people to talk to so she could resolve a situation.

Plus, there was that lunch with Adele, her grandmother Sylvia's much younger half-sister. She'd only met this relative a few weeks ago when Adele had rung her doorbell. She'd bought Ben's house, she'd said, and carried on about how nice it was they were going to be neighbors, and didn't Tootsie remember when they'd last met: twenty years ago, at Beverly Greenberg's wedding?

With one more too-distracting kiss…this one held promise for later…Steve was gone. He had a meeting with a prospective client who wanted ex-cop, ex-SWAT team leader Steve—who was also an expert in all things personal and professional security—to take a look at his headquarters building and let him know what changes Steve thought should be made to harden it into a safe and secure location.

After giving the last dish a good scrub, she stuck it in the dishwasher. Steve had made breakfast using one of her copper frying pans, and she hung it back with its mates in the display of copper pots above her kitchen island.

As she started to head toward the stairs to shower and change into something luncheon-like, she paused and thought about the woman she was lunching with. Adele was as different from her older half-sister as she could be. Sylvia had spent her life whining about the wrongs committed against her. Adele had taken life and wrestled it to the ground. She was a firecracker and a force. She'd taught history at Teaneck High for forty years. After she retired, she'd reinvented herself as an author and had written several well-regarded books on how to teach children to love learning about history. She had a new book on the subject coming out in the spring.

The sound of heavy clumping coming down the stairs and toward her heralded Chris's arrival into the room. "Hey," he said, and made a beeline for the fridge. "I won't be home for dinner. I'm having pizza in town with…" he reeled off the names of his friends… "and then we're going to the library to study. Anything you need me to take next door to Aunt Adele?"

"I'm seeing her for lunch, so if there is something, I'll take care of it myself."

Sixteen-year-old Chris Hart was now living with Steve and her, since Ben, who was his grandfather, had sold his house to Adele. Chris's parents…well, they were not in the picture. Now that Ben was in an assisted living facility, to keep the boy from living on the street or in a foster home, Tootsie and Steve had taken him in. It was the right thing to do. Besides which, the boy had very sneakily crept into Tootsie's heart. Then, the moment Adele had moved in, Chris had adopted her as his aunt, too.

"Old people are chill," he'd said soon after the movers had arrived with Adele's things. He'd gone to his grandfather's old house to see if there was anything the new owner needed that he could help with. "Besides, I like to listen to her talk," he'd said one day when Tootsie asked him what he liked about Adele. "She knows things I don't."

Chris walked across their joined lawns, every day, twice a day. Adele was not only happy to entertain Chris for however many minutes his first-thing-in-the-morning visit lasted, but she was tutoring him in Language Arts, a subject he needed a little help in.

Though Adele had taught history, she was a stickler for writing in top grammatical form.

Chris reached into the fridge, took out the sandwich Steve had made for him the night before, and slammed the door behind him so hard, the whole fridge shimmied.

Tootsie said, "I think we're having lamb chops with mint sauce for dinner."

"I love lamb. I'll eat leftovers when I come home," Chris said, and waved goodbye.

Tootsie stepped into the dining room that she and Steve had converted into an office for her hellraising operation and his security business. She needed to prep some notes for Fern Burke, their office manager/friend, before Fern showed up later that morning, and she wanted to update her on the French drains at Glen Allyn's senior living complex.

The flooding in the complex's basements had gone beyond the nuisance stage and was now dire. She'd told Genene Cohen, Glen Allyn's mayor, that she would be on the case, making sure the county officials who were supposed to be supervising the situation didn't drop the project like it was balls on fire.

Genene, who had been assistant mayor, took over the job from Neal Morgan who went to live in a minimum-security prison for white-collar criminals because he'd made the mistake of hanging out with the wrong people.

She had a lot to do, cleaning up the mess Neal left putting Glen Allyn's public projects up for grabs to the bidder with the best mob connections. But Tootsie knew Genene would find time to talk to Tootsie about the problem with the French drains.

Or more accurately, the problem with the people in the swamp on the Potomac. The Department of Housing and Urban Development was sitting on the money...idiots. Didn't they recognize the longer they waited, the more mold the seniors would have to put up with in their basements? Her job today was to get them off their tuchuses and send the money. Finally.

She wasn't sure what the plural of tuchas was. If not tuchuses, could be it be tuchi?

Wait. That was Latin, not Yiddish.

When Genene picked up, Tootsie thought she sounded like she was busy shuffling through paper. "Have you seen this, Toots?"

Since Tootsie didn't have X-ray vision, she had no idea what 'this' was. "No, I haven't."

"It's an article I downloaded from today's Montclair Daily."

Tootsie loved the paper. The new e-broadsheet was covering local news in the wake of the big papers in the state forgetting there was such a thing as local news.

Tootsie opened her laptop and hunted over to the article Genene was talking about. "Who or what is this group, Parents for Righteousness? I never heard of them."

"I don't know who they are. But I do know who the organization's president is, a woman named

Melanie Mangold. She spoke at the Glen Allyn library board meeting last night and they're calling a special meeting next Monday night to discuss what she brought up. It's made quite a stir."

"Who could possibly make a stir at a library board meeting?" Tootsie queried, but as the words fell from her mouth, she paused. "We're not talking about book banning, are we?"

"Not quite. At least I don't think so. This Melanie complained about some books she wants moved to a less prominent place in the adult section of the library."

Tootsie resisted pulling the phone away from her head and going to look for a Q-tip stat because she needed to clear her ear. "Wouldn't that be all but the same thing as book banning? Who is this woman? What does she really want?"

"She says if kids wander into the adult section and find what she calls these disgusting books they'll be scarred for life, and yes, she did say scarred."

For a hot minute, Tootsie's frontal lobe closed for business. When it opened back up, she said, "Children have their own section of the library. Did no one tell this Melanie person about that?"

Tootsie paged down, looking for info on Melanie's organization and not finding it. "The only other thing I've found about Melanie Mangold is this little article that appeared in the Daily, welcoming her and her husband to Glen Allyn. It seems she made a hefty donation to the library foundation, which everyone is grateful for. It mentions she has two children, a boy and a girl, both under the age of ten. Is Melanie Mangold going to be one of those people who just has to be a pot-stirrer?"

"Allegedly she's on a mission to reform Glen Allyn, starting with the library."

Tootsie's eyebrows took a hike up her forehead. "Seriously?"

"Yes, seriously. After that business with Neal, the last thing I want to deal with is more fuss in town. So, I read this piece, and then I reached out to the library. I asked which books we were talking about. I was told there were a bunch, but the ones this Melanie was concentrating on were romances written by some woman named Candy La Plume.

Tootsie opened her mouth. And then closed it. "Well, I'm not fond of romance novels. But they are for adults, aren't they?" Then on a sharp exhale she said, "Someone needs to talk sense into this woman."

Genene said, "I was thinking you could."

"Me?" Tootsie's frontal lobe was getting tired of being challenged. "I'm a hellraiser, not a therapist. Besides what's wrong with the librarians? Do they have a terminal case of laryngitis?"

"Librarians are usually very shy."

"Not that I think that's altogether true, but excuse me," Tootsie said in her driest voice. "They're adults. By now they should have outgrown their shyness."

"Spoken like a woman who wouldn't know shy if it hit her in the face."

"Okay. You're right," Tootsie admitted. "But...still."

"Never mind still." Genene cleared her throat. "You would be doing a good deed for Glen Allyn. It would be like hellraising in reverse."

Which, as Genene said it, made a weird kind of sense, but not so much that Tootsie would agree to help. "Someone needs to tell the librarians they should pull up their big girl pants and make like they're defenders of the word, public, in public libraries everywhere."

Genene sighed. Which of course made Tootsie feel guilty. Which was Genene's intention.

Tootsie wasn't letting herself fall for that. "Oh, wait. I just remembered. Why don't I ask my Aunt Adele to help? She has the street cred, being the author of some serious pedagogical books. What could Melanie say to her that my aunt wouldn't use to make her look like a fool?"

"I like your idea, Tootsie. I bet the librarians will, too."

Relieved she wasn't going to be pressed into action, she said, "I'll ask my Aunt Adele to call you. My aunt is your woman."

"I'd love to meet your aunt if for no other reason that I'm amazed that someone her age has so much energy to write all those amazing books of hers."

Someone her age... First Steve and now Genene were talking about age when age was the last thing Tootsie wanted to talk about today, or any day. Because what had she accomplished in all her years? Of course, considering the success she'd had hellraising these last few months, if she said that out loud, no one would understand what was really upsetting her.

Since the subject had come up twice in one day, what was required was a change of subject. "So now that we've resolved that issue, can we talk about the French drains? This job has got to get done before the next drenching rain floods those basements."

Yeah, floods of oversize proportions made for a more pleasant topic than anything to do with birthdays.

CHAPTER TWO

After Tootsie made a phone call to the HUD people—and hallelujah, things were starting to move in the right direction—she went upstairs to shower.

Dressed, she decided she had time to treat herself to something that might make her feel a little better about her impending birthday. She drove Viv, her beautiful, new gray Volvo to the nail salon that had opened next to the Salt n Peppa deli on Glen Allyn's town square. Viv had replaced her beloved Marge who had gotten totaled after Chesty Kowalczyk's goons shot at her and she'd crashed Marge against a tree. The salon did the usual: manis and pedis, regular and special, and waxed various body parts. She stopped, parked, and stepped inside.

When she came out, an hour later, not only were her eyebrows waxed to perfection, but the woman who had wielded the wax and then the tweezers to snatch away any stray hairs, had colored her eyebrows a lovely, medium brown to match the curls on Tootsie's head.

Those few silver hairs she'd seen nestled in her eyebrows were gone. She planned on keeping them gone...and pretending her fifty-first birthday wasn't around the corner.

By the time Tootsie was back home, she'd begun to think about where she could find someone professional to tattoo on permanent eyeliner. But all thoughts of tattoos went on the backburner when, as she walked into her house, she realized her aunt was inside waiting for her.

Adele and Fern were sitting at her kitchen table, sipping tea and chatting so loudly that Tootsie heard them before she'd opened her front door.

"...the boy is smarter than he thinks he is. What a shame that someone made him feel like he doesn't have a brain in his head."

Tootsie knew Adele was talking about Chris. As she stepped into the kitchen, she said, "And how's the tutoring going for our boy?"

Adele turned from where she was sitting at the kitchen table. "*Mamaleh*, you're back. I was a little afraid you forgot our lunch date, but then I walked over here from my house, and Fern and I got into a good talk so I thought I could put off the worrying."

Adele had communicated in flawless English during her teaching career, but when she was with friends and family, she spoke in that immigrant just off the boat Yiddish accent or speech pattern.

Tootsie bent to give her aunt a kiss on her papery cheek. "I would never forget our lunch date." She tapped her watch face. "Is it 12:30 yet? That was the time we said we'd meet."

Fern snickered. She and Tootsie had worked together at the radio station and known each other for years. These days Fern managed Tootsie's and Steve's business. Thank goodness. Because otherwise the State of New Jersey tax people would come to collect because Tootsie had forgotten to file. The IRS would be right behind.

Fern rose. Today she was wearing a royal blue skirt with downy peacock feathers decorating the swishy, floor-length cloth. "I told Adele by the time we finished our tea, you'd be back."

Adele held up a hand, as if to second that motion. "She did. And now..." She braced both hands on the table and levered herself up. "*Oy,* such a curse, this arthritis. But I shouldn't complain. I can still walk, even if I look like an old lady when I do. I must remind myself that I'm ninety, not seventy."

"Aunt Adele, in your case, ninety is fifty," Tootsie said. And in a way, that was true. Adele was tiny, an inch or two under five feet...if she was wearing her sensible square-heeled shoes. Tootsie had no idea how long ago Adele had started to dye her hair red. But it wasn't just red, it was the red of a hot chili pepper. Somehow, the color went with her sweet, round, wrinkled face, the smile that seemed a permanent feature, and the hazel eyes that were always kind. And warm. And knowing.

"You're paying me such a compliment?" Adele gave Tootsie a tap on the arm. Which wasn't such a tap. It was more a *zetz*. Tootsie was used to the little slugs coming from Adele at this point. She knew they came from love.

"It is a compliment. I don't know anyone who does as many things as you do and does them well," Tootsie said.

Unlike her. Who'd stumbled into doing good things. Who hadn't planned to do good things. Who'd missed years when she should have been doing good things.

Adele said, "Well, I do have another book coming out in the spring."

Tootsie grinned. "See? That's what I mean. How many women of fifty, let alone ninety have written as many books as you have?"

"And award-winners at that," Fern piped up.

"Enough, children, enough." Adele held up a hand. "And now lunch, Tootsie-leh. It will be time for dinner if we don't get going soon."

When they were in the car, Adele chattering away about Chris's progress learning not just grammar, but proper writing style, she changed direction. It seemed there was an award dinner Adele was scheduled to speak at in New York just before Christmas, her new contract with her publisher was coming and... Tootsie's mind started to wander.

Adele was so accomplished. She was an award-winning teacher, and an acclaimed writer. What was Tootsie?

She was a hammer. Black Windbreaker had pointed that out to her. Her hammering had solved three different mysteries this year. But so what? What had she done in the entirety of her life before this year? Not much.

She glanced at her Aunt Adele. What would people say about Tootsie if she was lucky enough to reach her ninetieth birthday? Given all her flaws—and she knew she had many—the jury was way out.

"Tootsie."

Tootsie blinked at the intrusion into her poor-me pity party. "Sorry, Aunt Adele. I was daydreaming."

As Tootsie steered into the tapas restaurant's parking lot, she said, "Listen. There's something disturbing going on in Glen Allyn. I think you'll be interested in helping to make sure it doesn't get out of hand."

"Tell me."

So, Tootsie did.

"Her name is Melanie Mangold?" Adele powered down her window and leaned out. Cold air swirled into the car.

Tootsie grabbed Adele's coat sleeve. "What are you doing? Close the window."

"What, you wanted I should spit on the floor?"

No, she didn't want that. Viv still had the new car smell.

"So, I'm spitting outside. On the pavement. '*Lig-in in drerd un baken bagel.*'"

Tootsie knew Yiddish curses. This one she wasn't familiar with. "What does that mean?"

"This woman, this Melanie, should go to hell. She should bake bagels every day, smell how delicious, and not be permitted to eat one."

Tootsie snort laughed. "I love it."

"This woman thinks it's a good idea to tell people what they can read and what they can't? It's a good thing, when I was teaching, I didn't tell my students what they could read. Why limit intellectual curiosity?"

Good. Adele was disgusted, as Tootsie knew she would be. "So, you'll help with the situation, right? This woman wants the librarians to move certain books from where they're shelved now in the Glen Allyn public library and put them where they won't be so easily found."

Adele made a scoffing sound. "Of course, I'll help. This crazy Melanie woman…she will be sorry she ever met me. Which books does she want to move?"

"Some romance books. They're written by an author named Candy La Plume."

There was a heavy, prolonged silence.

"What's the matter, Aunt Adele? Have you already changed your mind? You don't want to help?"

"I can't."

"Why not?"

"Because I'm Candy La Plume."

CHAPTER THREE

Tootsie's first reaction was to laugh. Not a ha-ha laugh. A 'this is too crazy for the room' laugh. "You want to say that again?"

So, Adele did.

Tootsie pulled the car into a spot and shifted into park while her brain looked for answers to yet one more bomb lobbed her way today. "I definitely want to hear what you have to say about this."

Adele gave her a one shoulder shrug as they walked into the restaurant. "Why not? I'll be happy to tell you."

After the server took their order, Tootsie said, "Start with why you never mentioned that in addition to the researched-based instructional books for teachers you write already, you write something wildly different." She opened her napkin and placed it on her lap. "And why you picked such a suggestive pen name to boot."

Adele raised one of her sculpted, darker red than her hair eyebrows. "When I began to write as Candy, just a few years ago, I decided I wanted a name that matched what I write. In other words, a certain type of romance."

Their *Patatas Bravas* came. Tootsie served her aunt and took some for herself. "Certain type?"

Adele put her fork down and raised her chin. "Candy writes what they call erotica."

Tootsie was already having a problem looking at her ninety-year-old aunt and believing she wrote something other than tips and tricks for how to teach history to high schoolers. Now she had to process that Adele was writing saucy romances that had serious sex in them.

"Okay." *Hmm.* Not the sharpest response but her mind faltered as she tried to think of another one. "Erotica is popular. Always has been. Think D.H. Lawrence. Anaïs Nin. But what made you decide to join those ranks?"

She wouldn't add *at your age.*

"It pays very well."

Their *Gambas al Ajillo* arrived. Their little shrimpy selves looked cute and precious all nestled together in their gold-orange garlic sauce on the little plate they were served on. Unfortunately, she couldn't appreciate the dish as she usually did.

"Not that I'm counting your money, but why do you need another source of income? If you're having a problem, you should have let me know. You do know that Arlo won a huge lottery a few years ago, and when we divorced, he had to give me half. I can help you with any money problem you have."

"*Mamaleh*, you are so sweet." Adele indulged her with a smile. "I don't have a money problem. I was already well-fixed. But what, can you tell me, is wrong with making more?"

She speared a shrimp and popped it in her mouth. Chewing, then swallowing she said, "I have found that people turn their nose up at making money only if they already have a lot themselves."

"Is that what you thought I was saying?" Tootsie's cheeks heated. "I'm not judging you."

"No, no. Not you, Tootsie. But others." She took another shrimp and placed it on her plate. "Basil will judge me if he knows. And not only about the money."

"Basil?"

"Basil Jernigan publishes A. S. Silverstein's books. He only publishes educational works. That means he would never publish Candy La Plume's books. But Basil is also a snob. He would hate to hear that I write such books as Candy writes."

"So, you keep your two lives separate because of Basil?"

Their next dish, *Albondigas*, was placed on the table. Adele gave Tootsie an impish smile. "Who wants to hear from that *schmendrik* Basil that Candy writes smut? Who wants to hear from that *farbissineh hoont*, Melanie?"

Tootsie knew Yiddish—her beloved grandma Hannah, her mother's mother, spoke the language. Tootsie had picked up enough that she still mixed Yiddish into her everyday speech, mostly adjectives and nouns. And curse words. But now that Adele was living next door, and because Adele was a native Yiddish speaker, Tootsie had been learning a whole lot more. She didn't know this one.

"You're calling him a *schmendrik*...a fool. But a *Farbissineh hoont*...that means...?"

"A loose translation: bitch."

"That's a good one, Aunt Adele. I'll have to remember to use it. When appropriate." She grinned, which immediately became a frown. "I understand why you don't want to go face-to-face with Melanie at the meeting, then."

As Tootsie said it, she knew she would have to go herself. Something she wasn't looking forward to. She had the French drains to tackle, and Fern had a whole lot of hellraising ideas for her to consider.

Still, Candy La Plume was her Aunt Adele. Or should she put that the other way around?

Which was what she said to Steve when he came home later that night. "Who would have thought a woman her age would write all that steamy stuff?"

"People who make assumptions."

Psych. She'd been told.

Then she gave him the outline for Monday night, when she was planning to show Melanie up.

He put a hand to his ear and rubbed. "Did I hear you say you're going to a meeting and planning something that might be a little crazy? Not that I'm judging or anything, but your idea may be a little out there."

She slammed her arms across her chest. "What are you saying? You don't think I can pull it off?"

"If anyone can pull it off, it's you."

"Then what's the problem? Because I know you think there is one."

"Babe, I have to compliment you. You've been working really hard the last few months to make a whole bunch of positive changes. You've been thinking before leaping...okay, most of the time. That's an improvement."

She gave him a death glare.

"You haven't jumped down your mother's throat, not once."

"Though she's given me reason to," Tootsie amended. "I need more than a compliment for that. I deserve five gold stars."

Steve ignored the self-praise and continued. "Best of all, no one has threatened to kill you...that I know of." He raised one eyebrow. "No one has, right?"

She sighed. He was making valid points. Was what she had in mind truly a good idea? Or was she about to step over the line? This was a case where she wasn't sure where the line was. She might be about to step over it by inches, which wouldn't get her aunt what she needed. Stepping over it by miles wouldn't either.

"I'll tell you what. I've got a few days to think about it. I promise what I plan on doing will work. All I'm going to do is get people to laugh at Melanie."

Both eyebrows went up. "All? It's that *all* part I'm worried about."

"Well, if you're that worried, you better come to the meeting with me and my aunt. You can keep an eye on me. If I get too crazy you can give me one of your looks and I'll just back myself down. How's that? But just so you know. Wild horses will not keep me from that meeting."

Tootsie had never understood the wild horse analogy. Seriously, what would wild horses have done? Galloped in a circle around her? Like they didn't have anything better to do?

There were no wild horses at the Glen Allyn Elks Lodge. The library board usually met in the community room in the library. Not tonight. Because Glen Allyn had heard there was going to be a meeting. With a capital M. Which meant they needed a bigger space to accommodate everyone who wanted to be where the action was.

Steve had left the house with Adele seated in the front seat of his black Ford F-150. Tootsie didn't just climb into the back seat out of respect for Adele's age. It had to do with how Tootsie had kitted herself out.

He slowed as he came to the lodge. The parking lot was full. Naturally. Meeting with a capital M. There was a lot of salivating over what was about to go down in Glen Allyn tonight.

"I'll find a place to park down a side street. You ladies wait for me in front."

Turning in his seat, he gave Tootsie a pointed look. "I mean it. Wait for me. We'll walk in together."

Of course, he said that. In his mind, she'd need his protection considering what she was wearing.

"But I have my coat on over the dress. No one can see it yet," she complained as she shut the door. He shook his head and drove off.

Tootsie smoothed her coat down and the dress underneath. Which crackled. She stopped. Fern had said keep the touching to a minimum.

"Hey Tootsie," someone said and side-eyed what was visible underneath her puffy coat's hem.

She smiled. She repeated the smile as others she knew walked past her. There were more greetings. And a lot of looks.

She shuffled from one foot to the other. To Adele she said, "Steve's probably having trouble finding a space. You go in. Save us seats."

Adele toddled away.

As she was getting ready to walk in by herself, Steve strode up and took her by the arm. "Let's go," he murmured. "Promise me you'll stay away from any open flames."

The Elks Lodge had been around since the animals had marched off the ark. The low-ceilinged room was paneled in pine that had darkened with age. The ceiling tiles had stains of an indeterminate origin, and the floor sloped. There was a bar. Behind it, was an array of new and shiny bottles of every kind of liquor known to the drinking public. The Elks obviously put their money where it was most needed.

The smell of beer in the air had Tootsie saying, "I think I'm already drunk."

Steve grunted and led her to the side of the room where Adele was sitting in a row halfway back in the room. Two eight-foot tables at the front were set side by side to accommodate the library board members. Who were shuffling in with the crowd and making their way to their assigned places behind the tables.

Tootsie sat, gingerly, and rustled. She hadn't taken her coat off yet, but she still drew the curious stares of everyone around her.

Aunt Adele leaned in. "*Mamaleh*, I think the next time you need to go to a wedding or a bar mitzvah you should wear this dress. Just be careful how you sit."

"Because it will disintegrate," Steve said, arms folded, leaning against the wall and studying said dress with more skepticism than he had when she'd told him she was going to wear it and why. "I'm going to call Chief Stafford and see if he can send someone to stand at the back of the room. You know. In case."

"As if something bad could happen." Which Tootsie had to admit could, considering her reputation.

More heads turned in her direction. To her Aunt Adele, sitting with hands folded in her lap, she said, "You think the dress is too much?"

"It is too much. But if you think this will stop the *hoont*, then it's not too much."

As most everyone who had decided attending the library board meeting on a Monday night talked amongst themselves, Charlie Fortenberry, chair of the library board gaveled the meeting to order. He looked around the room, an oily smile on his face. "Welcome everyone, welcome. How nice to see so many people interested enough in the Glen Allyn Library that you've come out to learn about the important work we do."

He motioned to his side where three women sat, dressed in black suits with white blouses. "Ladies, if you would please stand..." Which they did. He turned to the audience. "And please give these members of the board the recognition they deserve for their volunteerism."

Everyone dutifully clapped. The ladies sat again. Charlie took off talking about something called millage. But Tootsie had stopped listening because someone sat down in the seat Steve should have been sitting in...if he hadn't gone to make his phone call to Chief Stafford.

Tootsie didn't have to turn her head to figure out who it was. The woman's scent, Calvin Klein's Eternity, worn as if the wearer had bathed in it, gave her away.

"Hello, Helene," Tootsie murmured to Helene Benson.

Helene was not exactly a friend. Nor was she just an acquaintance. She fell in the middle ground between.

"I would say nice to see you, Tootsie," Helene whispered. "Except I don't know what I'm seeing. What is that dress beneath your coat?"

Tootsie wiggled on her seat. She wasn't careful enough this time and Toni Morrison fell to the floor. "Drat," she muttered underneath her breath.

"I actually made this dress, with the help of a friend." She toed the piece that had fallen and thought about bending to pick it up, but Mark Twain had begun to hang in a dangerous way from her right seam. Bending was out of the question.

Yes, Fern had helped. In fact, because she was an artiste when it came to her own strange and awesome attire, Fern was the one who had sewed and stapled all the pieces of Tootsie's dress together on the full slip...the one Tootsie had all but forgotten she had.

"I don't know," Fern had said as she worked all afternoon on the design of books that had been banned at one time or another. With Tootsie in it. "This is out there even for you."

31

Which was what Tootsie surmised Helene was thinking. With a dubious look in her eyes, Helene asked, "Are you making a statement?"

Helene, who was a crayon box with some of the crayons missing, got it, which for Tootsie was a yay. If Helene guessed, then others with crayon boxes that were full of colors, would get the picture.

She was saved from having to explain, because it looked like Helene wanted an explanation when Adele gave her an elbow. A new arrival appeared. And Tootsie did mean arrive. Because the newcomer paused in the doorway. All heads swiveled in her direction.

Ta da, the *hoont!*

Oh boy. Tootsie knew right then she'd have to fine tune the image she'd had of Melanie Mangold. Tootsie had thought she would be tall, as in WNBA tall, and that when she entered a room, she'd take up a whole lot of square footage with her presence. How wrong Tootsie had been. Melanie was a woman of short stature.

As the *hoont* who was not a lover of Candy La Plume's books sailed ever so slowly toward the front of the room, as if she was oblivious to the fact that every eye in the room was on her, Tootsie decided that like herself, Melanie was cuddling up to the underside of five-foot-two-inches.

Tootsie rustled as she leaned toward Aunt Adele. "I bet Melanie wears the max size at Chico's."

Chico's was one of Tootsie's favorite stores.

"Tootsie! That's terrible! Next Yom Kippur you should keep praying for forgiveness even after the final prayers are over."

Tootsie pressed her lips together. Okay, so what she'd said was mean and she felt a stab of shame that she'd said it. Yes, Melanie weighed more than Tootsie, and yes, Tootsie had said what she'd said under her breath to her aunt alone. It was still mean. And a sin. Yom Kippur couldn't come soon enough.

Melanie kept walking right to a seat that must have been saved for her in the front row. She glided into said seat, eyes trained on Charlie as he continued his lecture on millage.

Helene tapped Tootsie on the shoulder. Tootsie cringed. The shoulder seam was the one she and Fern had had the most trouble with. It was where they'd sewn J.K. Rowling.

"Oh, sorry," Helene whispered. "I just wanted to ask you if you knew what millage was."

Tootsie didn't. Nor did she want to get into a debate on what it might be. But then Charlie's lecture came to an end so no need.

Melanie raised her hand and Charlie recognized her.

"Good evening, Mrs. Mangold," he said in a voice Tootsie could only describe as smarmy. "We're so glad you decided to join us for the meeting tonight."

Then turning to the crowd, he added, "Mrs. Mangold has agreed to take Lucius Pisco's place on the Board. Because of a family concern, Lucius need-ed to hand in his resignation earlier this week. We're relieved she was willing to step up since there are so many important issues that will be coming before us in the next few weeks and months. We welcome Mrs. Mangold."

Again, with the desultory clapping. Nobody cared about the niceties. The message in the under-tone in the room was *get on with it, already. We're here for the show.*

Nodding to the crowd, Charlie added, "I'd also like to thank Mrs. Mangold for the very generous do-nation she has made to the Glen Allyn Library, mean-ing we don't need to worry about millage all that much this year or next. Now, as a little favor to her, I'd like to give her the microphone as she has some prepared words she'd like to share with us this even-ing."

Bodies shuffled and necks craned for a better view as Melanie stood and made her way around one side of the long tables to a spot next to Charlie. And the microphone.

Melanie turned to Charlie and smiled. "Thank you, Mr. Fortenberry." She looked back at the crowd with wide-eyed gaze, snub nose, and pretty bow-shaped mouth. Tootsie didn't trust the innocent look in the woman's light-colored eyes. Nor did she like that her hair was cut in bangs that marched straight across her forehead as if someone had put a bowl on her head and snipped away from one side to the other.

But none of that was all that startling. It was the voice, the Betty Boop, Jessica Rabbit voice. Tootsie bit her lips to keep from snort-laughing.

As Tootsie stifled herself, the *hoont* continued. "It's such a great pleasure for me to have been made a member of this illustrious board after only being a resident of Glen Allyn for such a short time. The honor is just"—she placed a hand over her heart—"so overwhelming."

On Tootsie's left, Helene said, "Wow, she sure is gracious."

On her right, Aunt Adele snorted, *"Gay kokn afn yam."*

And wasn't that one of her favorite curses, Tootsie thought. Go do it in the ocean.

In her teeny-tiny Boop-ish voice, Melanie said, "Over the last few years I have made it my mission to understand how best to serve the needs of our children. They are our future, aren't they?"

She looked around the room. For affirmation that she was right? For the green light that she could go on saying whatever was about to come out of her mouth? "As a mother myself"—and once more, she placed a hand over her heart— "I have become diligent, and I might even say unrelenting, in my pursuit of protecting our young ones from harm."

She turned to Charlie and gave him a sweet-as-honey look…with powdered sugar sprinkled on top... and said, "I want to thank you from the bottom of my heart, Mr. Chairman, for allowing me to join the library board so I can continue the righteous battle to keep books that should never be placed on library shelves, away from where children can find them."

There was more than one gasp in the room.

Hello! The *hoont's* mission was out there. In full view.

"Excuse me, Mrs. Mangold." A voice on the other side of the room spoke. "To which section of the library are you referring? The children's section?"

The *hoont* raised her eyebrows and widened her eyes. Gazing at the person who had spoken up, she made her voice even sweeter than before. It was so sweet it wouldn't have been a surprise if in that one instant every person in the room became diabetic.

"Oh no, sir," Miss Sweetness and Light crooned. "I don't refer only to the children's section of the library, although once I'm on the board formally, I intend to review every book that is shelved there. To answer your question, unfortunately, there are books in the adult section of the library that...oh my goodness..."

She gave a fake shudder. "I'm not saying they should be outright removed. I would never suggest that. That would be book banning and I don't believe in that."

Tootsie threw up in her mouth.

"But I do not think these books should have a place of prominence on the library's shelves."

A murmur traveled through the room. Tootsie couldn't tell what the tenor of that murmur was. But it didn't matter. She was readying herself to do her thing. And make Melanie look like the fool who should have probably kept her mouth shut before she broadcast her mission statement for the Glen Allyn world.

The person who had spoken, a man, came to his feet. "Let me make sure I understand. Are you suggesting that there are books in the adult section of the library that should be removed from sight?"

Melanie looked all around. She fluttered her eyelids. "Why yes, sir. That's what I'm saying. Just think about it. Your child, in all innocence, comes along and thinks the spines of the books in the adult section are so pretty. And you know how children are drawn to pretty things. So, he or she, out of curiosity, decides to pick one out to look at it. What do you suppose happens when he or she picks up that awful book by…"

The *hoont* fashioned her face into thinking mode. "Let's say, for example by that foreign man, Kafka. His book was about a bug."

"Not really, but I don't want to confuse you just yet by saying so," Tootsie muttered and looked down at her right knee where she and Fern decided to sew in the copy they'd made of the book page on Amazon for *Metamorphosis* by yeah, that 'foreign man' Franz Kafka.

Melanie went on, though whispers were filling the room. "Don't you think that would be an awful experience for that child? I want to guard against that happening. Surely, you can see why."

"Actually, I can't," the man said, raising his voice. "Since you're standing up there at the microphone and Charlie has given you a position on the board, I'd like to know more about your agenda. But before that, I'd like you to tell us what your qualifications are for becoming a member of our library board?"

And that was Tootsie's cue. She shot up and yelled, "Melanie! Where have you been?"

Every eye in the room swerved around to fasten on her. Including Melanie's. Better said, both her eyes. Which now didn't seem so 'I am so innocent and honest'. Instead, they narrowed with suspicion. "Are you talking to me?"

"Who else would I be talking to?" Tootsie lifted one leg at a time over Helene's to get to the aisle. She rustled toward the front, past rows of wide-eyed Glen Allyn-ites.

Despite Fern's best work, she was dropping parts of her dress beneath her puffy coat, even as she prayed it would hold together. She said excuse me and sorry a couple of times, until she stood smack in front of Melanie, whose hand seemed to be no longer able to hold up the mic.

Smile on her face, Tootsie said, "I was hoping I could undress in front of you and then you could tell me and all these people behind me"—she kept her eyes firm on Melanie but held an arm out behind her to encompass the crowd— "which parts of my dress should be stuck somewhere in the back of the library."

She laid a hand on her forehead, as Melanie's eyes grew wider. "Oh, no. I didn't mean my dress. I meant the design on my dress. Or maybe not the design but the representations...of books. Pictures in other words."

As Melanie's eyes became saucers—they were light blue, Tootsie confirmed for herself—Tootsie ripped off her coat and dropped it on the floor. Along with a couple of pieces of her so-called dress that Fern had sewn to the lace on the bodice of the slip. "What about this one, here? It's *The Handmaid's Tale*. You've heard of it, haven't you?" Tootsie slapped it down on the table right in front of Melanie.

Through gritted teeth, Melanie leaned her head in Charlie's direction. "Who is this woman?"

Charlie was well-acquainted with Tootsie. It was nothing for them to exchange pleasantries when they both found themselves grabbing a sandwich at the Salt 'n' Peppa deli.

Now, he looked at her like they were strangers. "I suppose you two ladies have never met."

"Oh, Charlie." Tootsie smiled and batted her eyes at him "You're so cute."

Nope. Never. Not even close.

In a plaintive voice, Tootsie went on. "I've got more to share with you, Melanie." And she ripped off *Lolita* and *Grapes of Wrath*. "Seriously, I get why some of these books are disturbing to you. That's because they're disturbing."

She tore off *The Kite Runner*. "Terrible things happen in these books. You kind of want to look away, right?"

Her voice was rising. She snatched off the part of her dress with *The Color Purple* on it. "But these books show another world, show us adults that we're not on our own little islands where everything goes just the way we want it to go. That there are places and times when it goes so far from how those people wanted things to go that they must learn how to cope and live with themselves, maybe overcome tragedy. But somehow, they do go on. Or not."

In the back of the room, someone started to clap.

Melanie's face was brick red. Charlie was sputtering. The three ladies sitting at the table looked like they wanted to bolt.

Tootsie wasn't through.

With both hands she ripped and ripped at the papers that had been sewn so carefully onto the slip. Taking handfuls of the papers she threw them on the table in front of Melanie. "You're entitled not to want to read *Catch 22* or *Beloved*, or *Huckleberry Finn*, which are classics. You're entitled to not read any book you don't want to read, whether it's a classic or not." She ripped a piece of paper that she and Fern had sewn onto the center of the slip's bodice. "Like this one."

Holding it up in one hand, she swerved around to face the crowd. "It's called *Dangerous Love* and written by the author Candy La Plume. It's got sex in it, lots of sex."

As she'd turned, Tootsie had seen that whatever sweetness had masked Melanie's face was gone. Her blue eyes weren't so warm and her mouth not so sweetly bow-shaped. Her round face now had become more sharply angled. But those damn bangs remained unmoved on her forehead.

The man who had asked those questions of Melanie shouted out, "Mrs. Mangold, why don't you tell us if you've read *Dangerous Love?*"

Tootsie looked behind her at Melanie, who had recovered and somehow found the strength to pick up the mic again. "I have not, but why should I? Like this woman just said..." She gazed with contempt at Tootsie. "It's got sex in it. That's disgusting."

"Maybe to you, not to me," someone in the audience shouted.

At which point, the laughter started. And then continued. And got louder.

Raising her voice, Melanie said, "These books of Candy La Plume's must be removed if we are to protect our children from their terrible content."

And there it was, thought Tootsie. She didn't want books moved. She wanted them *removed*.

"Where are these kids' parents?" someone else in the crowd yelled out. "They need to be with them. In the children's section."

"Yeah, leave the adult section as is. No need to change anything there," said yet one more person, who added, "I don't know about anyone else in this room, but I don't want someone making it hard for me to locate the books in our library I want to read."

Tootsie raised her hand. "I'll second that. If I want to check a book out of the adult section and it's a romance that has a lot of sex in it, or something about a serial killer, then that's what I'm going to do." She turned to look straight at Melanie. "There's nothing wrong with murder...I mean murder in a book. Right?"

Message delivered she told her inner voice which had decided to raise *its* hand to say *maybe this is when you sit down?*

Then, the man who had first spoken said, "Lady, with your opinions about what books shouldn't be found in the adult section of a library, you shouldn't be on the library board."

As the murmur of voices grew, Tootsie decided it was time to listen to her inner voice.

By the time she got back to her seat, she was convinced she'd made Melanie a laughingstock. Which wasn't necessarily the best thing, she had to admit. Sometimes people who are laughed at came out swinging. Which, for a change, she hadn't considered. That was okay with Tootsie. She could take it. As long as Melanie left her aunt alone.

Steve was back from wherever he'd gone to call Chief Stafford, who after all hadn't sent an officer to keep the peace.

He eyed her as she sat down next to him. Helene had left. Adele gave her a broad smile but continued the conversation she was having with a woman next to her. Charlie Fortenberry was trying to bring the proceedings to order. Melanie had slunk back to her seat in the front row.

Steve helped Tootsie get into her coat. "I never thought I'd have to help you get dressed in public, Toots." And wasn't he making a good point? Yeah, she had on leggings beneath her slip, but not anything else besides her bra. It was November and she was shivering and just this short of naked.

"What do you think," she said, smiling up into his serious eyes. "How did it go?"

"I think you just made an enemy."

CHAPTER FOUR

Come the Wednesday night before Thanks-giving, as they were putting the final touch-es together for their feast the next day, Tootsie was still thinking about what Steve had said. "I haven't heard a word from Melanie. I think she's gotten the point."

Steve rifled through the pages of one of his fa-vorite cookbooks, looking for a pecan pie recipe he'd seen, because he decided with seventeen people sit-ting around their dining room table, the two pies he'd already made, weren't going to be enough. "Don't say that. The *malocchio* hears all."

Tootsie was setting the table. "Since when do you believe in the evil eye? Besides which I think evil *eyes* don't do much *hearing*."

"A technicality. And who said I believe in it? I just don't like to call attention to it."

Wasn't that interesting? It seemed the man wasn't an entirely rational human being. Good to know.

"When Fern and I put that dress together…and if I must say so, it was a brilliant idea…I knew Melanie and I weren't going to be BFFs afterwards. That was a price I was willing to pay to keep her from going after my aunt. And another thing…from the response in the room, she must know there are a whole lot of people in this town who she won't be BFFs with, either."

There was no discussion on Thanksgiving Day about Melanie. The food on the table took up most of the conversation. Which was the star of the day? Was it the turkey, which Steve had glazed with maple syrup, or the sweet potato casserole with nuts and marshmallows? No one would have voted in the brussels sprouts mash, though it was excellent. Nobody ever voted a green vegetable the star of any day.

However, everyone was in agreement about the pies, all three of them: the apple pie, the pumpkin chiffon, and the pecan pie Steve had baked at four o'clock that morning.

Adele had seated herself next to Steve's mother, Aurelia, who had charmed everyone at the table, even Francine, Tootsie's mother. Toward the end of the meal, when it seemed everyone was laughing at something, Tootsie happened to glance at Adele and thought something wasn't quite right. Like all her aunt's pistons weren't firing.

It wasn't until after hangers-on had all left…with doggie bags…that Tootsie walked across their joined lawns to check in with her aunt.

When she answered the door, still dressed for the day's festivities, Adele gave Tootsie a tired smile. "I'm all right. It's been a long day."

As it had been a long day for Tootsie, too, she readily accepted Adele's explanation.

When Monday came around, Tootsie checked to see if there'd been an attempt at the library to remove Candy La Plume's books, or any other books on Melanie's blacklist and put them elsewhere.

To Steve, who was in the process of leaving for a job, she said, "I'm thinking Melanie heard how everyone reacted and she's decided to back down. This situation is resolved."

"The *malocchio*, Toots. The *malocchio*." And he left.

"The *malocchio* should take itself elsewhere," she muttered. Then she added, "*Kenahora*" to ward off any other evil eyes.

For the rest of the day, she ignored the presence of any supernatural curse, if in fact any existed. She crossed her fingers. Annoyed at herself, she uncrossed them just as Chris came tramping into the house.

After slamming the front door—why couldn't boys just *close* the door—he made his announcement. "Something's wrong with Aunt Adele."

Tootsie frowned. "What makes you say that?"

Chris walked into the kitchen. Tootsie followed. "I just came from there. She's not her usual schmoozing self."

Answer delivered, he opened the refrigerator door and peered in.

The world could be coming to an end, but boys had to eat. Happily, he was able to locate the foil package with leftover turkey and a loaf of bread Tootsie had stored on the bottom shelf in the fridge.

Tootsie reached into the cabinet, lifted out a plate, and handed it to him. One of her few rules, since Chris had moved in, was whatever he found in the refrigerator, he couldn't stand there in front of the open door and munch down. He had to plate it and eat at the table.

Tootsie mused, "She didn't seem like herself the other day, either. I think I'll go over for a visit."

The foil package spread open on the island in the middle of Tootsie's kitchen, Chris was selecting eight or nine slices of turkey and four slices of bread. He needed the fuel because dinner was three hours away and he might starve between now and then. "That sounds like a good idea," he said, around a mouth filled with turkey as he stepped over to the kitchen table.

Tootsie donned her puffy jacket...the weather had turned unseasonably cold, even for November, and headed across to Adele's house. The house...she still couldn't think of it other than as Ben's since he'd lived there longer than she had in hers...was a mirror of hers. Every one of the Tudors on this street had been built at the same time by the same builder back in the 1930s.

Slowing to glance through the living room window, she frowned. It was dark inside. As if no one was home. But Tootsie knew that wasn't the case since Chris had just come back. She rang the doorbell. No answer. She rang again. And then again. Fear trickled down her spine. Good thing she'd brought the key. As she inserted it into the lock, she prepared herself to find what she didn't want to find.

"Adele?" she called out with trepidation. "Aunt Adele?"

There was the scrape of a chair. The sound came from the kitchen. Tootsie let out the breath she'd been holding.

"I'm here, *mamaleh*." With shuffling steps, Adele came from the kitchen through the dining room to the foyer where Tootsie stood. "I'm fine. Just a little depressed."

Adele was dressed as neatly as if she was headed out to her job as a history teacher at Teaneck High. There wasn't one wrinkle in her white blouse. On her collar, she'd pinned a cameo brooch. Her muted black and brown plaid skirt hit her leg just below the knee. On her feet were a pair of low-heeled black patent-leather shoes.

While some women who'd reached an age that was ten years shy of the one-hundred-year mark were casual, meaning a total *schlump* about their appearance,

Adele made it her business to always dress as if company was coming. It could be four o'clock in the morning, and she would be up, neat as if she'd come out of a bandbox, and ready for whatever.

"Would you like a cup of tea, darling?"

"With all the hydrating I've done today, whether coffee, tea, or water, I'm ready to float. I think I'll pass. Thanks. Shall we sit?" Sharp-eyed, Tootsie could see something that was not depression was going on.

She turned toward the living room and hit the switch for the overhead light, banishing the shadows in the room. Positioning herself on her aunt's maroon upholstered sofa, she patted the cushion. "You know, we haven't had a good talk since we went out to lunch. That was weeks ago. How about you tell me what's going on with you lately?"

Adele shrugged. "Who said there has to be something going on?"

Tootsie rolled her eyes. "Please. Maybe you've only lived next door to me for the last month or so and maybe we didn't see each other for years before that, but you haven't been yourself for days. Even Chris noticed. So how about sharing."

Adele heaved a big sigh and looked around the room. Which had Tootsie doing the same. There were the usual pictures on the wall...bucolic landscapes and the occasional still life of fruits and vegetables in bowls.

Adele stood. "For this I most certainly need fortification. Even if you won't have a cup of tea, I want one. Just in case you change your mind while I'm still in the kitchen, I'm bringing you a cup, too."

As she walked toward the kitchen, her voice floated back with, "You want green tea, right, *mamaleh?*"

Tootsie smiled. At least Adele was okay enough that she was telling Tootsie what she wanted, whether she wanted it or not.

While Tootsie heard her aunt fill the teakettle with water, take cups and tea out, Tootsie stepped into the dining room to look at what her aunt had on the walls there. No bucolic scenes here. Instead, there were decades worth of class pictures. Each one showed groups of kids in rows with Adele sitting in the middle of the bottom row. At the bottom of each picture was a legend that told what year the picture had been taken... *World History 11ᵗʰ Grade, Mrs. Silverstein, THS, Class of 1975, of 1995,* etc.

The plaques and the occasional statuette commemorating her aunt as Teacher of the Year sat on her aunt's mahogany sideboard. On that same piece of furniture were copies of her best-selling books on how to teach history to high school students. One time, after Adele had moved in, Tootsie had gone on YouTube and listened to a TED talk her aunt had given a few years previously on the subject.

"You must train yourself to be a storyteller," she'd said, standing on that big stage, with what looked like hundreds of people in the audience staring raptly up at her small figure.

"Telling the story is your first obligation. You must always paint a picture with words. History doesn't matter if you don't, and your children won't learn. Yes, you must teach the facts, but you aren't teaching history if you only ask students to tell you what year Waterloo took place. You must teach them what led up to Waterloo, how that fateful day happened and why.

"You should be able to breathe life into the adventure of how Napoleon was able to sneak past his British captors on the island of Elba, escape to Paris and regain the support of the French people. And then the battle of Waterloo itself…this deserves the painting of a very large canvas.

"Say the place names: Ligny, Quatre Bras, the village of Waterloo itself. Help them see the lines of cavalry as the French, the Prussians, and the English charged each other, sabers flashing in the air. Paint the picture of the foot soldiers and how they advanced and retreated, and how Wellington and the Prussians almost lost, but in the end were victorious. You must bring history alive. Otherwise, you are feeding your students dry facts, which are soon forgotten."

Adele came back from the kitchen. She carried two mugs and set them down on the table in front of the couch. "Drink. It will be good for you."

Tootsie pressed a smile back behind her lips. "You know, now that you made this for me, I realized how much I really wanted one."

Adele gave her a weak smile and then sighed. Again. She studied her fingers, gnarled with arthritis, one sign of age, though there were a few others that would tell someone meeting Adele for the first time that she was a nonagerian.

"Sometimes I wonder if I know what's good for me."

Ah. An opening.

"I'd love to hear what you think. I can learn plenty from you."

Adele sighed yet again.

Whatever was bothering her must be a heavy burden. The fear that it could be something terrible came roaring back. In the few weeks since Adele had moved in, Tootsie hadn't just grown fond of her aunt. She could say without equivocation that she loved this woman. So now, her heart turned into a boulder as she wondered if she'd lose Adele just as she'd gotten to know her.

Plus, if Adele was ill, Chris would be devastated. He'd made Adele a big part of his life, now that his grandfather was only peripherally in it. Adele represented a steadiness in his life that he needed.

Adele placed her hands on the couch cushions and levered herself up. She walked across the room to a table where an iPad lay. She swiped at the screen and brought up an image. Retracing her steps to the couch, she gave the iPad to Tootsie.

Tootsie gave Adele a long look before glancing at the screen. It was an image of Candy La Plume's author page on Amazon. She looked up. "This is the page for *Dangerous Love*. I don't see anything wrong."

Silence.

Tootsie frowned. "You want to tell me something, don't you?"

"I have followers."

"You mean like the Pied Piper of Hamelin?"

"What nonsense is that?" Irritation raised the color in Adele's papery cheeks. "No, Tootsie. I'm talking followers, Candy La Plume's readers who love every single one of my books. There are at least 20,000 of them. Some of them are in my Facebook group. Some of them get my e-newsletter, some are my reviewers."

And that was when Adele's voice disappeared. Tootsie heard the words on some level somewhere, in a kind of undefined burbling.

Because she'd just heard the news that her ninety-year-old Aunt Adele didn't just write a lot of books. There were 20,000 people out there who identified themselves as her obsessive readers. If Adele knew of 20,000, Tootsie couldn't imagine how many more there could be.

A lot. A whole lot.

"...and continues to— Tootsie, are you listening?"

Tootsie recalibrated herself. "Yes, I'm listening." And thinking about how her Aunt Adele, who had been born while there were still rotary phones, computers were the size of city blocks, when arsenic and sulfa drugs were still being used to treat infections, had a Facebook Group. She was the total package.

More than that, her ninety-year-old Aunt Adele was a freaking star.

"Tootsie-leh, have these people nothing better to do with their lives? Couldn't this one be…"

Once more Adele's voice faded into the background.

Tootsie had been a marketing manager at WCLS. She was small beer compared to Adele. All those years she'd wasted that Adele had not. Those thirty years when she was feeling sorry for herself and could have done something good for someone else, could have made a difference, like she had finally done these last months, when she'd gotten over her ridiculous self and used her abilities to do the right thing for others. Instead of hiding behind fear.

Unlike Adele. Who never had.

And had 20,000 followers.

Adele was rapping a knock-knock on the table. "Tootsie, if you're not feeling well, because *mamaleh* I can see you don't with your sick face, maybe you should go take a nap?"

Tootsie blinked herself out of her pity party. "I'm fine, Aunt Adele. "Tell me about your followers."

Adele's forehead creased as if confused. "But I'm telling you about the troll."

Tootsie laid a hand on one ear. She must be losing her hearing…not that she would admit it because it was one more thing that reminded her of her age and how she'd… "What troll?"

"That's what I've been trying to tell you and you haven't been listening," Adele said, "I have a troll."

Tootsie opened her mouth and closed it. "Are you getting nasty messages from this person on your Facebook page?"

She gave Tootsie a one-shoulder shrug. "Yes, and I delete them. They're silly and childish. But some of my followers are telling me they have begun to see terrible, awful things this troll says about Candy on message boards and Reddit and in some Facebook groups."

Tootsie hadn't known what a message board was before Chris had burst into her life. She knew what a Facebook Group was. She'd ask Chris to tell her what Reddit was later. "When did it start? Do your followers know?"

"I asked that very thing. The ones who answered me aren't sure, but they think it started last week."

She would have smacked her head, but that would have been high drama. "*Malocchio*," Tootsie gritted. "I should have kept my mouth shut."

"What?"

Tootsie shook her head and came to an instant conclusion. "This troll has something to do with Melanie. I'm willing to bet that's so."

Adele took a sip of her tea. "This person is doing me damage. Now, Basil knows."

Tootsie's brain cleared because there it came, the awakening. Just like it had at the radio station when things had gone awry, just like at the townhall when

Neal initiated his thievery, and just like when Sage Rust was hurting Chris. Something bad was going on. Again.

You need to take care of this, Tootsie.

She did. French drains taken care of, she had more hellraising to do. This was personal.

Adele sighed and said, "Yes, Basil. I told you what a snob he is. He will hate that he's associated even if only secondarily with Candy. Even if somehow, he doesn't know now, he will know, soon."

Tootsie waved Basil away. "Let's talk about him later. Let's talk about whether we think there's some connection, if this troll became active around the same time as last week's meeting took place."

Adele made a scoffing sound. "Meeting you call it? More like a spectacle."

That was true. "Not to play devil's advocate here," Tootsie reasoned, because for once she wanted more than her intuition to be on board with this latest development. "Isn't it possible that this troll is someone who just thinks like Melanie? Or maybe Melanie is the troll?"

"I don't know," Adele said, "But I don't know enough about how the internet works."

Compared to what Tootsie knew, Adele was Steve Jobs.

Adele took a sip of her tea.

Tootsie took note of the sigh that went with the sip. Her aunt had a long face, and it wasn't altogether about the troll. "You're afraid of what happens if Basil finds out you also write as Candy."

It was like her aunt's chin decided on its own to raise up in bravado until it fell again. "Yes, *mamaleh*, that's right. Someone will tell him his precious A.S. Silverstein has a pen name and it's not a good one. Then he'll tell everyone he knows because he's a *yenta* and my phone will start to ring and not stop. No one will believe it when I say I'm on deadline for the next Candy book. They'll say how much deadline do you have to worry about when you write one of those books with sex in it? Two minutes it'll take you. Such arrogance...I don't have the strength to explain how wrong they are, and I don't want to."

Tootsie stood. She picked up the empty teacups. "Let's not think the worst. Maybe he won't."

"Maybe Tevye will move back to Anatevka." Adele came to her feet. "I think now it's time for me to tell my children about Candy, so they don't have a conniption fit when someone else tells them first." Lips turned down, she sniffed. "Not that I want to call them. I don't like when they yell at me."

She walked Tootsie to the door. "Maybe I'll call them next week."

Tootsie put her hand on the doorknob, prepared to leave for home. She did an about face. "Would you like me to call them? I don't mind. Besides, I've never spoken to my cousins. They are my cousins, aren't they?"

They were, and no, she wouldn't mind if Tootsie made those phone calls. Adele patted her hand. "You're a wonderful niece. Now I see I made the best choice when I moved next door to you."

Tootsie had once thought to ask Adele why she had but had gotten distracted and never brought the subject up again. "Why don't you tell me now."

"Your cousins, my children, Larry and Jennifer, I think I didn't do such a good job raising them, which, looking back, I'm ashamed of. I was more—what is it you youngsters say now—more invested in the welfare of my students than I was of my own children. So, now my children don't want to have anything to do with me. I thought if I moved by you, I would have someone in my life. So here I am."

Tootsie's sinuses grew thick with tears. Saying not a word, she took Adele's hand and gave it a gentle squeeze.

Adele turned away from Tootsie to stare out the back window. "Larry is in Seattle. Jennifer lives in San Diego. We speak on the phone." She shrugged. "Once a month, maybe twice. But no more. This I think, tells you what they think of their mother."

CHAPTER FIVE

Tootsie left Adele with a kiss on the cheek and a piece of paper in hand with her cousins' contact info on it. She called Jennifer first.

Jennifer, who lived in San Diego, answered on the first ring. After an introduction, Tootsie got down to it and asked the question of the moment. "Do you know that your mother has a pen name and besides the books she writes as A.S. Silverstein, she also writes erotica as Candy La Plume?"

"My mother writes erotica?" Jennifer had a frog of a voice. Smoker, Tootsie presumed. Then after a juicy cough, she added. "I have no idea what little things my mother does with her time."

Little things? Tootsie wondered if her cousin would dismiss her mother's erotica so cavalierly if she knew her mother earned a serious income from those books every year.

A sharp laugh came through Tootsie's phone, the sound of voices in conversation somewhere in Jennifer's house. "Oh," Tootsie said. "Do you have company?"

"Some friends from my complex are here for coffee, so, I'm sorry but I need to go. But no worries, I'll give my mother a call sometime over the next few days, maybe by the end of the week."

Tootsie knew what a bum's rush felt like, and this was one. But she wasn't going to be rushed. Until she was ready to be. "But, Jennifer, maybe you want to give her a call before that?"

"I will." Impatience colored every syllable her cousin uttered.

Tootsie wasn't finished. "Your mom is dealing with an online hater, a troll. Don't you want to let her know how much you care and are concerned that this is happening and how sorry you are that she has to put up with such a thing?"

There. Guilt. But good guilt.

Jennifer made a dismissive sound. "My mother has been dealing with issues as long as I'm aware, which is forever. She doesn't need my support. Besides to be completely honest, I'm so busy, now that I'm retired, that I have no time to have any deeper conversations with her. But I have to say if she's Candy La Plume, I'm impressed. Who knew my mother had it in her? Not," she added hastily," that I've ever read anything by Candy La Plume."

Riiight. The daughter doth protest too much. The daughter might even be a *hoont*.

There was a loud, inhuman screech. Jennifer yelled, "Crystal Anne, I told you to leave my orangutan alone!" And then more directly into the phone, she added, "I have to go. Nice to talk."

Tootsie stared at the phone, put it down and stared out the window. "I should have asked for the orangutan's name, shouldn't I?'

The phone call she made to the son resulted in less interest and…here, read *no*…satisfaction. He was very busy at work, he said. He'd give mom a call when he got a chance.

Which, if Tootsie knew anything, was probably going to be never.

"She could be dead, and he wouldn't know," she complained to Steve that night.

Steve was in the middle of sautéing a piece of cod. As he pushed the sweet potatoes, flecked with thyme aside, which were nestled there in the pan with the fish, he said, "Your cousin is an asshole."

"I take it back. I'm not counting him as a cousin."

The spatula paused mid-air. "What?"

There was no point relating the convo she'd had with Adele about Jennifer and Larry, not the one before Tootsie had called them, and not the one after when she reported back to Adele. Which saddened Adele but didn't surprise her.

Steve resumed his spatula-ing. "You did the right thing, calling them, Toots. Don't aggravate yourself about what you can't do anything about, like getting Adele's children to care about her."

"I agree." She came up behind him with a fork in hand and speared one of the pieces of sweet potato.

He gave her the cop look.

She grinned at him. Then, grin fading, she said, "What do you know about finding online nuisances?"

Steve asked for an explanation of what kind of online nuisance. "I know a guy who might be able to find this individual. Let me ask. In the meantime, I've got a piece of information for you that I think you'll find interesting."

The cod ready to be eaten, and the potatoes done, he filled two plates only—Chris was out with friends.

"What will I find interesting?"

They sat down to eat. "Last Monday night, Melanie's husband wasn't there."

"Oh?" Tootsie cut her potatoes into small pieces. "I didn't think about a husband. Should I have? And why are you bringing it up, now? Would he have ripped my dress pieces off or stamped on them? Would he have called me bad names?"

"I don't know. I know his name, though. Remington Carlisle Mangold III—Trey is what he goes by. He's in the trucking business. It's a third-generation family business."

"Trucking, huh?" Tootsie popped up to get the iced tea carafe out of the refrigerator. She came back to the table and filled both their glasses. "But after how this Trey's wife has been acting, I'm not inclined to like her husband no matter what business he's in."

"I'm giving you background, Toots. Trey moved his family here from Flemington. "You know where that is, right?"

She rolled her eyes at him. "It's in New Jersey. You and I should take a ride down there. So, you know where it is, too."

He ignored the shot. "Trey got a promotion to company vice president—"

"Of the family business?" Tootsie interrupted. "Promotion. I wonder how that happened?"

"You think you can wait for me to finish a sentence here, babe?"

She buttoned up her lips...and her impatience.

"As I was saying, he was put in charge of all their service centers, nationwide. The CEO needed him to be in the office in downtown New York and available to him on a moment's notice."

"The CEO, probably his father."

"When you're right, Toots, you're right. Except sometimes you're not."

Tootsie stopped squeezing lemon onto her cod and glanced up into her man's gorgeous black eyes. "It's nice that you think I'm right. But I don't like the second part of what you just said. What brought that on and what does it have to do with Trey Mangold?

Because I know you. You've brought him up for a reason."

"Now that security is my business, it's important for me to read about what all manner of companies do, and what their security needs might be because some of them could be clients one day."

Yup, and there it was. Her man didn't just wait for his ship to come in. He swam out toward it and boarded. She gave him a kiss of admiration. Smack on the mouth.

He gave her one of his little smiles. "Thanks, babe."

"You're welcome. And now that you explained that little sidebar, get to the part about Trey Mangold."

"After I heard why Trey had moved to Glen Allyn, I reached out to Bert Schwimmer."

Tootsie knew Bert. He was someone her Black Windbreaker worked with on occasion in his new security business. "What did Bert tell you?"

"First, he asked me if you'd done a Google search on the Mangolds. You did do one, didn't you?"

Okay, so everyone in her life knew she was not brilliant when it came to doing anything online. But… "I do know how to do a Google search."

Steve ignored her huffiness. "The first thing Bert did was run a criminal background check on both Mangolds. Then he looked at the national registry of sex offenders. Trey Mangold did not show up, so we assume he's not a pervert."

If Melanie's husband was a sex offender, Tootsie would have had to go to bat for her. It would have given her indigestion like she'd eaten too much chopped liver, heavy on the *schmaltz*, but she would have done it because no woman should have to live with a sex offender. "So, the Mangolds are super clean. How annoying."

"I wouldn't go so far as to say they're clean."

Tootsie perked up. "You wouldn't? How far would you go?"

That brought one of her man's secret smiles out from its hiding place, behind his usually deadpan lips. "We know the answer to that, don't we?"

And didn't that bring out her own blush? "Let's not change the subject," she said with haste. Rushing on, she said, "Tell me what Bert found that wasn't so clean about the Mangolds?"

"It was Trey."

"Trey the trucker?" Tootsie snorted a laugh at her use of Ts.

"Trey was dishonorably discharged from the Army."

"Bad boy Trey. Did Bert find out why?"

"He didn't. But a dishonorable discharge is something that follows you through your life. It's a good thing Trey is working in the family business."

"I'm happy for him. But...? And yes, I know there's a *but*."

"While the Mangolds were living in Flemington, Trey coached his daughter's' soccer team. He got kicked out of the league."

"Oops."

"It seems he didn't play well with the parents. Or the refs. Trey's a bully. He isn't afraid to use his fists. He got into it with a father who didn't like that Trey wasn't giving his daughter any playing time."

"So, Trey can be violent, can he?"

Steve, who was the neatest eater Tootsie had ever met, but could also be the fastest when necessary, rose to take his plate to the sink. As he rinsed and loaded the plate into the dishwasher, he said, "He had something on Melanie, too. Nothing that rose to Trey's level, but it does tell us something about why she got involved with the library board."

Tootsie's curious mind wanted to ask more about Trey but, it was way more interested in Melanie. "I'm listening."

"The Mangolds lived in a big old house on a big piece of property off Route 202 north of Flemington. Melanie became a frequent guest in the tax collector's office down there."

"Why, she wanted to know what all her neighbors were paying?"

"Yeah."

Tootsie could feel her eyebrows go up and her mouth quirked up on one side. "I was joking."

"The neighbors didn't think it was a joke."

Tootsie brought her plate over to the sink. "From just that one time at the library board seeing her in action, I'm getting that Melanie has a reason for doing everything."

"You're right. She thought she and Trey's taxes were too high when compared to others with properties like theirs. But that wasn't all. She also raised issues with the county because some people said their land was agricultural and taxed at a lower rate because they had farm stands on the road during the summer months. She didn't think they should have any breaks because of some little table out front with tomatoes on it for sale to tourists. Stuff like that."

"So, Melanie has a long-standing reputation for judging. That's not a surprise. But what is Melanie's problem? What makes her want to make trouble for people?"

"I don't know. You're on your own with that one."

She wandered into the great room. Tootsie didn't fancy herself a psychiatrist. But it would be nice if she could figure out what made Melanie tick. In the meantime, she had a thought that didn't involve the Mangolds and she wanted to do something about it. It involved Candy La Plume.

"I do appreciate you sharing all that info about the Mangolds." She reached up for a book she'd placed on the mantel. "To show you how deep my appreciation runs, I thought I'd read you a page from Candy La Plume's very first book, *Dangerous Love*. According to my aunt, she was just getting her feet under her when she wrote it. So, she says it's not her best work. It doesn't have a lot of sex in it. Or said another way, it has less than her later books have. It's pretty vanilla."

Steve raised one brow. A look of deep interest filled his black eyes. "I've never heard sex at any level described as vanilla."

"I just bought it and I've only read a few pages. I would describe them that way. But I paged ahead and what I found was... Well, why don't I read it to you, and you can be the judge."

He sat on the couch, stretched out his legs, and leaned back, hands behind his head. He didn't answer with words. He didn't have to. His face did the answering for him.

He remained silent while she read to him, standing there by the mantel, like she was doing a poetry reading at a café. After reading the last word on the page she'd picked to read to him, she closed the book. And then looked up.

He was smiling. It was a smile she'd never seen before. She wasn't sure it was a smile. It might have been a wolf grin, as if pouncing was involved.

But seriously, what was wrong with her that she hadn't thought he would have that kind of reaction when reading him something about how dangerous love could be?

It was good that Chris wasn't home.

CHAPTER SIX

Tootsie decided she needed to do a little more investigation into what Candy La Plume wrote. Which was why she drove Viv over to the Woodland Park Barnes & Noble.

The romance section was on one side of the store. The U-shaped shelves created a haven where readers of romance could peruse in comfort. Snug armchairs and some long benches were arranged in the belly of the U. The store had thoughtfully provided stools, so short people could reach the top shelves.

Tootsie approached, wondering how many of her aunt's books she was going to find. She had no clue what to expect.

What she hadn't expected was to see a stack of Candy La Plume's books right there on one of the benches, as if someone had just been looking for one to read.

The book on top was entitled, *Two Can Tango but Three Is Better.*

Wha...?

Had she said that out loud?

The way one of the helpful employees in the store peeked into the U and asked if she needed any assistance said she had. Tootsie waved her away and then sat herself down and picked up *Two Can Tango.*

She opened it to a middle page, as she always did with books she was considering buying. She didn't get halfway down the page when her face began to burn. She clapped the book closed.

Revelation...Tootsie was mortified to think her nice little old lady aunt knew things about how bodies could intertwine with each other that she hadn't even imagined because her imagination didn't travel that far.

After patting her chest into a state of calm, Tootsie sampled another book in the pile.

If her face had been red before, now with this next book and next passage...and yes, what she was reading and what her aunt had written fell into the category of BDSM...Tootsie broke out into a hot flash.

"How do you know about this stuff, Adele Silverstein? I hope not from visiting some of these..." Tootsie's breath failed her. But then she sucked it back in and whispered, "Clubs."

Her helpful friend was back. She peeked back in and said, "I see you're looking at Candy La Plume's books. She's very popular. We shelve every one of hers because there's a big demand for them." She gestured behind Tootsie where there was not one, but two shelves loaded with books by Candy La Plume.

That evening, as they were preparing for dinner, Tootsie reported to Steve on what she'd found. "I spent a good part of the day doing background work on Candy La Plume."

If paging through books that featured love à la BDSM, could be called research. "There are some in the world who wouldn't want to read erotic love and BDSM. I'm fine with that. We should all be fine with it. Each to his own taste."

She put two plates on the table. "Have you been able to speak to Bert? Can he tell you anything about how to uncover a troll?"

"He found him."

She blinked at the news and put the cutlery next to the plates as he slid dinner, a piece of grilled salmon with dill dressing, on each plate. He returned the pan to the stove and checked to make sure the gas was off before moving back to the table. "Bert says whoever this guy is, he's smart. He uses an avatar."

Steve pulled out Tootsie's chair for her to sit and then sat himself. "His handle is @bygeorgewashington."

"Wow, an historical reference. Adele would like that." Tootsie wouldn't mention it. Since that was her being sarcastic.

"The account's only been around for a few weeks. I checked his posts myself," Steve continued. "He posts all day long, every day. Most of them are aimed at your aunt. He's got a thing for her. He's nasty. Real nasty."

Tootsie put the fork with a piece of salmon on it back down on her plate. "Does he say why?"

Steve chewed, swallowed and then said, "He says Candy La Plume is a disgusting human being."

Tootsie paused, then said, "That sounds up close and personal."

"I'd say he's met her. Or he knows someone who has."

"How did he find her?" Tootsie demanded, no longer making any effort to eat. "Candy La Plume is a pen name."

"Information about who publishes her books is right there in the front of every one of her books. With that information and a little knowledge about searching the internet for the answers you're looking for, it wouldn't have taken much effort for someone with an ax to grind to find her."

Pushing away her plate, because what Steve was saying was ruining her appetite, Tootsie said, "Is there any way to hurry this investigation along? My aunt is afraid the guy who publishes her educational books will find out. She doesn't want to have to deal with his disapproval."

"These things take time, Toots."

And didn't she know that?

The following morning, Tootsie started out the day promising to figure out what was motivating Melanie. She tried doing a Google search. But after the third page and seriously not knowing what search terms to look for, she gave up. The best thing for her now, was to keep her eyes and ears open. If Melanie made any preemptive moves at the library, Tootsie would make it her business to know.

She sat over her coffee and ticked off the things she knew that might or might not be important. Number one, Melanie and Trey were pot-stirrers. Number two, Trey could be violent if pushed. There was no number three, drat it, helpful or not.

She stood. Maybe she needed to go in another direction. Maybe it was time to find out more about what made Adele tick.

Her aunt answered her knock right away.

After Adele's usual greeting…kisses on both cheeks…and the usual like what's up, how do you feel, have you heard from Basil …Tootsie followed Adele into the kitchen. "You've never said what got you started writing for publication."

Adele sat at her table. There was a cup of tea that she'd been drinking when Tootsie knocked. Next to her cup was a plate with slices of Mandelbrot on it, which she offered to Tootsie. Linking her hands together on the table, she said, "As which writer? A.S. Silverstein or Candy La Plume?"

"Is there a difference?"

Adele's indulgent smile told Tootsie that yeah, she recognized snark when she heard it. "I'll start with what came first. Some of my fellow history teachers, in my school and others, wanted to know my secrets. How did I get my pupils to be such wonderful history whizzes? Some of my colleagues asked me to write down how I taught them."

"From there to attracting the attention of a publisher…there must have been a connection."

"There was. A fellow in Teaneck whose kids had been in my classroom called me one day. He worked at a publishing house in New York. He asked if I would consider writing a book on my methods. The rest is history."

Tootsie grinned her approval for the funny. "Awesome story, Aunt Adele. For most people a new career like A.S. Silverstein's would have been enough. But it wasn't enough for you. You had to invent another persona, write something completely different. Why?"

Adele gave her a mysterious smile. "Because I could." She held up a hand to forestall what Tootsie was about to say.

"Let me say it this way. I write my books on how to teach history for a reason. It's essential for all of us to know what people who have come before us did with their lives and how their actions affected others. To know the triumphs and the tragedies of nations, the longing for everyday people to make things better and how leaders made it happen or suppressed it. For me, teaching history will always be the essence of who I am. I want to be able to share my knowledge and my ideas as long as I can." A sad smile just ticked the edges of her lips. "If I couldn't, it would hurt me. Deeply."

Tootsie could just imagine. The passion driving her aunt was amazing. Then, to have her work so valued… "Um, Aunt Adele. Your phone." She pointed at the cell phone on the table next to her aunt's teacup. "It's buzzing."

Adele looked. Her face fell. "It's Basil."

CHAPTER SEVEN

Tootsie sat up straighter. "Will you put it on speaker so I can hear?"

Adele's mouth worked for long seconds as the buzzing phone insisted *answer me*. Then she gave Tootsie a sharp nod and pressed Talk. "Hello, Basil?"

"Hello, Adele." Basil spoke through his nose. How charming. He continued, "I'm glad I caught you. I wanted you to know what I've done before you hear it from someone else."

Adele and Tootsie looked at each other.

"I'm halting production on your spring release."

The silence that followed had an echo to it. Like the words were repeating themselves, though they couldn't be heard.

Adele said, "Why?"

"You should know."

Again, his words lived in the silence.

Worry in her eyes, Adele glanced once at Tootsie. Then she bent to the phone as if that would make her words clearer. "I think you're making a mistake."

Basil snorted his disdain. "If you think so, you've forgotten what I told you long ago when we first started doing business together. Reputation of my writers is everything. I will not tolerate one that has been sullied."

A low hum began in Tootsie's ears. Her heartbeat reset into speed mode.

Adele's face turned the same shade of red as her hair. She bit her lips hard. "I do not have a sullied reputation."

Basil snorted. "Candy La Plume does."

More silence.

Tootsie wondered. What exactly did Basil expect her aunt to say, that she wasn't Candy? She'd stop writing as Candy if only he would put her newest book back on the schedule? If he did, did that mean Basil believed in blackmail?

That's what it meant.

Tootsie's neurotransmitters charged to their feet.

She speared a determined look at her aunt. But her aunt wasn't looking at her. She was staring at the phone.

Basil cleared his throat. "I don't like to do this, Adele, because we've had a long and fruitful partnership, but you have transgressed."

Transgressed? Was Basil's full name Basil Cotton Mather?

"I might have to sever ties with you," Basil was saying. "I'll have to let you know."

He hung up.

With a shaking finger, Adele hit End. Then she said, "Perhaps he won't do it. Perhaps his lawyers will look at our contract and tell him he can't cut ties with me because of the provisions."

Tootsie had heard and she knew. Pigs would fly. Basil intended to go on as he said he would.

With a big sigh, Adele picked up her cup and carried it to the sink.

Tootsie searched for something to say, to sympathize. She came up blank.

Adele started toward the front door. Tootsie followed.

"I'll give him some time, then I'll call back."

Tootsie didn't tell Adele that would do no good.

Her aunt went on. "Perhaps then I can talk sense into him."

Tootsie knew her aunt was reaching. "Perhaps you can," she said anyway, and with a goodbye kiss, knowing Adele's attempt to change Basil's mind was doomed to fail, she headed home.

"There's a new situation with my aunt," Tootsie told Fern as she tramped into her house.

"Hmm." Fern handed Tootsie a report that had come in on the fax machine. "Before you tell me anything, here's good news. You've conquered the French drains."

Tootsie read the report that had come from her HUD contact. It closed with a handwritten note on the bottom:

I thought you'd want to see your persistence has paid off. The project has been completely signed off on. Thank you, Tootsie, for never giving up.

Hmm, nice. Now, if only there was a way to persist with Basil. Like *he* was a French drain.

She told Fern about the phone call. "My aunt is devastated."

Fern picked up the report and stuck it in the top drawer of their file cabinet. "I agree. It's why now that the French drain project is in your *Hell-raised Successfully* file, you're free to do your thing and fix things for her. Melanie has already done too much damage. You need to go full steam and find out why she seems to have singled out Candy's books and make sure she can't do more to hurt Adele than she already has. You need to go after this troll, too."

Biting an annoying cuticle on her thumb, Tootsie said, "Yeah, I know. Only, so far, we don't know enough about the troll for me to go after him."

Fern sat herself back down in front of her laptop. "Don't look my way. You're the one who's good at asking questions and getting answers."

Tootsie's cuticle gave up the ghost. She snatched a tissue from the box that sat in the center of the table and wiped her hands. "You're right. I am. I might not be able to do anything about the troll right now, but I'm about to ask some pointed ones about where Melanie did her thing before she began to do it here. Tomorrow, I'm taking a ride to Flemington, where the Mangolds lived before moving here."

Fern brightened. "Good idea. Take Steve with you."

Naturally Fern would invoke Steve's name. He knew how to keep Tootsie from going all the way off the rails when she asked her questions.

"He might not have time to go with me," she hedged. "He's got some new clients."

When she asked him later, he surprised her. "Yeah, I'll go. Know your enemy," he said as they got ready to stream their favorite series. "There's a good chance we'll come back with more than we know now."

Which was why, though it was threatening to snow, the next morning early, they got in Steve's Ford F-150 and motored their way toward southwest Jersey.

Flemington had charm. The town, located near the Pennsylvania border, was crisscrossed with narrow streets lined with vintage Victorian houses, complete with bright white gingerbread curlicues decorating the columns that ran the width of their front porches. Each house was renovated, refurbished, and painted in pale colors.

"We'll admire the architecture some other time," Steve said, as Tootsie gave a running commentary on which houses she thought were more spectacular than the others. He added, "Let's start our investigation in a logical place."

Like the library.

To see if Melanie had worked her magic there, too.

The Flemington library was a charming, squarish, red brick building with white pilasters that adorned the brick front and ran down from the flat roof to disappear behind the bushes on each side of its main door.

They stood aside at the main entrance to let exit a gaggle of harried moms shepherding their kids away from what looked like story time. As the last of the moms with kids passed her by, Tootsie stepped in and scanned the interior. Tomes of every size stood upright on the all-wood bookshelves that rimmed the walls of the room. In the center space were long white wood tables and square-backed chairs pushed up to each, just waiting to be pulled out and sat on by library visitors.

She poked Steve. "Doesn't this feel like every library you've ever been in?"

Before he could answer her, she heard the squeak of rubber-soled shoes on the tile floor.

Tootsie turned in the direction of the squeaking.

"Can I help you?" The woman who spoke was older, roundish, with salt and pepper curls hugging her head. Her brows creased with curiosity. She wore a half-smile on her lips. "You look like you've got questions."

The woman introduced herself as Virginia Page, head librarian. She followed with, "Yes, I know. Page being my last name, I was destined to be a librarian." She chuckled as she made fun of herself. "You can call me Ginny."

Ginny suggested they seat themselves at one of the tables in the middle. Once ensconced...poor Steve had issues with where to put his legs, since the chairs were mostly meant for people shorter than his six-foot-three-inch frame. Tootsie gave him a sympathetic look and got started on her spiel. "We're from Glen Allyn. Our library is in a state of flux." She paused inside her head. She just loved that word, flux. As in flux capacitor. An image of Christopher Lloyd's character in *Back to the Future*, bushy-haired and wild-eyed, filled her brain and her pause became a full stop.

Steve cleared his throat. He knew. He was reminding her to focus.

Good thing he'd come along on this field trip.

She coughed lightly. "A woman who just moved to town has been chosen to fill a spot on the library board. We don't think she's qualified."

There. Out there. No soft-soaping or being circumspect.

Ginny Page got a knowing look on her face. "Let me guess. We're talking about Melanie Mangold."

Ta-da!

She gave Steve a triumphant look. "What can you tell me about her?"

Ginny's entire upper lip curled into a sneer. Her nostrils flared. "What I can tell you about Melanie Mangold is nothing good and before you ask, yes, she was on the library board here, too. We did not enjoy the experience and, frankly, were ecstatic when she and her family left town."

That was good to know. In a bad way. "We need to stop her from doing more damage in our town than she already has."

Ginny crossed her legs as if she was settling in for the long haul. "Why don't I tell you what I know. I think you'll drive back home with plenty of ammunition." Eyes widening, she said, "I meant information, but I said ammunition, didn't I? My bad."

"Don't give it another thought. We'll just sit here and listen."

"Melanie was not in love with the scent of books. When she first joined the board, she told us we needed to open all the windows, even in the winter, and get rid of the odor. What person who loves books doesn't like the smell of them?" Indignance colored her face pink. "That was one of the first signs we had that we were in trouble with this woman."

Oh yeah. This was going to be good.

Ginny wrinkled her nose. "It wasn't long after she started coming into the library…the family hadn't been living here more than a few months. It was before she became a member of the board. We librarians came to dread it when she opened our front door and immediately after, opened her mouth and offered her opinions about how we were running our library."

Into the stillness of the room, Tootsie said, "What kind of opinions?"

Ginny's hands, which she had folded together in front of her, tightened up. "The opinions where she spoke the words of a higher authority, and don't ask me if I know what higher authority that was."

Back that night of the board meeting, the first time Tootsie had met Melanie, it had taken her one hot minute to get that vibe from her. "I assume they covered more than the scent of the books."

"They did."

A woman with a little boy perched on her lap two tables away glanced up.

Quieting down, Ginny murmured, "I want to be clear with you. Melanie never outright suggested that any of our books should be banned. We would have known how to deal with that. But what she did want us to do was move books she thought were suspect to where they wouldn't be so easy to find."

Which was what Melanie had suggested the night of the meeting in the Elks Lodge.

"Wouldn't that have screwed up your Dewey Decimal System ordering of the books you were shelving in places where, numerically, they belonged?"

"At the very least, of course, it would have."

Tootsie nodded. "And wasn't moving the books the first step to what might come next, what she really wanted was to get rid of those books altogether?"

"Yes, except..." Ginny's face took on a pained expression before hardening.

Tootsie straightened. "Something else happened. Is that right?"

Uncrossing her legs, sitting forward, Ginny slapped one hand on the table in front of her. "It was something I thought I would never see and to this day I am still horrified that she did it. Do you know of the author, Candy La Plume?"

Tootsie blinked. She felt Steve stir next to her. "I believe I do, yes."

"We had her books on our shelves."

Had. "Let me guess. Melanie didn't like them."

"There you're wrong. She *hated* them. In her mind they had no redeeming characteristics and so she said. Over and over again. Candy La Plume's works were the subject of a diatribe she treated us to at more than one meeting."

"I'm going to assume Candy La Plume's books were among those she wanted moved."

"That would be the least of it. One day she came in here with her husband and her two little children. I'm positive the kids had no idea what their parents were about to do, which was to pull every Candy La Plume book from the shelves."

Shocked, Tootsie asked, "Where were the librarians?"

Ginny made a face. "Trey Mangold has an over-whelming physical presence. He stood guard while his wife and kids took all those books outside and threw them on the ground. Then, with people standing by and not lifting a finger, Trey left his post, walked outside, and grabbed a very big barrel. I'd never seen it before. The Mangolds must have brought it with them. The barrel was like what you see on TV during baseball games, like when someone hits a homerun, and his teammates pour a barrel of water over him at home plate. That's what he did. Poured that whole barrel of water over all of Candy La Plume's books. Every last one was destroyed."

CHAPTER EIGHT

As they drove back to Glen Allyn, Tootsie shivered, as if a phantom dump of ice-cold water was pouring down on her like she was one of her aunt's books. "There aren't words for what Melanie did."

She felt Steve's anger, too. It was in his voice. "She brought her children. Who the hell does that?" He paused on the question and then said, "Destruction of public property." The man who'd spent a good part of his life in service of the law, had nothing but contempt for those who broke it. Worse, used their children as they did.

Tootsie said, "If this was personal before, it's more personal now."

Steve turned up their street. "We're going to stop this bullshit before it can metastasize. You do what you need to do. I'm going to delve deeper into who

Trey Mangold is. If he's more than meets the eye, I'll find out."

First things first. Tootsie had to decide how much to tell her aunt about what they'd learned about Melanie from Ginny Page. She could just imagine how upset her aunt was going to be to know her books had been destroyed by that...*hoont*.

Fern voted for telling her. "She's no shrinking violet, your aunt. She can take it, probably better than most."

Which was why, later that evening, on the visit she made after crossing their lawns that Tootsie laid it out for Adele. They were sitting in the living room on Adele's sofa. Her aunt's eyes took on an angry glint. "I don't like that woman."

With a sharp nod, Tootsie said, "I don't know why she seems to have it in for you. Why did she destroy your books and no one else's?"

"I don't know. Could it be that she knows me?"

Tootsie blinked. She stood and walked into the dining room. Adele followed. "Is it possible Melanie was one of your students?" She leaned close to one of the pictures, a later one, chronologically.

Adele came up to stand next to her. "There was no Melanie Mangold in my classes."

"Mangold is her married name." Tootsie continued to scan each picture. Not that she thought she'd recognize Melanie if she were in one of them. People changed over twenty or so years. Especially their hairstyles. Nobody in these pictures had godawful bangs like Melanie Mangold had.

After they looked at each picture and came up with nothing, they returned to the living room. Sitting, Tootsie said, "Even if we can't figure out if she knew you, we still have to figure out how to stop her from pursuing this vendetta she has against you."

The sound Adele made was filled with disgust. "She's already she's done plenty. How much more can she do?"

Tootsie knocked her fist on the coffee table in front of the couch. "Don't say that."

Adele nodded. "I take it back."

"Okay," and Tootsie meant okay. Except… "Aunt Adele, over the last few weeks you keep parceling out bits and pieces of your life as if you'll share only what's necessary to share. It's like not only do you have a secret life, but your secret life has secrets. When are you going to tell me everything?"

Adele lifted her chin.

Tootsie held up a hand. "Don't misunderstand. I only want to know what will help me figure out how what the deal is with Melanie."

Adele fiddled. "Haven't I been trying to figure it out?" Her voice held a plaintive edge.

Tootsie folded her arms across her chest. "All right. I know this is tough. So let me do the figuring. Meanwhile, why don't you tell me more about what decided you to write as Candy."

Adele gusted out a sigh. "It happened when Basil asked me to write another book and I didn't want to. I was bored writing about methodology. I'd always read romances. I decided to see if I could write one."

"When was that?"

"About five or six years ago. I started doodling some ideas about a woman who wanted to escape a bad marriage and decided the plot would have her figuring out how to get away from her abusive husband. So, I came up with my first main character, Delores De La Vigne. I made her the heroine of *Dangerous Love*. In the book she learns that sex, when it's not about violence and control, can be good. But only with the right man."

There'd been no violence in Tootsie's marriage with Arlo. But she understood the part about how sex could be good with the right man. "La Plume, De La Vigne...is there a reason why you choose French names?"

With what Tootsie might have called a Gallic shrug, Adele said, "Who knows more about love than the French?"

Maybe an Italian ex-cop, the one with whom Tootsie enjoyed great sex? "Go on. Tell me more."

"I was enjoying the doodling. Before I knew what was happening, I began to think of Delores as a real person. I wrote sentences about her and then paragraphs and before I knew it, I was writing chapters about her life. Then lo and behold, I had a whole story about her. Then to make it truly complete, I gave her story a happy ending, just like the romances I've always liked to read."

"And you went to Basil and asked him if he would publish it, right?"

Adele gave her a look that said *are you hitting the vodka before lunch?* "Basil? That publisher? They only publish…" she made air quotes, "serious works, never romance. That would be beneath them."

"So, you found another publisher who wasn't opposed to making money from your Candy books."

"I did. Right away. This publisher tells me stories about her sexual experiences I don't want to hear." She grinned, imp-like. "Maybe I should listen. I could learn something."

Tootsie's blinked yet again. Whoever thought ninety-year-olds couldn't have bawdy thoughts was an ignoramus.

As Tootsie kept absorbing, Adele kept talking. "No, Candy's publisher is very happy with me and I'm happy with Candy. Her stories are easy to write, and I keep on writing them. They're always about the same thing: a woman has a bad experience with her husband or sometimes it's her boyfriend. She realizes it doesn't have to be that way. She has agency." Adele patted Tootsie's hand. "That's what we writers say when a character takes the reins, meaning she takes charge of her own life. One of the things she decides is she wants to have better sex."

"Which, based on what I learned on that visit to Flemington is what Melanie objects to."

The shine in Adele's eyes that had been there since she'd begun telling Tootsie about Candy, faded away. It was replaced by a hardness that Tootsie rarely saw in her aunt's eyes. "That's too bad. Candy's books aren't about sex but about women choosing who to have sex with. If the one they originally chose treats them like *dreck*, then they can find a man who won't." She raised a finger. "Especially because the woman would be in charge of the sex."

Which Tootsie could appreciate.

"And that, *mamaleh*, is the real reason I write Candy's stories."

Tootsie smiled. "You write them because women should be in charge of sex?"

Which was an appealing idea. She liked when her Black Windbreaker wanted her to be in charge of their nightly shenanigans. She liked it just as much when he was.

"No. It's that Candy has changed the life of more than one of her readers. For the better. Before you ask me, I know because they tell me."

"One of your 20,000 followers does, right?"

"Yes. One morning when I was struggling with a plot point in my then latest story, I got an email from a reader who told me that my books allowed her to escape from her struggles. She was working three jobs, none of them paying enough that she could give up even one of them. In the few moments she had between her work and caring for her young children—and no, her husband didn't help around the house—she read my books."

Adele paused and then continued. "In that email, she said she was transported to another, better place. She loved that Delores had started out like where she'd started out. She liked that Delores had agency..." She tapped Tootsie on the arm. "Remember, agency is about taking charge. Anyway, this reader saw how Delores faced the trouble in her marriage and stood her ground against that good-for-nothing husband of hers. That encouraged the reader to stand her ground against her own good-for-nothing husband. She told me those few minutes with Candy La Plume's stories gave her the strength to do that one thing she'd never been able to do before.

"At first, I thought how silly. But then I realized that it didn't matter if I thought it was silly or not. Candy's book about Delores De La Vigne's life was out there in the universe. It wasn't Candy's story about Delores anymore. It was Delores's story. This lady made it her own."

This made sense to Tootsie in a way that it never had before. Basil and people of his type, snobs all, were dismissive of her aunt's spicy, steamy stories. Because they weren't literary fiction. Yet they had a positive impact. Did readers of literary fiction write to literary authors saying how much their words had changed their lives?

"Was that the only email you ever received?" she asked, but already knew the answer.

"I've received others. When I go to book sign-ings, people tell me how much my writing means to them."

"This is exactly what I have to talk to Melanie about. She needs to understand that though she may not want to read a book like yours, others do. And value them."

"You know, Tootsie…" The smile that had warmed Adele's face faded again. "Sometimes I think about that woman, the one that sent me that email. I wonder if she figured out how to keep her children from sapping all her energy. Has her husband relented and now helps her around the house? Has she found a wonderful job that allows her to work one, not three? I don't know. What I do know is at least for those few moments when she's reading my books, she is weathering her storms."

The next morning, when Fern arrived—along with more snow—Tootsie told her about Delores De La Vigne. She also told her she had a plan she was about to put into action.

Sitting in front of her laptop, page open to her favorite online bookstore, Fern said, "I think I need to read your aunt's *Dangerous Love*." With a flourish, she submitted her order. Then, task complete, she glanced up at Tootsie. "Now, what about your plan?"

"I'm going to another library board meeting at the Elks Club. To reason with Melanie."

Fern's eyebrows shot up. "Is reason in her vocabulary?"

"I trust my powers." Tootsie also trusted her ability to talk in circles so eventually, just to get her to stop, her target agreed to do what Tootsie wanted.

"Make sure Steve goes with you."

Tootsie bristled. "What? Do you think I can't handle myself?" Besides, Steve had a meeting down in New Brunswick.

"I know you, Toots. You'll be fine. Until she says something that gets under your skin. Then I worry."

All of which Tootsie knew to be true. *Keep your cool*, she cautioned herself as she walked into the Elks Lodge that night, which unlike last time was empty of people. But full of chairs.

"Look at this, Charlie Fortenberry, you idiot," she muttered to herself. "You could have held this meeting in the community meeting room at the library instead of this old, decrepit place. People have lost interest in your precious Melanie."

People were fools. They had short attention spans. She didn't.

Tootsie was surprised that the man who'd been so vocal at the last meeting was not present. She wasn't surprised that Melanie was sitting at the table with the other board members.

On purpose, she took a seat in the front row, so Melanie would know she was there. Tootsie knew it rankled because Melanie refused to look at her.

Too bad for you, Mel.

Charlie banged his gavel, calling the meeting to order. He launched into the subject of state support and bemoaned the reduction of funding they'd gotten this calendar year.

The whole time, Melanie sat, hands folded in front of her, eyes wide, staring at Charlie as he spoke. As if his words were golden. Every once in a while, she'd nod. Adoringly.

Tootsie did not throw up.

When she'd heard as much about the library's budget as she thought she could stand, Charlie got to the part of the meeting no doubt Melanie had come for.

Turning toward Melanie, Charlie gave his best harrumph. "Now, it's my honor to complete a task that I was prevented from completing at our last meeting."

His gaze slid Tootsie's way. She gave it right back to him, eyes open as wide as she could stretch them without her eyeballs dropping on the ground in front of her.

Quick as a mouse escaping a predatory cat, he jerked his gaze away. "Ahem. Mrs. Mangold, if you'll just stand for a moment..."

Looking lady-like in addition to innocent...and Tootsie wanted to know how she did that...Melanie rose. She didn't just rise, she took herself over to where Charlie stood. Because center stage was better than off-to-the-side, right?

For a moment, Charlie was nonplussed. How to regain attention to himself was the question. He managed. "I'd like to welcome you as our newest board member. I'm sure not only will we benefit from your thoughtfulness, but with your input our meetings will become so much livelier."

He stuck his hand out to shake Melanie's. As he did, the other board members weakly applauded. Tootsie folded her arms across her chest in case her hands did the automatic clapping thing, too.

The meeting broke up soon after. The few people present, other than the board, exited. Melanie and Charlie, heads together, remained in what looked like a world-shaking conversation.

Their little conference didn't stop Tootsie from stepping up to the table. "Excuse me."

Charlie and Melanie turned toward her as one. Melanie forgot to put on her 'I am just such a lovely and delightful person' face. Instead for that instant, before she realized she shouldn't, she showed Tootsie her demon face, the 'I am capable of ripping your heart out' face.

Then, like magic, she became sweetness. "Yes, hi."

"I know you two are seriously busy, but I was wondering if I could get a minute with you, Melanie."

Melanie didn't bother to look at Charlie. Why would she? Now that she was a member of the board, she could act the part of Charlie...ahem...Charles in Charge. "I'll just tell my husband I'll be a few minutes."

Hmm. Trey was here?

How had Tootsie missed him? She looked around and there he was, him and his Schwarzenegger-sized body...on top of which was a tiny head. Everything in the head was small, too. His eyes, his nose, his pursed lips, and his teeny-tiny chin. He gave his wife back the nod she'd given him and then turned those little eyes on Tootsie.

And wasn't that a moment for feeling a deep chill. It was based on two points. Point A: Trey, the husband, wore an expression that declared he did not like Tootsie Goldberg. Point B: if he could get away with it, he was thinking it would give him a lot of pleasure to rearrange her face.

This, she knew, was one of those times Steve had mentioned where beating a fast retreat might be best. But even though pretty much everyone had left, and she was alone except for the *hoont*, the *hoont's* husband, and useless Charlie Fortenberry, Tootsie needed to ...like she'd told Fern...reason with Melanie. Because she still didn't know why Melanie had it in for Adele. Until she did know, reasoning with the woman was her only option.

So, she was staying and would let the chips fall where they may. Or if not chips…she glanced at Trey…and shivered.

"So, Melanie… If you don't mind, I'd like to ask you something for clarification."

Melanie smiled.

"You've made it a point that you don't like Candy La Plume's books. Can you tell me why?"

Another smile. This one seemed like it hurt her face. "Because they're smut."

Said with spite. Though she was still smiling.

"But not everyone thinks so, do they? Some people like them, and they don't call them smut."

Melanie's smile became a grimace. "Those people are perverts."

Even though she'd expected Melanie to say something like that, she was startled. But not fazed.

"So, following your reasoning, people who like to read thrillers and police procedurals are hoodlums."

"No, they're heroes," was Melanie's prompt response. She turned to look at her husband, who had eased himself over to the side of the room. Where he was smack in Tootsie's line of sight. She was pretty sure he'd done that on purpose.

Her neurotransmitters stood, ready to do battle. She had to send out a caution about not getting too crazy because, as she reminded them, they lived in her imagination and seriously were not up to defending her against Trey Mangold, whatever they thought.

Melanie said, "There are many people in our world who think books are the be all and the end all. This is a foolish thing. You know this, don't you, and by the way, you don't mind if I call you Tootsie?"

Tootsie held up both hands. "Of course, I don't mind." But she did mind the "womansplaining".

"So..." And now the woman who Tootsie was pretty sure had perfected the art of condescension brought it out into full view. "We as a society have gone downhill. We Americans are not the strong, righteous people we were back in the day and books are responsible for our fall."

"Hm..." Tootsie nodded. "That's a pretty broad statement, don't you think?"

Melanie treated her to a lovely, tinkly laugh. "Oh, that's funny, Tootsie." She wagged a finger at Tootsie...who had the urge to grab that finger, turn it around, and jab it in Melanie's nose.

"Back in the day, we lived more simply. Happily. Books in the library were wholesome."

Tootsie's eyebrows flicked up and back down. She'd come to this meeting *to reason with Melanie.*

Reason had left the room. It might never have been present. Like Fern said.

Tootsie said, "Back in the day?" She tried to keep the snap from her voice and failed. "Back in the day, you' weren't alive so you couldn't know whether all of them were wholesome."

Melanie's nostrils flared. Okay, so she didn't like to be dished the "womansplaining" the way she liked dishing it. Which was not going to stop Tootsie now that Melanie had opened the subject up. "If you're referring to the 20th century, it was not a simple time and for sure it wasn't happy. Had you asked many millions of people, living then, they would have told you that you were mistaken. You know, wars. Atom bombs dropping on peoples' heads. The Holocaust."

Now was not the time to bring up her Grandma Hannah, a survivor of the Holocaust, who was the reason Tootsie was standing here in front of this holier-than-thou *hoont*, trying to do the right thing for her Aunt Adele.

She leaned forward in her chair. "You should study your history more, Melanie. In all of history there were never simpler, happier times."

Trey took that moment to move away from the side of the room where he'd stationed himself. Melanie turned for a moment to track his steps, which took him to the back of the room. Then to Tootsie, she said, "Well, that's your opinion."

"Yes." Tootsie nodded so hard she was afraid she was going to give herself an attack of vertigo. "But it's also the *opinion* of ninety-nine point ninety-nine per cent of historians everywhere." She made air quotes around the word, opinion.

Melanie speared her with a 'drop dead' look. Tootsie gave her what she called her 'psych' look. Except, even as she did, she held onto that one forlorn hope: that she could still get what she'd come for.

Dialing down, she said, "Melanie, you're probably going to do a great job on the library board. But really, while you're making sure the library is funded so it truly can be a library for everyone, why not allow people to read whatever they want, whether James Patterson or Daniel Silva or Candy La Plume."

Melanie jumped to her feet. "Thank you so much, but no. People must be protected from themselves and protect them I will. Candy La Plume..." Her lip curled. "That woman writes things that are worse than disgusting. She encourages women to leave their husbands."

"Yes, there's that story where her main character, Delores, leaves a real nogoodnik," Tootsie cracked, realizing, finally, that all was lost.

Melanie turned red and snatched her purse, which she'd laid on the chair next to her. "You have no right to talk to me about how a woman should leave her husband." She pointed right at Tootsie's nose.

That blasted finger again. Now, Tootsie wanted to break it...if she could have caught it. But Melanie was waving it around so wildly, there'd be no finger catching tonight.

Eyes filled with righteous fire, Melanie shouted, "You're a divorced woman and you live with a man out of wedlock!"

"Wow, out of wedlock. I don't think I've ever heard anyone use that expression. Although Thomas Hardy probably did. Thomas Hardy. English novelist

who was born in the 19... century. His books are no
doubt in the library. Oh, and by the way, at one time
Hardy's work was banned."

Who knew it would happen, but Melanie was
now all but apoplectic. Her bangs were bouncing on
her forehead, her feet stamping rhythmically on the
Elks Lodge's tile floor. "I think you just better shut
your mouth! You have no standing in a proper world.
You're worse than Candy La Plume."

Okay, so now they were back at it. "Which
brings me to another question. I know what you did
at the library in Flemington to Candy La Plume's
books. Why? What have you got against her?"

"Why did I?" Melanie screeched. "She...she..."
Red-faced, sputtering, Melanie was spinning out of
control. "She could have, she should have...she..."

"She what, Melanie?" Tootsie shouted as Melanie
stormed away, stumbling once before righting herself
and grabbing hold of the door leading outside, she
slammed it behind her.

Which was when Tootsie realized.

She was alone in the Elks Lodge.

She felt a breeze.

The lights went off.

CHAPTER NINE

Stuck in the pitch dark of a room that smelled of hops, old wood, and cracked leather seating, her heart leapt into her throat. Her pulse beat so hard that a headache stabbed like ice shards at her temples. She fumbled for her purse, which she'd hung on the back of her chair. It wasn't there.

Maybe it dropped? She felt around on the floor with one foot. No purse. Could it have disappeared like magic? "Like what, Tootsie," she said into the darkness. "Like David Copperfield came to Glen Allyn just to take your purse for his new act?"

Swallowing hard she tried to remember. Maybe she'd left her purse on the first chair she'd been sitting in? She felt around the chairs on either side of her. Nothing. Then, she felt her way back, retracing her steps as much as she could in the pitch black. "Why," she whined, "Could the Elks not have one of those red exit signs? Wouldn't that have been helpful?"

Wouldn't it also have been helpful if she hadn't left her coat in the car? She was beginning to shiver. And then she remembered another disaster. She'd left her phone in Viv's console. "You couldn't have put it in your purse like a normal person?"

She felt around on the chairs. No purse. Which was when she remembered the breeze. Could someone have whisked her purse away in the breeze? Maybe it *had* been David Copperfield.

Arms extended straight out, she set out toward what she felt had to be the back and the door to outside. When she got to the last row of chairs, she paused. She recalled a void where the chairs stopped and a big space over to the door began. She thought about getting down on all fours but the idea of putting her hands on a floor where who knew what had landed and been smooshed onto the tile was worse. Who knew what could have been dropped on it? A shudder rippled over her shoulders.

With not a whole lot of faith that she wasn't going to face plant, she stepped into space and thank God, somehow found her way to the door. Pressing her forehead against it, doing what she could to control her rapid breaths, she had a moment when she feared whoever had turned the light out had also locked the door.

But it wasn't locked. Relieved, she pushed it open and stepped out onto the Elks Lodge's single step. Patting her chest, like that would get her heart to stop thundering, she took a bunch of deep breaths. *Never again will I, Tootsie Goldberg, set foot in this Elks Lodge.*

There were no stars and no moon to illuminate the street. Bonus prize—The snow had turned to sleet. She slid her foot over the step, hoping it wasn't slippery. Which was when she saw her purse.

"Oh," she cried, bent, and picked it up. And then she said 'oh' again. Her fob to the car was gone.

But the wallet was still there.

"Yay," she grumbled. Because maybe she was locked out of her car and was about to freeze to death but at least she didn't have to cancel all her credit cards.

Ice pellets snuck under her turtleneck sweater as she set off toward her car, which she'd parked around the corner. Maybe she'd left the doors unlocked? "Please, please," she sing-songed, hurrying, hoping she didn't slip. Relief. Viv was still there, waiting for her in all her beauty in the darkness.

Yeah, Viv was a beauty. But…why was she sitting at such an odd angle? Tootsie slowed her approach and gasped. Someone had slashed Viv's tires. This was so not a good thing. But maybe she'd left the car door unlocked? It would be warm inside, and her phone was there. She could call for help.

She snatched at the front door handle and prayed. Her prayers remained unanswered. Because she lived with an ex-cop and he said lock your car doors all the time, she'd locked up Viv tight.

"Maybe you shouldn't do everything Black Windbreaker tells you to do," she muttered. There was a tremble in her voice, which she didn't want to acknowledge because now she was ready to conclude what had happened. While Tootsie had been in her fruitless talk with Melanie, Trey Mangold had gotten up, come outside, and done his thing.

And now she was alone.

She wheeled around, looking. Hoping. Nope. No one. That was because the Elks Lodge was located on a street with a series of low-slung office buildings. Not a single house in sight.

"You guys had to locate your lodge here?" she gritted. "You couldn't have found a place closer to civilization?"

From having driven past the lodge every once in a while—Tootsie had never had many occasions to visit this street before—she knew she was about a half mile from downtown and an equal distance from the street where her own house was located.

Through the sleet that was now caking her eyelashes, she narrowed her eyes at each office building. There was not one light lit in any of their windows. Well, yeah. Who would be working on a night when the weather sucked? Besides which, it was after nine o'clock on a weeknight and everyone was home streaming some fabulous series, unlike herself who was huddled next to her locked car, trying to decide what to do next. Which, if she'd been thinking strategically, she never would have had to. Since she never would have come to this meeting. Because what exactly had she thought would be the outcome, confronting a crazy woman?

But she had confirmed something. Melanie had some deep, very personal hate-on for Adele. It was even worse than she thought it would have been.

After a quick glance at her watch to see if she was right, that it really was after nine, she slid her sweater sleeve down to cover the watch so it wouldn't drown in the increasingly intense deluge of sleet.

Now that she'd tried and failed to find relief from the situation, she turned away from Viv and started up the street in the direction of home. Hunching in her now soaked-through sweater, her imagination, always vivid, decided it needed to wake up.

Was Trey waiting for her here in the dark? Was he about to accost her in a deadly way?

Over library books?

"But no, you wouldn't do that, would you?" she said, voice all reasonable, like she was talking to Trey himself. "And really, was it totally necessary to destroy four, perfectly good tires, which I now have to replace? Excuse me but your timing sucks. The last day to get the best tire deal of the year at Costco was yesterday."

She stumbled on a crack in the sidewalk and caught herself before she could fall on her face. Around her the storm's fury intensified.

"Black Windbreaker is not going to like this," she said talking and walking. "You've made an enemy, Trey Mangold." Because Steve was definitely not a fan of types that hurt her.

She trudged on in the wind and the rain and the frigid cold. The chattering of her teeth matched the cadence of the shuffling steps she took to keep from falling. She'd be home soon, wouldn't she? She'd peel off her wet clothes. Well, unless they were frozen to her limbs and then she'd have to cut them off, which she really didn't want to do because she loved these trousers. She'd bought them on sale two weeks ago at Chico's and they looked fabulous on her. Maybe she needed to get into the shower in her clothes and that would defrost everything and it wouldn't destroy the trousers.

Although... Were they washable? *Oy*, the thoughts that went through a majorly stressed person's mind.

She turned the corner out of the office park and came to the end of the sidewalk. This was the part of the walk home that she wasn't looking forward to. This was one of Glen Allyn's parks. In the daytime it was lovely. It had picnic tables, slides, and swings. She'd visited this park with Sam and Josh when they were little.

Off to the far corner was a baseball field. There was a light on over the diamond. In the light's downward cone-like beam there was clear illumination of how hard it was sleeting.

She came to an abrupt halt. Was that someone coming toward her? The figure coming toward her was holding an umbrella. "Oh, thank the Lord and little fishes," she whispered.

Except then she asked herself if she should be thanking the Lord so fast. She squinted. Why was he out at this time of night? What was on his mind? Did he have something to do with Trey?

The figure plodded on toward her, coming closer. And there it was: decision time. Should she continue, pass by the guy—because yes, she could tell it was a guy—and say something like *will you look at this? Not only are you crazy to be out in this weather but I am, too?* Or should she turn around and head back toward the office park and Viv? Like Viv would protect her against…what?

Well, there wasn't a choice, was there? She plodded on, putting one foot in front of the other. Umbrella man came closer. He was wearing dark pants. And was that a plaid shirt? And were his pants being held up by suspenders?

Now, she could see his pallid face. Perched on his head was a billed hat. With earflaps. They were pulled down over his ears.

She slowed. Then stopped. He slowed. Then stopped.

"Hey," she said., across the five feet that separated them. Like sure, this was a normal situation.

"Hello," he returned. "What are you doing out on a night like this, ma'am?"

She supposed she couldn't say that she had been locked out of her car by a pinhead with rotten intentions. She settled for, "I'm on my way home."

"Do you need some help?" He shifted from one foot to the other. Which drew her attention to his feet, clad in a pair of dirty, laced-up boots.

And just like that, out of nowhere, the theme from *Deliverance,* complete with banjos, surged into her mind.

"No, thank you," she said, squishing on soaked-through shoes, stepping around him, and hee-hawing a nervous giggle, "I need to get home before the weather gets bad." Like it wasn't beyond bad already.

"Would you like my umbrella?" He thrust it out, as if to hand it to her.

She did want it. But what if when she put her hands on the handle there was some kind of toxin and the moment the flesh of her palms came in contact, her nervous system would go wacko and she'd fall to the ground insensate, only to awaken later tied down with rope, and duct tape slapped across her mouth on a cold table in his garage while he sharpened his surgical instruments to carve her up.

"Uh, no," she said, waving his offer away and looking back toward him as she hurried past him on her sodden shoes. "Goodbye. Have a nice night."

The rest of the way…and she never ever remembered this park being as big as it was…she stumbled along on noodle legs, praying she wouldn't fall. The whole time she stumbled and bumbled, she felt his gaze plastered to her back. Any moment, she expected to be grabbed from behind and dragged into the trees, forget waiting to take her to his home to duct tape her up. He'd do the deed with his wicked scimitar...and no, she did not have to explain even to her inner voice that men with plaid shirts didn't carry scimitars. It was *her* fantasy. So there.

At last, she stumbled out of the wooded area onto a sidewalk at the head of her street. Only then did she slow and turn to see if the man had followed her. He hadn't.

If he were anywhere, she would guess he was on his way to get dry, just like she was.

Up ahead she could see her house. Steve's truck was in the driveway. She churned forward, relief warring with her slowly fading fear. Her trousers, she knew, no matter how much she liked them, were never going to be the same. Her turtleneck was sopped through. The curls on her head were flattened to her scalp and studded with ice.

She stumbled up her front steps and banged the knocker. She heard her lover coming at a clip toward the door. He yanked it open and eyes unblinking, stared.

"Shit." He pulled her inside, slamming the door behind them. "Where the hell have you been? What the fuck have you been doing?"

"Wow," she said, shivering all over. "How upset are you that you've raised your voice, which you never do, and used three curse words within less than five seconds when you hardly ever use one in five days?"

He grabbed her, ignoring her attempt to make light of his reaction, and all but carried her upstairs to the bathroom. "We need to get you out of these clothes now before you go into shock. And no, don't try to tell me what happened. Yeah, I want to know. But first things first."

The whole time he was talking, he was pulling her sodden clothes off her. Her teeth were clacking so hard...reaction to the cold or the scare, she didn't know...she couldn't have spoken if she'd wanted to.

She stood on the bathroom mat, shivering like a palm tree in a category five hurricane, waiting while he turned on the shower and it became moderately hot. He denied her request to make it boiling hot. He stood there, arms at his side, fists flexing, until she stopped shivering under the cascade of water. When she made to get out, he shook his head.

"You stay in there until I say you can get out." On that last word, he reached in and turned the knob to increase the temperature. "You can have your hot water now. Just leave it as is. I'll be back. I'm getting you something to put on."

He was back in a moment with one of her flannel granny nightgowns. He turned off the water and helped her out of the tub.

"Don't even think you're going to wear a sexy little number." He was busy rubbing her down with one of her over-size bath towels. "I don't get turned on by a woman with blue skin. You're going to wear this nightgown and say thank you, Steve, for finding it in the back of my dresser drawer. Are we clear?"

Wow. Black Windbreaker giving orders and going on and on. She knew he could do the first thing. That's the way they'd started their relationship with him giving her orders...that she ignored...but rant at length? That was a rare occurrence.

"Yes sir," she said, words muffled in the towel.

Dressed, with the shivers abating, slippers on her feet, Tootsie followed Steve to the kitchen where he pushed a steaming cup of Earl Gray tea into her hands.

He sat. "Okay. Tell me what happened."

She told him. The whole time she did, his face remained set in the cop look.

As she wound down, he stood and grabbed his cell phone from where he'd put it on the island. "I'm calling down to the station to ask the desk sergeant to send someone to check on your car."

After that call, he made another, this one to his friend, Johnnie V.

"Johnnie V takes phone calls after 10 o'clock at night?"

Steve had come back to sit down next to her. "We're friends. So yeah."

Okay, back to short answers. "Will he pick up Viv?"

"He'll send his flatbed for her tomorrow first thing. I told him I want her to be checked out, hood to trunk, to make sure Mangold didn't do damage we can't see."

Tootsie began to ask him if he really thought that was possible. She didn't bother. She was too tired. Too disappointed in herself.

She hadn't noticed he'd fixed another cup of tea until it was sitting in front of her. She heard his words on a weird delay.

"Normally I'd tell you not to drink this because you won't be able to sleep because of all the caffeine, but your insides still need something strong and warm."

She stared into the steam that rose in lazy figures from the cup. Did she care about having too much caffeine after her walk home from the Elks Lodge and her meeting with Deliverance Man? Yeah, that would be the name she'd remember him by, as opposed to Umbrella Man.

Steve took her hand in his. It was all warmth. And comfort. And safety. And the fright of the long walk home faded away.

"I need a different plan of action," she murmured, and took his other hand in hers so she could be on the receiving end of double the warmth. "I'm thinking I need to cease and desist."

"Really?"

She sighed. "I couldn't reason with Melanie tonight. How did I think I would?"

He tightened his hold on her hands. "You haven't been able to figure out how to get at her, how to make her stop. You were trying something. What you tried didn't work. So what?"

That perked her up. "You're saying so what?"

For the first time since she rang the doorbell and he'd opened the door to see her standing on the steps all bedraggled, his eyes sparkled.

That pissed her off. Her hands flexed in his. "You think this is funny?"

He raised both her hands to his mouth and kissed them. "No, babe. None of it's funny. But the things you say. How you say them. They tickle me. I like living with you."

And how exactly with his few words did he always manage to spike her guns when she wanted to go to war with him.

She bit down on the smile that wanted to come out to play. And failed when it bloomed on her face. "Do you? Really?" Like she wasn't saying that in her coy voice and didn't need to hear him say, *oh yeah*. Because she never got tired of hearing his *oh yeah*.

He placed their hands back on the table, leaned forward, and kissed her mouth. This was one of his sweet ones.

Aw, shucks.

"You love living with you. I love just about everything about you."

She couldn't even take exception to that 'just about' business. Because she knew what he meant. Her high drama had been a sticking point. When they first decided they would be in each other's lives, he said he'd have to get used to it. The thing was a man as orderly as Black Windbreaker was bound to have trouble with high drama. It had never been a part of his life before she was in it. It was one huge switcheroo for him.

Tonight had beenall about her high drama. Who besides her would ever challenge Melanie as she'd challenged the woman? Without thinking of the consequences and making Trey an enemy?

"I've been thinking." She took her hands from his and wrapped them around her cup. "What am I really accomplishing here?"

He raised one eyebrow.

"I keep telling myself that I need to make up for lost time all those years when I wasn't true to myself. When I didn't try to live up to the principles Grandma Hannah lived by. You know...doing the right thing. Maybe I need to let someone else do the right thing. After all, I've done the right thing a bunch of times, lately."

In low tones, he said, "Is that what you think?"

She began to answer. Stopped herself. Because what she'd said ought to feel right. Surely was right. Somehow it didn't. "Still..."

Her inner voice took over. It reminded her of a couple of realities that somehow, she'd forgotten.

"My Aunt Adele is not exactly hurting, money-wise. She mentioned that she bought that house outright. She can afford to live there for as long as she wants. No matter what Melanie says about her Candy books, truth is the more she says they're smut and filth, the more people will want to read them."

Because she was still staring down at her hands where they lay in her lap, she didn't see his smile...did he smile? But her peripheral vision told her he was nodding. He said, "Maybe that guy who spoke up at the last meeting will take on Melanie so you can take a step back for a little while. Rest."

Tootsie shrugged. "Maybe my aunt can sue Melanie. For harassment."

Silence.

The central heat switched on and a swoosh of warm air came at them from a vent in the wall close to where they were sitting. The fridge motor hummed. She shifted on her chair and one of the chair's legs squeaked against the floor.

Steve put both elbows on the table and leaned toward her. "What happened to always do the right thing? I thought that was your big guiding principle."

She stood up. She wouldn't look at him. "Let someone else do the right thing this time."

CHAPTER TEN

The following morning, with Steve gone to check in with a client, Chris off to school, and Fern not in yet, Tootsie found herself alone in her kitchen. She'd spent a night half-sleeping, half-awake, aware that Steve was doing his best to soothe her. Normally he was excellent at the job. Not this time.

She knew why. Yeah, she'd mouthed the words, let someone else do it this time, but even as the words left her lips, they felt wrong.

But she wasn't about to take them back.

For once, she decided, she needed to turn away. Last night, walking home in the pitch-black and the sleet, Deliverance Man showing up out of nowhere? As frightened as she'd been, she might have shortened her life span by a decade.

These days, with her Black Windbreaker, she wanted to savor every birthday, every day. Was that such a bad thing? Couldn't she leave the hellraising to someone else?

Except even thinking that still felt wrong.

She lifted the note Steve had left her. His message said he was going to take a look at Viv before he started his workday and check with Johnnie V on how long he thought it would take him to get Viv back to her.

Well, she could still be in the hellraising business. If she were to continue, she'd have to find things that were more about business and less about the hell part. Like going to bat for the people who lived in the senior complex. Making sure French drains got installed to prevent flooding. She'd done a good thing there. And no one had put a hurt on her car.

She was so into thinking about new, less dangerous ways to hellraise that she was all but jolted out of her chair by the sound of knocking on her front door. It was too early for Fern. There was only one other person who was up as early as Tootsie and would be knocking on her door.

Aunt Adele. Of course.

She opened the door.

Anger clouded Adele's face as she stepped inside and hurried past Tootsie's curio cabinet with the silly Meissen monkeys and hand-painted Limoges boxes. Tootsie's original monkeys and boxes had to be replaced after the thug Elwood Robinson had wrecked them all in order to scare her off from looking into how the radio station had gotten sold to the wrong people.

"That *pischer*." Adele kept walking until she reached Tootsie's kitchen table, pulled out a chair and dropped down into it. "He's decided not only will he take my new book off the print schedule, but going forward, he won't publish any of my books because my reputation as a writer of serious subjects is tainted."

She held up a finger. "Not that he'll give me back my rights, and don't bother to ask what that means."

Tootsie didn't need an explanation. Basil Jernigan, her aunt's idiot publisher, would still take profits from what books of hers sold, but he wanted to wrap himself in righteousness, telling anyone who was interested that he couldn't allow himself or his firm to be associated with someone who wrote what Candy La Plume wrote.

"I don't know what he thinks the big deal is." Tootsie sat down in a chair next to Adele. "It's not as if sex isn't a part of thousands and thousands of works of literary fiction."

"That's true." The anger that had hardened the lines of her soft, papery skin, morphed into glumness. "I pointed that out. He wouldn't listen."

What could Tootsie say to that besides what she was getting ready to say. "You know, Aunt Adele, I think you shouldn't let any of this bother you. Steve and I were talking last night..." And no, she wasn't about to tell Adele about what Trey Mangold had done and about her scary slog home. "It occurred to me that you're okay where you are in your life. Why not let all this go? Let the *hoont* wind herself up until eventually she'll be found out as the narrow-minded person she is. Life will take its course, she'll go away, and you won't upset yourself more than you already have."

The words weren't out of Tootsie's mouth before Adele reared back in her chair. "Esther Ruth! I never thought I'd hear you say those words. What has come over you?"

Tootsie opened her mouth to respond. For what seemed like too many times over the last couple of days, she found herself speechless. Because how could she explain her change of heart to her aunt?

Which was when she realized.

She couldn't. Change her heart, that is.

She stared at Adele, who stared back, unaware of the massive shift that had just taken place in her brain.

She was a hellraiser. She was meant to be a hellraiser. It was in her blood. It always had been, though she'd denied it. It always would be.

Finding herself in the dark in the Elks Lodge? Finding all four of her car's tires slashed? Having to walk home in the pitch-black and the sleet? Meeting Deliverance Man? She'd let herself get distracted.

"Aunt Adele, I take it back."

She jumped up and began to circle around her island. Because she was thinking and when she was thinking, she was walking. Until she stopped. "What do you think of TV reporters. Do you like them?"

Adele gave her the 'what difference does it make if I like them or not' look.

Tootsie amended, "What I mean is do you think it would benefit you to do a TV interview with a reporter about the nonsense going on at the Glen Allyn public library?"

"Hmm." Adele pursed her lips. "I've certainly done the occasional interview on TV, radio, podcast, and live on Facebook groups. It couldn't hurt. What did you have in mind?"

"There was a reporter that I recently befriended. She did a story about Sage Rust that exposed him for the hypocrite he is. You know, the 'I am a rich man, and I can do things no one else would get away with doing'. She told me if I ever had another good idea for a story, I should let her know."

"Well, restricting access to books in a public library would make a fabulous story."

"Then if you agree, let's put our heads together and come up with a pitch, which is what, in the industry, they call an email or a message where you suggest a story idea you want the reporter to consider doing."

Adele's smile grew wide. But then her eyebrows came down, Angry Bird-like, and she said, "*Oy*, that's very good. My niece, she's some smart one. So smart, she explains to me something I already knew."

Tootsie had a good laugh at her own expense. "My bad. I should have said here's what I'm going to do. I'm going to pitch our story to my reporter friend. How's that? Better?"

No doubt pleased with herself that she'd given Tootsie a little *zetz*, Adele said, "Much better, *mamaleh*. Much better."

After only a few moments thinking about how to frame what she would say about Melanie's efforts to the reporter, Blaze Brotherton, Tootsie, with Adele's help, had it down to the sentence, noun, and verb level. With a flourish, Tootsie closed the lid of her laptop. "I don't believe in sure things, but it's going to be hard for Blaze to say no to this story."

She didn't say no.

The plan was for Blaze to meet Adele at the library. Adele should be sure to have a copy of one of Candy La Plume's books that she could hold up for the camera.

"You think maybe *Dangerous Love* because it was my first? Or what about one of my ménage books, since they're newer."

Yes, she'd be just as guilty in a way as Melanie was if she self-censored and said one of the ménage books might have some people saying, well, that's a little too far out there. Which it wasn't. Because they were talking adult reading. Still...

"Bring a copy of *Dangerous Love*. Yes, it's your first and there's a story there to tell, the one you told me about you trying something new. And it's Delores' story. That one will pull at people's heartstrings. You know that whole agency thing you explained to me."

CHAPTER ELEVEN

Agency was what made Adele good at her interview with Blaze. Standing on the sidewalk in front of Glen Allyn's library, she held up *Dangerous Love* and spoke assuredly about how writing as Candy was her starting something new while she was in her eighth decade. Adele spoke about the impact Candy's words had on readers. And she spoke about how wrong it was when a single person elected themselves arbiter of what books should be shelved in a public library and where.

Blaze was her usual enthusiastic self. At some point, after she'd gotten Adele to talk about the impact Melanie's efforts could have on the choices people made about what books to read at the library, her cameraman turned the camera back on Blaze. Having fluffed up her long, dark brown curls, and reapplied her lipstick, she looked into the camera and spoke her summation.

"Here in Glen Allyn, it seems that one woman is on a crusade to change the reading habits of Glen Allyn residents. She wants to make it harder for certain books, like those of author Adele Silverstein, writing as Candy La Plume, to be found in the local library by those who want to read them. All because this woman, Melanie Mangold doesn't like them. We reached out to Mrs. Mangold for comment. She hasn't responded."

Of course, from what Tootsie could tell, that might not have been true. Yes, Blaze had reached out. But Tootsie knew, because she'd been standing there, that Blaze had called Melanie's cell number—and how exactly she had gotten the number Tootsie didn't know and didn't ask—gotten voice mail, suggested Melanie call her back. And didn't wait for her call.

"If she wants to call the station and let me do a phoner with her tonight before I'm off at seven p.m., then I'll give her an opportunity to talk."

Then, as her cameraman stowed his camera in its carrying case, she winked. "But I might not be available."

Was that fair? Tootsie thought Blaze was the kind of person who listened to both sides of an argument before deciding which side to come down on. But, it seemed, not this time.

Adele shook hands with Blaze and the cameraman. "Thank you for telling this story." She held a copy of *Dangerous Love* firmly in her other hand. "No one person should decide what others can choose to read in a public library. I emphasize the word public, here." She held up her hand, thumb, and index finger close together. "What Mrs. Mangold is suggesting comes dangerously close to book banning."

"Oh, I get it." Blaze nodded, all seriousness. "I'm looking forward to putting this story together." She turned to Tootsie. "I'll text you later and let you know when the package is going to run."

Which she did. And surprise, surprise. Blaze's editors decided to have it be part of the morning show the next day.

"You should let your followers know you're going to be on the news talking about Candy," Tootsie suggested.

Adele agreed. She posted in all her social media and even sent out a quick e-blast to her newsletter subscribers.

Tootsie had joined Adele in her office in front of her laptop while she sent all her messages winging in the right directions. She said, "I'm hopeful that this will do it. Get Melanie to back off and leave our library and your Candy La Plume books alone."

Swiveling around in the state-of-the-art chair she wrote in, Adele looked up at Tootsie and gave her a thumbs up. "I can't wait to hear what Blaze does with the story."

The story, when it aired, was to be positioned as the last one in the morning show. Tootsie decided that Adele should come over and they would watch together while eating an excellent breakfast, courtesy of Steve, who decided to delay the start of his workday so he could watch with them.

"I'm *plotzing* I'm so excited," Adele said, though she hadn't been too excited to eat. Her plate, on the TV table set up in front of the couch in the great room so they could dine and view at the same time, was scraped clean.

Of course, any meal Steve made would be consumed forthwith. This one was an awesome Spanish omelet with a side of sliced avocado, which was studded with garlic, cilantro and a spritz of lime, a kind of guacamole without the mashing part.

The hosts of the show were their usual bright, chirpy selves, and altogether annoying. They related news items as if they happened in some other universe, certainly in the one where the outcomes of those items affected people in their viewing area. The stories they spent lots of time on were of the *happy, happy, joy, joy* kind. Which was a reason why Tootsie had never watched.

"And now here's a story out of a small town in New Jersey," the male talking head, whose name apparently was Ross, said to his co-host, Marisol. "Our Blaze Brotherton tells all."

And there was Blaze in a shot with her microphone in Adele's face with Blaze doing the voice over. "Adele Silverstein, a long time, well-regarded teacher of history at Teaneck High, found herself a new career long after she retired from that position and one that not many women even half her age would aspire to. Adele Silverstein became an author, but not just of academic books for teachers to learn Adele's skills after her many years teaching history."

The camera morphed to Blaze's face. "It turns out that the whole time Adele was writing her serious books that fall into the area called pedagogy…" And here she treated the camera to a little smirk. "Pedagogy is one of those words we don't exactly use every day. No, that whole time Adele Silverstein, who will be ninety-one on her next birthday has been leading a secret life, just recently uncovered. It turns out that Adele writes steamy romance under the nom de plume, Candy La Plume. Plume…" Blaze winked. "Get it? Plume as in a pen name. Because Adele didn't want the world of pedagogy…" And here, she over-pronounced the word. "To know that she'd fallen into an area of fluff fiction, otherwise known as romance, and an area within that genre."

"What!?" Adele dropped her fork on the floor.

Steve, who'd been crouched down behind the couch, his arms folded over the couch back, came to his feet. "Was that part of what she videoed at the library?"

Tootsie bent to pick up the fork. "No, it wasn't," she said, biting off each word like it hurt her to say them. Which it did.

They all kept their eyes on the big screen on the wall. They hadn't missed much the few seconds it took for each of them to react. Because Blaze was still talking her talk. "And now Mrs. Silverstein finds herself having to defend what she's been writing all these years. This is what she had to say, the other day when we trekked out to Glen Allyn to speak to her."

Trekked out to Glen Allyn, fifteen miles from the George Washington Bridge? Steve and Tootsie exchanged WTF glances.

"Our libraries are a precious commodity," Adele was saying. "We are at peril if we choose to make books that we, as individuals, don't like, unavailable to the reading public."

"You're not talking about book banning, are you?" Blaze stuck the mic back in Adele's face for her response.

"Not yet. Although that could be the next step."

"But some might argue that the public library is that: public, and everyone should feel that it's a safe place, where controversy has no place."

"Why is controversy a bad thing?" continued Adele, looking patient. Like she was explaining a concept to one of the students in her history class at Teaneck High. "Controversy births ideas, some of them good, some not so good. But we can't always tell which one is which, not right away. We Americans pride ourselves on ideas, or the inventions that spring from ideas. We've made controversy, ideas, and inventions that have benefited not just us as a nation, but the world. The library, this one...," she turned halfway and pointed to the library's front door, "like every other public library, should be a place for anyone to read about ideas. Or controversy for that matter." Adele smiled. "Or for pleasure."

This next was the one that Tootsie had liked the best about the interview. She held her breath now, given how Blaze's approach to the interview was, so far, not what they'd expected.

"Even if it's a controversial book like one of yours?" Blaze was asking.

Was there a tinge of the tricksy there in Blaze's words that Tootsie hadn't noticed when Blaze was interviewing Adele?

Confused, because they weren't sure where the danger was coming from, Tootsie's neurotransmitters looked at each other and said *huh*?

In the interview, Adele said, "Even the person here in Glen Allyn who has made it her crusade to move books from one section to another where they can no longer be found readily, yes. Nothing says she has to read any book she doesn't like. Or finds unpalatable. But those books might be the very thing someone else would find palatable."

Blaze said, "I guess you're saying one man's poison is another person's pleasure."

"Have you ever heard of Helen Keller?"

Tootsie had *loved* this part of the interview.

To Blaze, she said, "As children we all learned about how Helen Keller overcame the disability of having neither sight nor hearing and made a full life for herself, including as a writer. Helen Keller spoke up during the 1930s when the Nazis began to ban certain books they deemed *un-German*. She wrote an open letter to the college students of Germany, too many of whom were becoming Nazis. They were all for banning books. Ultimately, they were among those who burned books. To them, Helen Keller said, 'Tyrants have tried to do that before, and the ideas have risen up in their might and destroyed them.'"

The camera came back to Blaze's face to do the part of the interview Tootsie *hadn't* seen. "Adele Silverstein says Melanie Mangold doesn't know history if she doesn't know about what happened in Germany in the 1930s. But is that really true? Or are Candy La Plume's books just about sex, not controversy. Is that truly controversial? Back to you, Ross and Marisol."

"Well, that's what you get for writing a steamy romance, I guess," said Marisol, her smile so broad as she said it that it spread across her rouged cheeks to her ears.

"Yes, you bring controversy into the picture," Ross intoned. Like he was sharing a thought that had just popped into his tiny brain and his mouth decided it was more than a perfect time to spit it out. "And now, let's hear from our trusty weather guru, Sandy Storm, who will look ahead to Christmas and tell us what the National Weather Service, and yes, Santa, says about whether we'll have some of that white stuff on the ground come Christmas morning."

Steve clicked the TV off.

Silence.

Until Tootsie broke it with, "You were talking about book banning and using Candy La Plume as an example. Why did she ignore that part of the story? Based upon what a great story she did on Sage Rust, why would Blaze do such a hatchet job on you, Aunt Adele?"

Adele, whose face had fallen in resignation said, "May I remind you that when she did that story, she was doing a hatchet job on him, too?"

"You're right." And it was what Tootsie had loved back then—a way to get back at Sage. She didn't love it so much now.

Adele said, "I thought the interview was going well. But even then—and I should have said something to you—there was a certain undertone that I didn't like. It's a known fact among us writers of steamy romance that reporters love to focus their brains on the part where there's sex."

"Which most people seem to enjoy."

Both women turned to the man in the room who'd just made that observation. As if that was all he had to say on the subject, he came around to the front of the couch, grabbed Adele's plate and headed for the kitchen.

"I'm leaving, now," he threw over his shoulder. "Today has been an eye opener." He stopped and turned. "And Tootsie, just one word. Be careful."

"That was two words," she called out to his retreating back.

But she knew what he meant. Whatever she decided to do next to clean up after this interview that had gone sideways, he wanted her to watch herself. Not do anything that would put her in one of her usual predicaments. Like the other night when she needed to walk home in the dark from the Elks Club. And met Deliverance Man.

By this time, Adele had slouched back against the couch cushions. "I had a feeling, even when she was interviewing me that this might happen."

Tootsie sighed heavily. "You're right and I don't know what I was thinking. I should have realized. There's a reason I stopped watching TV news. Because it's not news."

"Well." Adele stood. "I'm sure I'll hear from my supporters. Those who have seen this interview will be upset for me and say very nice things to make me feel better."

She walked over to the banister and retrieved her coat and purse from where she'd hung them on the newel post. Placing the purse on the first step, she slid her arms into her coat. "I'm sure Basil is relieved that he had already severed our relationship before this story aired."

"Your best revenge is writing more books as Candy La Plume. You already know that Candy's stories have made a positive difference in some people's lives. Why not write more books just like that?"

She held the front door open. Typical December frigid air whooshed in. "What I really think, Aunt Adele, is every book that you write is about fixing something."

Adele brightened. "That's a wonderful point, Tootsie-leh. You try to fix things, too. We're both hellraisers it seems."

Tootsie could go with that, which was what she told Chris when at last he came down to go to school. With a mouth full of the omelet Steve had left for him in a panini of sorts and which Chris had stuck in the microwave to warm up, he said, "Yeah, I asked one of the librarians, Mrs. Feinstein, why she was moving Aunt Adele's books the other day when I was in the library looking for information on Ukraine. She pretty much told me it wasn't any of my business."

Plate scraped clean, he stood. "She knows I live with you, Tootsie. I love that she's afraid you might come in and have things to say to her." He hoisted his fifty-pound backpack over his shoulders and flexed his elbow. And then he was out the door.

"How do we not have to take you for Tommy John Surgery," she muttered, grinning ruefully at the thought, as he slammed the front door behind him.

By the time Fern arrived, Tootsie already knew she wasn't going to have to relay much about the interview. Fern had already texted her disgust over how it had gone down.

"That Blaze must have trouble looking herself in the mirror."

"She probably had to contend with an editor," Tootsie said, as she followed Fern into the dining room/office. "And the editor had to contend with his or her producer. Who has to answer to management, or to the owners of the station who want what they want and if they don't get it, might fire them."

"Well, now that it's out there, I guess there's nothing you can do." Fern opened her laptop and began to sort through the papers she'd left in a pile next to it the evening before.

But that wasn't what Tootsie was thinking as she drove toward the library in a Viv with four, spanking new tires. She was thinking about what she would say to Mrs. Feinstein, who according to Chris, had already started moving books. Tootsie was looking forward to confronting her, especially after Chris had mentioned the woman was afraid of her. Advantage her.

Mrs. Feinstein was at the front desk checking out a young woman with two toddlers clinging to her knees. She looked up from what she was doing as Tootsie breezed by. The smile she'd bent on the mom disappeared as she saw who the newest visitor to the library was.

Tootsie ignored her and went directly to the place in the library where Candy La Plume's books should have been shelved. She spied Serena Summers, the librarian Adele had said was a nice young lady.

"Good morning," Tootsie said, probably a little too loud for a library. Serena threw her head up, startled. When she saw who it was, the practiced smile that she'd put on her face, faded to wariness. Obviously, she knew who Tootsie was, too.

"So, I'm just wondering. Where are all the Candy La Plume novels?"

"Oh." Serena popped up from where she'd been sitting. She smoothed her hands down her navy-blue skirt. "I'll show you." She set off toward the back of the library, Tootsie following. But that was not where she stopped. They came to an exit sign and an emergency door that led to the outside. There was also a staircase going down. Serena took Tootsie there. All the way. Two flights down.

This was a part of the Glen Allyn Library Tootsie had never been in. It was damp and cold and dark, even with the lights on. There were rows of wooden shelves filled with old books, books with worn spines and torn covers.

Fury steamed in Tootsie as she followed Serena toward the back of the long room. "Here they are." Serena pointed to the last shelf, and yes, there they were. Every single copy of Candy La Plume's books.

"How on earth can anyone who wants to read one of these books going to be able to find them?"

Tootsie did not bother to keep the sharpness from her voice. She'd heated into the red zone.

Serena shrank into her pale blue sweater set. "I-I don't know. But this is where Mrs. Feinstein told us to move them."

Adele might have thought Serena was a nice young woman. Tootsie had another word for her: spineless. "Didn't you think it was wrong?" Tootsie snapped.

She spun around and marched toward the steps, up into the library proper. She didn't stop until she was standing in front of Mrs. Feinstein. "Why did you do it? Did Melanie Mangold tell you to?"

Glen Allyn's head librarian adopted a disapproving pinched-lip look. "What we do in the library and how we display books is library business."

"Not hardly," Tootsie barked. Red hot steam flowed out her ears, her nose, and her mouth like she was a bull about to tear into a matador who had no idea what trouble he was in.

Feinstein had picked the wrong person to tease with a red flag this morning.

Tootsie punched her finger onto the desk to make a point. "Here's what's going to happen. You're going to put those books back where they belong and you're not going to discuss whether you should or shouldn't with Melanie Mangold."

"You have no sway in this library."

The teeny part of Tootsie's brain still functioning recognized that this was what Feinstein would say.

And that Tootsie did not have a Plan B once she'd said it. Which was when she lost that last part of her functioning brain.

She reached into her purse and, with fingers trembling with rage, she fished out her library card. With her neurotransmitters rioting inside her head, she ripped the card into a gazillion miniscule pieces.

Throwing the scraps down on the desk in front of the Feinstein woman, she yelled, "Take that, you puny, pusillanimous.... y-you *farbissineh hoont!*"

She stomped off, but not before noticing there'd been a man with a pile of books behind her. As she bellowed the last word, he set them down on a corner of the desk and held the outer door open for her as she stomped outside.

When she halted in order to give her lungs a chance to work without seizing up inside her chest, he halted with her. He said, "That was impressive."

She snorted a laugh though she was still shaking with fury. "You think?"

"Yes, I do." He was an older man, probably in his 70s. "I heard about the meeting where you dressed up to show how dangerous it is to free thought when someone tries to restrict it. If we're to take back the public in public library, we all have to make a statement. Mine is I won't borrow any books until that Mangold woman is thrown off the library board."

Tootsie perked up. Because as her new friend spoke, she realized she knew exactly what her Plan B was.

Mrs. Feinstein wasn't going to like it. Neither would Melanie.

CHAPTER TWELVE

It took her a good part of the day to do it. It was expensive, but that didn't matter. She hit pretty much every bookstore in the area, big and small. At each one, someone was more than happy to help her out with her purchases...every Candy La Plume book in stock.

While she was busy hopping from store to store, Fern hustled over to the FedEx in Clifton where they said no sweat. For a good customer, which Fern was, they could do her a solid and make the sign she needed: one, two, six quick.

In the phone call she made to Tootsie to let her know she was finished and had the brand-new sign in tow, Fern said, "Where are we meeting?"

"Wait for me at the library," Tootsie said. "I'm in the garage cleaning off my old card table."

"This is crazy, Toots. But I like it. Even if It's cold. And gray. Even if it might rain or snow. While I was standing at the counter waiting for the guys to finish the sign, it brought me back to that day at the radio station. I thought you were crazy then, too. But you weren't."

Tootsie smiled and scrubbed the table harder. "Look at the result. The radio station is back in the hands of its rightful owners: our old colleagues."

As Fern called out a thank you to her FedEx peeps, Tootsie took a trip down memory lane.

She hadn't called herself a hellraiser back then. That came later. But it was when she remembered the life lesson Grandma Hannah had taught her. Stand up. Speak out. Do something. Do the right thing, which she had put that aside for too many years.

The smile faded from her face. Not taking a stand on anything all those years continued to eat at her. It was why she didn't want that birthday party Steve was planning. It would remind her of what she wanted to forget.

Over her scrubbing, she heard the ding-dinging that told her Fern had opened up her car door and was getting in. She said, "How long do you think until you're back from Clifton?"

Fern started her car. "No more than ten minutes."

"Good. I'll be there about then, too. I want to set up quickly before Feinstein gets a clue what we're doing."

Fern pulled into the library parking lot just as Tootsie stopped Viv by the library's front door.

Trundling up with the sign in tow, Fern said, "You're parking in front? The cops will come and make you move."

"They can't. It's a legal parking space." Tootsie was Glen Allyn's resident expert on legal and illegal parking spaces. Her protest that there weren't enough, and then her purposely parking in illegal spaces so she made her point...and got tickets, all five hundred of them...had been her first attempt at hellraising.

She held up a roll of heavy tape she'd purloined from her kitchen junk drawer. "Besides, where else would we be able to put up the sign except on the side of the car if people are going to see it as they come to the library or even drive by?"

Still-dubious, Fern helped unload the bags of books Tootsie had bought. "Are we going to pile them on the table? Or are you only going to have one book of each of the different titles standing up so people can see what's available?"

Tootsie stood back and studied the table surface which, though now clean, was still a card table and not as big as she remembered it. "This is a lemon situation, Fern. We're about to make lemonade."

She dragged all the bags behind the table. Not that there was a lot of room, but she and Fern, working together, did their best.

"Each bag has to have at least one sample book on the top so people can see what's in the bag. That way people can look and decide which ones they want. We'll hand them out one by one."

"That sounds good." Fern put her hands on her hips. Underneath her menopause blue puffy jacket, she was wearing a knock-your-eyes-out circus barker red and white striped ankle-length skirt. Tootsie didn't want to imagine what shirt Fern had paired with the skirt. Knowing Fern, it might have been red and white plaid. At least, today there were no feathers or sequins.

"How long do you think we'll be out here?" Fern had that look on her face that told Tootsie though she was going along with the program, there was that one part of her that let anxiety take over.

"Until I make the point that needs being made. Don't worry. We'll be fine."

Bags where she needed them to be, Tootsie hefted up the sign and began to tape it to Viv's street-side windows. As she taped the last corner in place, she stood back, hands on hips, and admired her handiwork. And the sign.

Bold black letters proclaimed *Books you can borrow for free and never bring back. Come and get them.*

Fern nudged her chin in the direction of the sign. "One of the guys at FedEx told me he would drive by and beep."

"Those FedEx guys…we should thank them." Tootsie observed. "This sign will definitely get people stopping."

"We'll see, won't we," said Fern in a dark voice. She pulled her ever present fan from her coat pocket and turned it on.

"You're having a hot flash?" Tootsie patted Fern's shoulder. "Don't let your nerves take over. I promise it will be all right."

She pointed to one of the two folding chairs she'd brought with the table. "Sit yourself down and wait. Our first customer…," she pointed, smiled, and squinted at a man coming toward them from the parking lot, "is about to show up."

And then she caught her breath. It was the man she'd run into at the park the night Trey had slashed her tires. Deliverance Man.

Tootsie stopped pointing. Her shoulders tensed up. Yes, those were suspenders. Yes, that was a plaid shirt, and he was still wearing a pair of dirty boots. *Was he stalking her?*

Slowing as he came to the table, he looked down. He raised his head, which had no cap on today, and directed his quizzical expression at Tootsie. "What's all this?"

She took a step back, held up one of the books toward him, and prepared to run. "This is a flash giveaway of books from the romance author, Candy La Plume."

"I don't read romance." He seemed to think about that. "My wife does, though."

He had a wife? Like a normal person? Tootsie hefted the book in his direction. "You should give this to her. Take it. Take more than one. Take as many as you want."

He stared at her. Like she'd spoken in tongues. Just like that, she was back in the dark of the park, shivering with fear.

Mutely, she held the book toward him with *both* hands. "Maybe I didn't make myself clear. It's free." *Go, she wanted to shout at him. Go away.*

He was still staring. "I guess you made it home safe."

He remembered her and he was asking after her safety? She took a good look at him. He had very kind, very dark brown eyes. And hello. She knew. Deliverance Man was a nice man. She'd overreacted. For a change.

How was she ever going stop with the high drama?

Fear sloughing off her, a hysterical laugh threatening to bubble up, she reached into one of the bags that she and Fern had stowed behind the table. "This is *Catcher in the Rye*". It's one of the most banned books ever."

He looked at the book…as if it would speak. "Why is it banned?"

"It's because of what some people call obscene language."

His eyes widened. "Damn."

The word made her chuckle and lost whatever doubt she'd had about whether Deliverance Man could have been a danger to her. She shoved another Candy book into his hands. "Obviously, you're not going to object to the language in this book. I'm guessing your wife won't object to the sex."

Tootsie grabbed a couple of other titles and shoved them into the man's now willing hands. "These are great books. Some people don't want to read them because of what's in them. Some have decided they should make it hard for everyone else to read them, too. All the books we have here today are being relocated in our public library, so people browsing find it difficult if not impossible to find them. If some in Glen Allyn..." She stopped herself and held up a hand. "No, *one* person. If she has her way, the only place you'll find them is in the basement."

His eyes widened further. "Adult books?"

"Yes, adult books." Tootsie reached into another bag and grabbed another one of Candy's books. "Take another book, okay?"

Deliverance Man hadn't resisted her gifting him with books to begin with. He was willing to take more.

"We're here to say if you're an adult and want to read *Dangerous Love* or any other book, including books like *Catcher in the Rye*, you shouldn't have to look for them in the basement."

That was enough for the doubting Thomas...or John or Fred or whatever Deliverance Man's real name was. He took one of each of the other titles Tootsie offered him, turned back to his car, stowed his stash, and drove off. As he drove past the table, he waved.

Fern waved back. "That was a promising start."

Tootsie waved, too. "More like a happy ending."

Fern frowned. "Huh?"

Like Tootsie was going to explain. Not.

Almost immediately, people walking by stopped, listened to Tootsie's spiel, and left with an armload of books. Some people driving by slowed, powered their windows down, gave them a thumbs up, and honked their approval. Others pulled over and came up to the table to see what was going on. And took books.

"We're doing some business," Fern said, as she handed out books from their dwindling piles. Now that she saw there wasn't going to be a riot—though a few people walked by with frowns or pointed stares—and that people would be happy to take the books and listen to Tootsie's tiny-TED talk, she was all in with the effort.

Tootsie smiled at a mother with a kid who looked to be in the eight- to ten-year-old range. The mom stashed the books she'd picked in her voluminous purse then urged her kid up the walk into the library. Smart mom. Candy La Plume's books were not for children. Just like most adult books weren't meant for children.

Though Fern's enthusiasm only grew, Tootsie knew it would only be a matter of time before their scheme would be discovered. Then it would be a question of how much longer it would take before someone would suggest they pack up what was left and head home.

"Hey, Toots."

And she'd been right. Tootsie turned. She hadn't heard Brian Stoddard come up to stand right next to her. Now, there he was, hands in the pockets of his dark blue serge pants, quizzical look on his face.

"Brian. Did you come to pick up some of my aunt's books for Katie? You're behind the times. I know for a fact that Katie has read most of these books already."

Brian poked one of the bags next to the table with a toe of one of the polished black shoes that went with his uniform. "No doubt you're right and anyway I know better than to buy something personal like a book for my wife. I like the idea of peace in the house."

Tootsie was always glad to see Brian. He'd gone along with her hellraising scheme over the lack of parking spaces in town...had been the one to give her most of those five-hundred tickets she'd gotten in the name of a righteous cause. There were more legal parking spaces now. Her scheme had worked.

As she handed a couple of Candy's earlier books to a lady who looked to be in her retirement years, she said, "So, if you didn't come by just to say hello, why are you here?"

As if she didn't know.

"Chief Stafford asked me to come down here and get you to move."

She raised an eyebrow at him, turned for a moment to Fern, and then back. "So, though we have a good reason for being here, he still wants us to pack up all this stuff and go home?"

Behind his rimless glasses, Brian's light blue eyes sparkled with rueful humor. "So, will you?"

She folded her arms across her chest and cocked her head to one side. "What do you think? Besides, why are you doing anything for that man? He was never much of a friend. You don't owe him anything."

He sighed. "Not to disagree with you or anything when you're on a roll, but I do work for him, at least until I put my papers in next month, and you don't have a permit to be out here on a public sidewalk, blocking traffic."

"It's a protest, Bri. I didn't have time to get a permit." Not that a little thing like a permit had ever stood in her way. "I needed to hit while the iron was hot."

"You probably haven't used an iron in a couple of decades. Why start now?"

She wouldn't tell Brian his interpretation of the idiom was wrong. It was more about blacksmiths and swords than ironing boards. What she was doing had nothing to do with ironing a shirt, which was good. As Brian had just pointed out, she was the least domesticated woman in Glen Allyn. Maybe in New Jersey.

"Besides, your favorite way of dealing is to act first, think second."

"Hiding books in the library is just about the same as banning them. Either way, it's not acceptable." She patted a pile of books on her table. "So, here we are. Making that statement."

"Well…" He looked around. "We've been down this road, you and I, making statements. Maybe this time you need to retreat a little."

"Nope. I don't think so."

He sighed. "I guess that means I have to call in the big guns."

Fern moaned.

Tootsie was afraid he would say that. Because she knew what he meant about bringing in the big guns. Or said more correctly, the big gun.

Black Windbreaker.

Who Brian must have called already because there he was, pulling up in his big, black Ford F-150. He took his time getting out. He took even more time ambling over to the table.

Fern came to her feet. "I'm getting really cold sitting here, Tootsie. I think I'll go sit in my car."

As Fern hurried into the parking lot, her bright red and white skirt swishing around her ankles, she gave Steve a teeny, little wave, but didn't stop for any social niceties.

Incensed that Fern would leave her in her moment of need...although what that need was, she wasn't sure, considering this was her lover strolling toward her...Tootsie prepared herself for a good rationalization that would hold him off until she could hand out more books to more people.

"This is some set up," he said, as he reached her. And of course, as he always did, he gave her a kiss. She liked that part even if she was getting ready to be steamed at him.

He stepped back and stared down at her. "You look a little cold, babe. How long have you been out here?"

"Not long enough," she said, all grumpy. "I've still got work to do here."

"Yeah, I know. But, babe, think. You're going to irritate Mrs. Feinstein. Maybe get her all hot and bothered. Maybe she'll call the police."

"That's already happened." She looked Brian's way. Who shrugged, held up his hands, and shook his head. "Nope. I'm retiring. I'm only here because nobody wants to escalate this thing. According to the chief, Feinstein is getting ready to call the state cops."

"Who aren't going to come," Tootsie insisted. "Because this isn't their jurisdiction."

"Don't bet on it," Steve murmured.

She turned back to him and gave him a death glare. "Remind me again why you just showed up? I mean other than the fact that my alleged friend, Brian, called you? Aren't you busy with a paying client, looking into their security needs?"

"Well, yeah." He ruffled her curls. And grinned outright, something he hardly ever did. "But I needed to pick something up and bring it down here for you. I thought you'd like that."

With suspicion, she gave him a squinty-eyed stare. "What would that thing be?"

He reached into his pocket and pulled out a folded-up piece of paper. "Here you go, Toots. Your permit for the demonstration."

Look at that…she wasn't ticked off at him at all.

Only much later, after they were all back in the dining room/office—and no, not one uniform had shown up during the rest of the time she and Fern—who wasn't so cold after all—with a cease-and-desist order—did Tootsie tell Steve the whole story. She started with where she'd found her aunt's Candy books, stashed away in the back of the library basement, to when she stamped upstairs and tore up her library card in front of the Feinstein woman. "I should stop calling her Feinstein and call her Flintstone. Maybe Wilma. She's definitely prehistoric."

"Yabba dabba doo," Steve murmured. "I just have one more question."

"Oh yeah?" She was back to the wary part. "What would that question be?"

"Are there any Candy La Plume books left in any bookstore anywhere in this part of New Jersey?"

"If there are, the store employees held them in the back, so they'd have some stock left."

"Remind me how many you gave out today."

"All of them. Who can resist a free book?"

"Does Adele know what you've been doing all afternoon long?"

Tootsie had a moment as her brain went into temporary lockdown. She hadn't even told Adele what she intended. *Oops.* Maybe she should have?

"Um, no." She pointed in the direction of her aunt's house. "I think I'll walk over that way and clue her in, so she's not surprised when someone calls and tells her how much they loved her book, and she asks where it was purchased."

"Make sure you're home for dinner. We're having one of your favorites."

"Oh?" She was all ears. "What are you making?"

"Country Chicken Captain."

She practically salivated. "I won't be long." And she headed across their adjoining lawns to knock on the front door.

Her aunt was home. Looking a little distracted.

"Hi." Concerned, Tootsie placed a hand on her aunt's forearm. "What's going on? Have you gotten a call from Basil? Is he being a jerk to you?"

"No." For once her aunt's hair looked like she hadn't combed it, an oddity because neat was her go-to. "I've been writing."

She looked beyond Tootsie, who was still standing in the foyer by the front door. "But I went outside just before and saw something that I wish I hadn't."

Tootsie's neurotransmitters jerked awake. "What did you see?"

She pulled the door open and stepped out onto the top step. Tootsie followed. "Do you see?"

At first Tootsie saw nothing. Because she'd cut across the lawns, not up the front walk. But then she saw them, scripted in dark red chalk. On Adele's front sidewalk.

Bring back the Salem Witch Trials.
Bitch.
Fucking Bitch.
Shut your maw.

The two women stood and stared in silence.

And then Tootsie said, "Well, at least whoever came by to leave this message for you knows their history."

"Not funny, Tootsie-leh," her aunt murmured. Gone was her usual zippiness.

Tootsie clutched her arms to herself and shivered. "I didn't mean it to be funny." Well, she did.

Because they had to lighten the threat of the words so they both didn't go screaming off in fright.

"We need to show this to somebody." Tootsie reached into her pants pocket for her phone. She called Steve. He hot footed it right over.

Hands on hips, he looked down and then he retrieved his phone and took a couple of pictures. Then he made a phone call. Minutes later while the three of them talked about who could have done it, a squad car eased up against the curb. One of Glen Allyn's finest—someone Tootsie didn't know yet, but Steve did—took out a pad and wrote a report. Or at least that was what Tootsie figured he was doing.

While she waited for him to finish, Steve sent Adele over to their house to wait for them to come home.

Tootsie called after her, "Tell Chris to bring a bucket of warm water and a mop."

Minutes later, Chris was there, the equipment she'd requested in hand. After a quick scowl, he went to work getting rid of the scary, disgusting messages. When he finished, he propped the mop up and leaned on the handle. "What are you going to do about this?"

He looked, as he usually did, to Steve for the answer.

To Chris said, "An old friend I worked with up in Fort Lee called me just before I came over here. He's been looking into helping us find out who the troll is."

He turned fully to Tootsie. "We have a lead."

CHAPTER THIRTEEN

"This is good news," Tootsie said, eyeing the sidewalk where the red had been obliterated. To Steve, she said, "What kind of lead did you get?"

"I told you, didn't I, that Bert volunteered to help us out? He doesn't have the whole picture yet, but he will soon enough. One thing he wants us to do is stop calling this asswipe a troll and start calling him what he is: a cyberbully."

"Yes, indeed." Adele was back. Apparently, Adele hadn't been willing to be stashed for safety in Tootsie's house. "I wonder if the cyberbully is the one who wrote these terrible words on my sidewalk."

Steve turned a fond gaze on her. "Aunt Adele, you really shouldn't be out here in the cold. You should go back to the house."

Adele was all but a child's height compared to Steve. But as she drew herself up to her full, inconsequential height, it was as if she looked him right in the eye. "I will not allow this *paskudnik,* this rude, awful person to make me hide away like a scared, little girl. If I should be standing on my own front walk with my family, then that's what I plan to do."

So there. And Steve did his usual. He smiled without smiling. "Okay."

Chris piped in, "There's this kid at school. He's kind of a nerd without any friends because nobody wants to be friends with him. I could ask him if he knows about cyberbullies."

Tootsie cocked her head to the side. "What makes you think he'd know? Do you think he could be one?"

"Nah. It's just that he's always in the computer lab after school's over. He's always bragging he knows more about everything on the internet than anyone. I could ask him. He'd be like all over it and happy I'm talking to him, since no one else does, just so he can show how he's all smarter than me."

Steve asked, "Does this kid have a name?"

Chris was Steve's creature. Meaning for Chris, Steve was a god. He could do no wrong. But this time Chris just had to roll his eyes. "Yeah, he has a name. Logan."

Steve ignored the eye roll. "What about a last name?"

Eyebrows down, mouth twisted up in his 'I'm trying to remember mode', Chris said, "I think it's Sausalito or something like that."

Tootsie bit back a grin. "Maybe you're thinking a location not a name?"

Adele prompted, "Though that's a place name in California. I suppose it could be a last name as well. Yes."

She gave the boy a pat on his shoulder. The boy gave her a broad smile.

Whatever she might have thought she stopped thinking when Steve said, "Then, yeah. You do that, Chris. Find out what Logan has to say."

"Maybe he thinks *I'm* the nerd," Chris said, glum-faced, when he came home from school the next afternoon having failed to get Logan to help.

Tootsie, busy chopping up onions, carrots, and celery for her minestrone, which Steve had asked her to make, looked up. "There are some people you just can't make friends with. Even if you ask, they won't help you, no way, no how. It happens that way with all of us from time to time." She hoped that would make him feel like he wasn't a total failure because he hadn't gotten this Logan kid to talk to him.

"Steve's friend Bert will get back to us in a couple of days," Tootsie continued. "I'm betting he'll either tell us who this jerk cyberbully is or be close to knowing."

This didn't satisfy Chris. But he was more easily distracted considering soup would be in his near future and there were some good leftovers in the refrigerator.

Chris had gone up to his room by the time Steve came in through the garage, car keys jingling in his hand. "You want to take a ride? I have to pick up a part at Auto Zone and bring it over to Johnnie V's. But first I want to stop at the 7-11 and pick up a couple of lottery tickets. The jackpot for the mega lottery is $500 million. That's a number we could live with."

She looked up from her cut-up veggies. "It might be bad luck for me to go with you. There's already been a winning lottery ticket in my life." She reminded him of when Arlo had won a $10 million dollar lottery and had to share it with her when they divorced.

"C'mon, Toots. I just want you to take a ride with me. Forget about bad luck and the *malocchio*.

Wiping her hands on a towel, she said, "Okay, I'll go with you. But stop mentioning the *malocchio*. *Kenahora*."

Calling upstairs to let Chris know they'd be gone for a few, she stuck the veggies in a bowl and put them in the refrigerator. She'd finish the soup when they got back.

Steve dropped her off at the 7-11, saying he'd be right back. The store was busy, as usual. There was a guy, his cap worn backwards, stuffing bags of ice into a rickety cart. Party time, Tootsie decided.

A boy about six or seven was standing in front of a candy display while his mother cautioned him that he could only have one. Meanwhile he had three bars in his hand already.

There was a short line in front of the cash register where the people who were feeling lucky—or maybe they were just doing what they always did—were buying their lottery tickets.

She stood in line behind a tall, muscular man. He turned slightly.

It was him. It was Trey Mangold.

She backed up on quiet feet. She could wait until later to buy her lottery tickets. The drawing wouldn't be until tonight and that would be on West Coast time. She excused herself to the woman behind her and headed outside to a bench which she decided was a good place to wait for Steve.

Even if it was threatening to snow.

Even if it was frigid cold.

Because for once in her life, Tootsie decided to give her 'tude a rest and not start a figurative fist fight in the 7-11 with Trey Mangold.

The slats of the bench were cold on her tush, but she could stand it. Which is what she told Steve when she called to tell him why she was waiting for him outside.

"Are you okay if I wait for this part at Auto Zone? Or do I need to come for you now?"

She gave a convulsive shiver. Because, hello...it was cold enough to freeze her brains. And she was still too near to Trey Mangold, though she was outside. In public. "Just wait for the part. I'm fine."

"Do not and I'll repeat myself, *do not* engage with Mangold. I don't care if he sits down next to you. If he does, you get up and walk away. Walk back into the store where there are people."

"Okay," she said, and he hung up, and wouldn't you know it...all the luck. That was the moment Trey Mangold plopped his big body down on the bench next to her.

Her knees flexed. She would do what Steve told her to do. Get up. Go into the store. She would move away from the taco.... uh, the danger.

But... That was a smirk on Trey's face. His mouth turned up on one side and his eyes filled with shards of contempt. For her.

Excuse me, but her neurotransmitters wouldn't let her walk away.

Not smart, not smart, not smart her inner voice, who was the one in possession of all her brains, sounded quietly in her...well, not her ear but somewhere inside.

Like she was going to pay attention to that? Uh, no. "Could you find another place to sit, please," she snapped.

He propped big, fleshy hands on his knees and swiveled toward her. "I need you to back off my family."

"Family?" She gave him the 'eyes-open-wide' thing. "What am I doing to your children?"

Disgust ripped across his face. "Not my children. My wife."

"Oh, your wife. Hmm." Tootsie's heartbeat began to beat a fast tattoo. Her neurotransmitters were up, swords drawn from their scabbards, preparing themselves for whatever she wanted from them, including launching a psychic attack on the man who was seated sitting next to her. Her mouth readied itself to deliver vintage snark.

Thank goodness, that was when she remembered Black Windbreaker saying it was not good to poke the bear. The fact that this particular bear was a really big bear put an exclamation point on that warning.

Which was probably why she shouldn't say something like if Melanie was a big girl, she would have delivered her own message rather than sending him to do it for her.

She pressed her lips together in case that smack-down slipped out. Not that Trey would understand her silence. But then, she couldn't help herself.

"If there is something I'm doing that your wife doesn't like, she should tell me herself. Believe me. I'm not hard to find."

Said that way, it wasn't too snarky. Or so she told her inner voice. Said voice pointed out that, given the

way Trey's face had morphed into something seriously unpleasant, her question was oh yeah, snarky and
oh yeah, so not acceptable to the Neanderthal next to
her.

Her neurotransmitters muttered a group *oy vey*.
She'd done what Steve had told her not to do: she'd
poked the bear.

She inched away from him.

His face had colored up an interesting shade of
red. Maybe mauve, maybe rose? She wasn't sure, because seriously…did she have a color wheel in her
head?

It was interesting, though, that his nostrils had
begun to flare.

It was time. To leave. Now. She began to stand.

He laid a heavy hand on her shoulder and pushed
her back down.

Her neurotransmitters took a stutter-step
back…the cowards.

Trey growled, "I'm not through with you. You'll
walk away when I say and not until then."

"Is this the way you talk to your wife?"

Oops. Words just couldn't help themselves,
could they?

There was no longer any question about the col-
or of his face. It was maroon. He hissed, "You fucking bitch."

Of all the names people called her, this one was
so not her favorite.

"You people." He gritted out the two words. Like they were poison and he needed them out of his system. "You think you can force your ideas down our throats."

You people? Which people? Tootsie wanted to ask. But the fact that they were alone on this bench, and that he still had his hand on her shoulder, way too close to her neck, for the moment it kept her from asking something that would have that hand moving to cut off her air supply. Besides, her neurotransmitters wanted to know what he meant.

"Back in the day, things were good. Life was peaceful. People got along. There was none of this…" He came to a stop, waved his free hand around. Then he made a fist and punched hard against the back of the bench.

Tootsie tried to lean away. His hand tightened on her shoulder, stopping her retreat.

"There was none of this filth that good people have to put up with these days, like what's in those books your aunt writes. You could send your kids to the library and not worry they'd come back poisoned."

"Poisoned?" Her head began to pound. "What is your deal?"

Trey's eyes began to glow. Like Satan was trying to break out. "You don't know? You are one dumb, fucking bitch."

"You're repeating yourself," she threw back at him.

He ignored the shot. "My wife and I know what those books can do."

"What?" she snapped. "Entertain? Maybe even help women feel better about themselves?"

He leaned into her. He was so close now that she could smell his sour breath.

"Let go of me," she gritted under her breath. She cast a look around. What was going on? Where was everyone? It was like suddenly no one wanted to buy their lottery ticket at the 7-11.

He pressed his fingers into her shoulder. He must have hit a nerve. Pain shot down her arm and up into her head.

"Her books are dangerous. I don't care what you say. My wife and I will do whatever we need to do to keep your bitch, Jewish lady aunt's books out of circulation."

"Huh. Oh, great," she snapped at him. "Like always. The Jewy part comes into play. Good to know that some things never change."

He ignored her comeback to that not-so-veiled bit of nicety. "That includes all those other books she wrote about teaching history."

He turned his head and spat on the sidewalk. "Teach...those books don't teach. They groom. You can say what you want. We know. Others know. Embedded in those chapters are instructions about how to make kids forget what their parents are teaching them—"

"You mean teaching as in don't confuse me with the facts, my mind was long ago made up?" she interrupted.

He shook her. Now the grip he held her in didn't just hurt, it burned, it throbbed. It had tears coming into her eyes.

"Shut up. You don't have any idea what facts are. We have the right facts."

"Yes," she wheezed, now finding it hard to breathe. "It's easy to believe that facts can be factual for some people and not for others. That's a misconception started by people like you who think they're puppet masters and puppetry is some kind of righteous thing. That is one big problem."

"No." His voice was a bear-like growl now. "We know people right here in Glen Allyn who think like we do. We'll be talking with them soon about the next steps we need to take to cleanse the library of all of Adele Silverstein's books and other books that are just as bad."

How it worked that those were the words that gave her the strength to work herself out from under his hand, she wouldn't question. Not when the best thing she could do now was for once in her life do that primal thing: take flight. Back to where people were. Inside the 7-11.

She stumbled inside and shimmied along the line of people waiting to buy their lottery tickets to the front, right in front of the clerk. Out of the corner of her eye, she saw Trey opening the door, coming toward her.

Surely someone in this line would protect her against him.

Uh, except they were all now ticked at her because it looked like she'd cut the line that was long enough already and what none of them wanted was to be standing here any longer than they already needed to.

So, no help there.

"Do you have the key to the bathroom?" she blurted to the clerk.

"On the hook," he said, without looking up.

"The hook where?" She was beginning to feel desperate. Because no hook was in her line of sight.

The first man in line tapped her shoulder and pointed. Right there in front of her. Duh.

She gave him a quick thanks, snatched the key, and hightailed it toward the bathroom, which was down a long hallway at the back of the store near the outrageously overpriced single serve cups of mac and cheese and other equally bad-for-you food.

She yanked the metal door open and stumbled inside, pulling it closed after her and sliding the lock into place. She collapsed against the door, struggling to catch her breath. "Well, that was a lot of fun, Tootsie," she muttered. Only then did she look around at her sanctuary.

If a public bathroom could be called a sanctuary.

It had the usual accoutrements. A toilet, a sink, a bar next to the toilet for people with disabilities to pull themselves up after they did their business, and a paper towel dispenser on the wall. Next to the sink was the garbage can. It was overflowing with paper. Naturally.

But shockingly, all the fixtures were clean. Somebody had not only disinfected...the smell of bleach lingered in the air...but they'd even washed the floor. Which meant, if she had to do her business, which she didn't, she could risk it without too many germs jumping up from the floor, and worse, onto the toilet seat to latch onto her naked, innocent tush.

Tootsie was not one for public bathrooms. But then, she was in this one not because she had to make use of it for the usual reasons. It was because though there were plenty of people on the other side of the door who might help her if they were so inclined, they were all pretty much involved in imagining what it would be like to buy a beach house on a Caribbean Island and a Lamborghini in which to tool around town. Which meant they weren't inclined.

Tootsie flipped her phone out of her pocket. She pressed her number one pre-set.

"Talk to me," came that wonderful voice.

"You need to get here, please."

"What happened? Tell me where you are."

She told him.

"I'm on my way. But I'm stopped at the train crossing at the end of Martling waiting for one of

171

these 100-car trains to pass. You stay where you are. Do you understand?"

She opened her mouth. And closed it. To keep from letting the 'duh, ya think' fly. "Yes, I understand."

"I mean it, Tootsie. Even if you think the son of a bitch might be gone, you don't move."

"I understand. How long will you be?"

"Minutes after this train passes, I'll be there."

"Okay."

He hung up before she could ask him if he wouldn't consider finding another crossing, but she knew there wasn't one, not for miles, and that would take longer anyway. But she was safe, wasn't she? Trey couldn't get in. She could wait for however long it took, couldn't she? *Yes*, her inner self spoke up. *So, stop with your usual high drama*, it told her.

Which Tootsie really didn't want to hear.

Except seriously. Was she in any immediate bodily danger? Nope. Except there was this one thing. It was weird that there was no heat in this bathroom. Or maybe it was just that it was at the end of the line and the heat didn't get to it. It had walls...cinderblock walls...so maybe no insulation.

Suck it up, the inner voice said. Her neurotransmitters had laid themselves down. They had never trained to fight in the cold.

She flexed her hands. She'd left her gloves in one of the cup holders in the console in Steve's truck, and her fingers were starting to turn blue. Well, not blue as in real blue, but imaginary blue.

"High drama," she muttered to herself. "Your fingers will turn pink again. Someday. They will. When your man rides to the rescue."

Hiding out in a bathroom, one that was pretty clean, as public bathrooms went, she'd do it. Wait. She folded her hands up into her armpits to warm her fingers and forget about frostbite. "Suck it up," she whispered. Then she said it, again.

Except the smell of the bleach was getting to her. Her sinuses were exploding behind her cheekbones. She'd never had a bleach headache. She hadn't known there was such a thing. But you learned something new every day.

She marched around in a circle. Her heels tap, tap, tapped on the tile floor. Her sinuses began to cry. Or said another way, her nose began to run.

She looked at her watch. It had been three minutes. She took out her phone. Her finger hovered over the pre-set. And curled back into her palm. She would *not* call him again. Like she was checking on the train's progress.

Besides, the likelihood that Trey was still out there was slim. Seriously, didn't he get that she was done with him? And wasn't he done with her? Besides which, what would he do if she stepped out of the bathroom right this moment? If he was standing on the other side of the door just waiting for her to open it, he couldn't exactly drag her out of the 7-11 without someone saying something, could he? Because there would be some people who'd already bought their tickets and the ones who'd bought the scratch-off kind, well they were scratching off that stuff to see if they were instant, if smaller, winners. Among all those people, surely someone would say, "Leave the lady alone, dude."

Was she willing to bet that one person among those many would do the right thing for her?

Yes. She was 97% sure. Which was when she came to a decision. She was not going to wait to be saved. She would save herself. By exiting this bathroom and standing her ground against Trey Mangold.

She slid the bolt out of the locked position at the top of the door, took hold of the knob and pulled. It didn't budge. Okay, so this door was a tough one. Good that it would remain shut when someone was inside. She pulled again.

Nothing.

Now, she took hold of the knob with both hands and yanked.

More nothing.

Once more with feeling and a whole lot of bracing her feet against the tile floor while she pulled as hard as she could.

She got nowhere.

Maybe she was going about the thing the wrong way? Maybe her angle was wrong?

She stood off to the side. Like she'd be pulling back against the opening. The only thing she accomplished this time was a sharp pain in both wrists. And her hands, though still cold, oddly starting to warm.

She stood back, put her hands on her hips and stared down at the knob. And knew.

The door was not about to budge.

She was locked in.

CHAPTER FOURTEEN

Just like that, it was time for hot flash city, which meant if she was going to manage her situation, she needed to get rid of what would broil her to an imaginary crisp: her coat. She flipped the buttons open and pushed it off her shoulders. For one teeny, little second, she told herself to drop her coat on the floor. She liked it a lot. She'd bought it on sale at Needless Markup.

Clean as this place was, if she did, she'd have to throw the coat away. There were germs that were bleach resistant. So, instead of dropping it where she stood, she hung it on the back of the door.

Now, she was prepped to tackle the knob once more.

She laid her hands on the knob again and took a big breath. As she filled her lungs with as much ballast as she could there was a knock.

She froze.

"Tootsie?"

Her curls shocked themselves straight. She knew that voice. It was Trey. After all.

She took a step away from the door. She did not answer by saying yes, it's me.

"Tootsie, I know you're in there. You need to come out."

She shivered, yanked her coat off the hook, slid her arms into it, and rebuttoned every last button right up to the neck.

"I've been waiting for you right here. If you don't come out soon, I'm coming in."

She barked a laugh. She couldn't help it. "You can't come in," she shouted. "This bathroom is in use."

She glanced down at her watch. Two minutes had passed from the last time she'd looked at it. How come it was only two minutes when she needed time to speed up like it usually did when she didn't have enough of it. But no. This time, time decided to take its own sweet—

She shut her eyes. "Time," she muttered.

He knocked again. "Why don't you come out and face me. Unless you're afraid."

The Tootsie whose back went up when she was taunted opened her mouth to tell him threatening her would not be a good thing because…because why? What exactly was she thinking? She zipped her lip shut.

But Pinhead Trey wasn't giving up. "You know I can push this door open anytime I want to."

Did those words sound enticing? Friendly? Cajoling?

None of the above. Tootsie reached up and shot the door bolt home. In case somehow Trey was able to shoulder the door open. The bolt slid into place with a satisfying *clunk*.

"You can't come in. The door's stuck. Now it's locked. So, maybe you should just go away. Besides, you should know that…"

No. She would not do it. She would not say that her lover, Black Windbreaker, was on his way. She was not going to let Pinhead know that she was a wussy, weak woman who needed to be rescued by a man. No way. She'd asphyxiate into a bleach-induced coma before she'd admit to that.

As that last phantasmagorical thought crossed her frontal lobe, he began to bang on the door with one steady thud after another.

"What the—"

Wasn't there anyone out there in the 7-11? Yeah, the bathroom was down a long hallway and away from the lottery action. Surely someone else had to go to the bathroom.

More thudding.

"What are you afraid of?" His voice crooned through the door crack. And didn't those words make her think there was a whole lot more to be afraid of than she'd already imagined?

She stared at her watch again. Time was crawling along, but she sing-songed in her head that her Black Windbreaker would be here soon.

Meanwhile, what would happen if Trey actually was able to slam the door open?

Tootsie's imagination, never of the shy, retiring type, went into overdrive. "He can and you know it, girlfriend," she gritted to herself.

"I'm giving you two minutes only and then this door is coming down."

She slapped a hand over her mouth and looked around for a weapon. Except for the towel dispenser, which she really didn't think she could rip off the wall, there wasn't one.

So, what were her options? She could step to the side and when he slammed the door open, she could wait until he was inside the bathroom, and slip out past him and then run like hell.

Sounded like a plan. Although, he might grab her and...

She stamped her foot. What in the name of all that was holy was she getting so torqued out over? They were in a public place, a store, for goodness sakes. What could happen? Besides, though he spoke like he was threatening her with bodily harm, why would he?

She clutched her arms to herself and stamped a foot, once. "Have you got amnesia?" She whispered to herself. "Do you not remember when he put that paw on your shoulder and squeezed? Yes, he would hurt you."

She would not look at her watch again. And she wouldn't call Steve to tell him to hurry. He already was hurrying, as much as that train would let him.

Besides, didn't she just say she was no wussy, weak woman? She could rescue herself. There had to be a way. Wait—there was a window! It had a lever at the bottom. She could just flip it open, climb up on the garbage can, which looked sturdy enough to hold her and voilà, she would escape to freedom.

Quick as she could she shoved the garbage can over to the window. Scrunched up papers leaked from beneath the lid and fell onto her hands. If her skin could have screamed it would have.

"When I get out of here, I am disinfecting myself all over."

She slung her purse around her neck and, to the sound of steady banging on the door, she scrambled onto the garbage can. It teetered in one direction and then the other. And then it went over. She jumped and stumbled back as the lid gave up the ghost and what seemed like thousands of used pieces of paper people had wiped their hands on...and hopefully nothing else...spilled out onto the floor.

She looked up at the window and swallowed a shout of frustration and rage.

The banging increased in frequency. "I'm coming in!"

No, no, no. She looked with hope at the lock which, though it was shuddering, held. She reached into her coat pocket for her phone. The banging continued without letup. She put her phone back into her coat pocket. She had to go with the only thing she had left. She had to be a wussy woman.

Dammit.

"Trey, you know Steve DiLorenzo, right?"

The banging stopped.

Heartened, she continued. "I just texted him..." Which, hello, was a fib but he didn't have to know that. "To let him know where I am. Do you really want to be on the other side of this door, when he drives up and comes inside this 7-11 to look for me?"

Silence.

Then Trey said, "I don't give a crap about him. You can text him back and tell him to bring it on. I'm ready. Anytime."

On that lovely boast, the door shuddered with what Tootsie now assumed was Trey throwing his considerable weight against it. It shuddered a second time. Then came a muffled sound, a single syllable, which Tootsie took to be a curse word. Which heartened her more than she could have ever thought.

Was the Pinhead starting to realize that he couldn't open this door no way, no how?

There was one more bang, a fist this time, and then, "I'm not done with you, lady. You're a menace to good people. If I was you, I'd think about keeping that piehole of yours shut."

There was another bang, and the sound of footsteps receding.

She took a deep breath. Only then did she realize that she'd been holding it. She patted her chest, where her heart was exercising itself in ways it didn't need to. "Good riddance to you, Trey Mangold. I hope I never see you again."

But she knew that wasn't going to happen, that with her luck, she'd see him way sooner than she wanted to.

Right now, planning for what to do when that happened had to take a back seat to the issue at hand. Getting out of this room. Now that she wasn't in imminent danger of harm, which she knew might be physical...meaning Pinhead might grab her by the turtleneck, pull her up, and shake her like she was a limp rag...she made her phone call to Steve.

"Talk to me. Tell me you're okay."

For sure no preamble, no hello.

Giving him no hello back, she said, "I'm okay, Trey left. But I'm locked in the bathroom, and I can't get out."

There was only a short silence and then came, "You're in the bathroom and you can't get out?"

Despite the fact that Antarctica had to be warmer than this bathroom, she felt another hot flash coming on. "You don't have to make like it's a meme. Just get here, already."

And she disconnected. Because though she couldn't hear it through the connection, she knew because she knew the man, that he was driving his truck as fast as the law would let him, maybe faster. And now that he knew she was safe, he was laughing himself silly over the *I'm locked in the bathroom and I can't get out* thing.

"Thanks ever so much," she muttered, and waved vigorously in front of her face. Like that had ever helped before or ever would help calm the wicked heat saturating her body. Or keep her warm.

Only minutes later she heard quick steps coming toward her refuge. "Tootsie?"

She took a deep breath. Her man was here. Her knees, which had done a yeoman's job keeping her locked in the upright position, decided it was time to leave her to function on her own. That hand clutching the doorknob kept her from falling to the floor. That would have been the end of every piece of clothing she was wearing if she did fall. Well, not her underwear. Although if there was any bleach smell remaining after she washed them, they were going, too.

She slipped open the bolt. "I think the door is swollen although how it would be so swollen in cold weather, I have no clue. You might have to get the manager who surely has been around when the door has gotten stuck before this."

"He's here with me," came Steve's voice. "Stand away from the door, babe. We're going to force it open, now."

She complied. There was the sound of some jiggling and then, without any loud banging, the door opened and swung back on some well-oiled hinges.

Gaping at the two men in the doorway—her Black Windbreaker and a short, skinny man she took to be the manager—she said, "How did you do that? I couldn't open it at all, no matter how hard I tried."

The manager, peering in, said, "There's only one way to open it. You need to know how, like I do. Then it's easy." When he saw the garbage can on its side, with paper and the rest of what people who had preceded her in this bathroom had strewn all over the floor, he gave her a dirty look.

Giving the manager her own brand of dirty look, she said, "Maybe you should have a sign on the door with how-to-open instructions. Maybe you should put up an out-of-order sign because from what you're saying, everyone who wants to use this bathroom is going to get stuck. You don't want anyone else to think the only way out is through the window."

Disbelief marked the man's face. The look on Steve's face said, *yeah, why not?* Of course, exiting through the window, which was seven feet off the ground and climbing up on a garbage can that wouldn't hold your weight being the only way to do it made all kinds of sense.

She wouldn't look at him. Instead to the manager, she said, "Please get someone in here to fix this door. I'll pay that person whatever they charge you."

That was all the man had to hear to become gracious. Well, almost gracious. "I guess I can do that. You're like the third or fourth person this week I've had to jimmy it open for."

Steve, who had not involved himself in that exchange, held out a hand to her. "C'mon, Toots. Let's go home."

Didn't those sound like the best words ever spoken?

Though Tootsie knew Steve had been laughing at her expense over getting locked in the bathroom, he didn't do any laughing, now. He glanced across the console as he backed out of the space in front of the 7-11. "You look like you need a hot shower."

"It will be the first thing I do when we get to the house." She'd snatched gloves out of the cup holder where she'd stashed them and pulled them on. She folded her arms around her torso and lifted her toes toward the floor vent where heat was pouring out. Not that any of it did any good. She was shivering almost uncontrollably. It was not from the cold.

He reached across the console, pulled one of her hands out from the pretzel she'd wound herself in and wrapped it in his big, warm, magical hand, his glove to hers. "Tell me the details. After."

"Yeah, the details. He threatened me. I'm doing something he doesn't like. I understood that part. What I couldn't understand was his reasoning. He talked in circles."

Steve tightened his fingers on hers. "Did you ask him to give you the details?"

She knew why she hadn't. "I didn't really have an opening for that."

Which as fibs went, was a big one. She'd had plenty of openings. She'd used each one to snark at him.

"I have something to tell you."

"After today and my delightful interlude in a room I never want to enter ever again, I hope whatever it is you need to tell me is going to be something good. Like Johnnie V has started to sell lottery tickets, you bought one and it's a winner. Oh, and there's a tropical beach vacation in my immediate future, like the next five minutes."

He gave her one quick look of reproach. "Be serious."

This flush that bathed her face was not of the hot flash kind. It was of the 'I'm still kind of shaken by that whole business in the bathroom' kind. "Okay."

Which, once said, she knew he would take the way she meant it. As an apology. "So, what do you have to tell me?"

"I know who the cyberbully is."

She pulled her hand from his and sat up straight. "Who?"

"He's Melanie's son."

It wasn't until the next morning, early ish, they finally got down to a full discussion about the son. Yeah, last night, before they turned in, Steve had told Tootsie the kid was seventeen years old and did not live with the Mangolds. This morning, the three of them— Fern came in early having heard what had happened to Tootsie at the 7-11 the day before— were sitting at the dining room/office table. Tootsie was in her morning casual togs, meaning sweats and Steve was sitting in front of Tootsie's laptop.

He turned it around so Tootsie and Fern could see one of the Instagram accounts that belonged to the kid. "This was the easiest one to locate. Once Bert had it, he could trace the others."

Peering at the screen, Fern said, "The boy created an avatar, so we don't know what he looks like."

"Bert's on it. He'll text over the kid's picture when he's got one."

"Where does he live?" asked Tootsie, reading through some of what the boy had posted on his Instagram account.

"Also, something Bert is going to find out."

Tootsie leaned her elbows on the table and stared at the screen. "I'm looking at these horrid words this kid uses and remembering that story the librarian down in Flemington told us about how when Melanie and Trey destroyed my aunt's books, they took their kids with them. How had she infected her older child, even if he doesn't live with her? Who does that?"

"You don't know?" Fern snorted her disbelief. "Someone who was standing in the wrong line when they handed out kindness and decency. And respect. Those little kids of hers…they don't have a chance. She's teaching them the wrong values. I just don't know why."

Tootsie nodded, still staring at the screen. "I want to know why the older kid doesn't live with his mother and if he doesn't, how she's gotten him to be in her corner."

Steve closed the laptop lid.

Tootsie turned her cup around and then around again. "I'm going to find out."

"Toots."

She glanced up at Steve and smiled. "You're saying my name."

Fern made a scoffing sound. "I don't think he's just saying your name. He's warning you."

Steve gave Fern one of his patented non-smile smiles. "Thanks, Fern."

Sitting back, Tootsie looked first at Steve and then at Fern. She folded her hands in her lap. "What, you think I'm thinking of doing something you think I shouldn't?"

Steve sat back, too. He folded one leg over the other. "That's a lot of thinking."

Like innocence was her middle name, Tootsie said, "It doesn't have to be dangerous."

One eyebrow cocked, Steve said, "It doesn't have to. With you, it always is."

She gave him her wide-open-eyed look. "How about if you go with me to do what I'm thinking of doing?"

Uncrossing his legs, Steve sat forward and put both hands flat on the table. "Maybe not."

"You don't even know what I'm thinking."

Fern took out her fan.

Steve got the Black Windbreaker look on his face. "Tootsie, you just had to be rescued from a bathroom you locked yourself in to get away from that SOB, Trey Mangold. You told me about what you two talked about. He made it clear that he wants you to lay off his wife. You think whatever you're planning now, he's going to let it pass?"

"For what I'm thinking of doing, he won't even know. Until after."

"Tootsie."

Tootsie smoothed back her curls. "You can say my name as many times as you want. This business has gone too far. I can't let these people do what they're doing. As far as I can see, the only way I can do that, without getting into this trouble you worry about me getting into, is to keep asking questions, so I can get to the root of whatever it is that makes the Mangolds tick. Once I do, I can expose them for the frauds they are."

Fern moaned quietly.

Steve sat back once more. "Are you that sure?" The Black Windbreaker look receded but not much. Tootsie knew she hadn't given her man a good enough picture of what was on her mind and that's where all his doubts were coming from. Time to clarify.

"When Trey was entertaining me on that bench outside the 7-11, he told me there was some kind of meeting coming up and that many people in town will be attending."

Steve's eyebrows met in the middle. He gave her a slow nod.

"What would happen if we went, you and I?"

"You mean what would happen when you raise your hand to say you want to speak? You know the answer to that one."

CHAPTER FIFTEEN

Tootsie couldn't ignore her doubting Thomas of a man and the too correct point he was raising. She held both hands up, palms out. "I know. You think it won't work. It's because you don't think Melanie will answer any of my questions honestly, right?"

"Why should she? She has a position to keep to. In public."

"Except I did get to her that night with my paper costume."

"You did. Which might have helped her make her point, that nobody should listen to a grown woman who dresses like it's Halloween when it's not Halloween."

"There were plenty of people who appreciated my dress at that meeting. They understood."

"Plenty of people doesn't include Trey Mangold, who has you in his crosshairs," Steve pointed out.

There were points she was willing to concede to Steve. Like this one, which was too true. "Plenty of people at that meeting, and plenty who heard about it after, know what's right and what isn't. Banning books is a terrible thing. Melanie and Trey are on the very wrongest side of this business."

Fern turned off her fan and laid it on the table. "I agree. But even if most of Glen Allyn knows what the Mangolds are up to, do people still care? Tootsie, did you ever think that most people just move on?"

Tootsie knew what Fern meant. Too many people were experts at ignoring controversy. "Some people. Not all. And standing up against the Mangolds is right on so many levels." But her arguments were losing steam, considering these two people who were closest to her were making points she had to listen to.

Reasoning it through, something she was getting better at…thanks to admonitions from her strategically minded man…she realized that she had to find a better place where she could at least attempt to get Melanie to talk truth to her. "Okay, forget me facing Melanie down at a meeting." She held up a hand. "I might know of a place where I can track her down."

"Tootsie."

"Just wait. I'll explain," Tootsie said to Steve. "It won't be dangerous. The Mangolds have a dog. There's a dog run at Brookdale Park. A few times, lately, when I've been walking the perimeter…you know, exercise…I've spotted Melanie there, watching her dog play with other dogs. It's always at the same time of day."

Tootsie knew this, and while she didn't know what kind of dog the Mangolds had, she was willing to bet it was a bully kind of dog. Like Trey. Not a thought she'd share with Steve and Fern.

Because warnings. And admonitions.

"I'm thinking when I make my first circle at the park, I should amble over to where the dogs are and suggest Melanie and I have a talk."

Fern pursed her lips. "You think, after the paper costume, Trey slashing Viv's tires, and yesterday's meeting with him in the bathroom, she won't get up and walk away?"

Tootsie sat back. "Hmm. She might. But she's not the first woman I've gotten to talk to me who didn't want to. I trust that I'll be able to come up with something that will keep her stuck to her seat while I do my magic."

Yup. Tootsie trusted her annoying, seemingly idiotic way, of asking questions and making statements that got people to make disclosures they hadn't had any intention of making.

Steve came to his feet. "Just promise me one thing."

She got herself ready for how to deal with his warning.

She clutched her hands together. Hard. "Yes? What one thing?"

"Don't go to the park at night."

If she hadn't been sitting, she would have collapsed with relief. "Remember? Melanie is in the dog park at a specific time during the day. Besides, I would never visit Brookdale at night. All those big, beautiful trees that encircle the park's great lawn look so majestic in the daytime but look eerie and mysterious at night. Besides I'd be afraid I'd meet someone dangerous like Deliverance Man even though he wasn't dangerous that night I met him when I was walking home from the Elks Lodge in the pouring down rain. Even though Brookdale is closed to visitors after dark."

The way he pressed his lips together, she knew he was thinking she could've just said *yes, Steve I promise*... four simple words. Nope she had to go into high drama mode.

Before he could say it and prove that he knew what she was thinking, she added, "Okay. I promise. I won't go to the park after dark. How's that?"

His black eyes sparkled with his non-smile. "That's what I needed to hear." He grabbed his jacket from the chair where he'd thrown it. "I'm gone. I have to do a quick check on a project. If you're going to go, try for earlier. It's December. It gets dark at five."

Wasn't that some serious mansplaining to ignore.

As he closed the door from the kitchen foyer to the garage, Fern gave her that look that told Tootsie she wasn't ready to trust Tootsie wouldn't try to figure out a way to go along with his wishes and still do what she needed to do if she had to do something different.

"What?" Tootsie gave her an '*I am innocent*' look.

Fern shook her head. "You should've been a lawyer."

Tootsie's smiled and said, "I know you don't mean that as a compliment. I'm going upstairs, getting my sneakers, and a warm sweater to throw on over these sweats and heading over to the park for a little exercise. I need to work out some of these mental kinks I've gotten myself into with all these situations with the Mangolds."

"Mental kinks?" Fern fastened a look of disapproval on Tootsie. "Does that mean you should keep on with the crazy stuff? Because this time, the people you're after know you're after them."

To Fern's words, delivered in a raised voice...Fern hardly ever raised her voice...Tootsie said, "I understand, and you know I don't purposely put myself in a place where something could happen to me."

Fern's eyebrows hiked up together. "Purposely? Really? Yesterday was the bathroom. Before that, it was the tires and you had to walk home in the dark in the sleet and you met that guy. If you're talking bodily harm, he could have bodily removed you to a place where no one would find you and when someone did, you'd be dead. That would have destroyed my day."

Grabbing up her coffee cup and marching into the kitchen with it, Fern said, "I think I'll make myself an early lunch and hope that while you're doing your thing in Brookdale Park, all you're doing is exercise."

As it turned out, Melanie and her dog weren't there when Tootsie got to Brookdale. She swallowed her disappointment. Did that mean Melanie didn't come to the park at the same time each day. Would Tootsie have to come back? Pretend she was exercising more than once a day? She was allergic to exercise. But she did like to walk and walking in Brookdale rescued her from worries that never went away. Like this continuing worry about Aunt Adele and what the Mangolds had in mind for her.

She set out to make her first trip along the path that encircled the park's great lawn, feeling not so good about Melanie not being there so Tootsie could accost her.

As Tootsie came back to her starting point, there it was, serendipity in all its glory. There was Melanie. In the dog park. With *hoonts* galore. Including, no doubt, Melanie's.

Tootsie put her hand on the latch to open the fence and step inside. She paused. It was some circus. The dogs present came big, small, in between, and in every color, including combos of colors. Some were running every which way, like they'd been let out of solitary confinement.

Some were barking, like hello, please notice me and give me something I want, although you can't guess and since I can't talk human, you won't be able to figure it out. Some dogs were lying down in a corner, bored with the whole scene. Naturally, some were peeing against the fence, and because they, too, couldn't help themselves, there was one canine couple humping.

The dog on the receiving end was a mutt, with brown and white spots and a narrow, little face. The dog whose back end was gyrating a thousand miles a minute was a black and tan German Shepherd, with a black snout and a tongue hanging out of the side of his mouth as he panted in doggie pleasure. Tootsie hoped when the two of them were done, the poor little mutt would be able to stand.

None of the dog owners seemed to be more than a little interested. Melanie was one of them. She sat there, cell phone up in her face.

Tootsie stepped inside and, having looked at each dog, decided which one was Melanie's. It was the big, black dog with the flat face, the one that just stood there in the middle of the dog run. No dog came anywhere near this big guy. He was all muscle and yeah, Tootsie knew it was a he because what made him a he hung like another kind of animal, namely a bull. This dog didn't have to say a doggie word. Everyone who saw his equipment knew he was the alpha dog.

Yup. That had to be Melanie's dog.

Eyes averted from Alpha Dog…someone had once told her not to look at a dog who might be your enemy because they'd regard it as a challenge…she walked over and sat down next to Melanie. Who jumped.

After she got over the shock of who was sitting down next to her, Melanie fashioned her oh-so-not-really-lovely face into a look that said *you are so beneath me.*

Tootsie wasn't fazed.

"What are you doing here, Tootsie," Melanie said in her Betty Boop/Jessica Rabbit voice. Still, she managed to infuse major disdain in it. "You don't have a dog."

"I don't. But I was walking." Tootsie looked over her shoulder at the path circling the park behind her. She took a quick glance at Alpha Dog, who remained stock-still in his dominant doggie pose, and then back at Melanie. "I saw you and decided I needed to come over here and apologize to you."

If Tootsie had expected that any kind of emotion would replace the scorn that Melanie continued to wear in her eyes and on her mouth, it was good Tootsie hadn't taken a bet.

"I shouldn't have said those things about you that night at the library meeting, the one where I dressed up as banned books and intimated that you were...well, a book banner."

One of Melanie's eyebrows twitched. Her lips pressed themselves into one disappearing line.

Tootsie powered on. "Everyone is entitled to their opinion. Isn't it the American way?"

It was amazing to Tootsie that even when Melanie's lips were pressed so close together, they could still send a message of contempt.

Tootsie got herself ready. Because that little response of Melanie's was about to go away and be replaced with something Tootsie could actually work with.

"I get that when your husband slashed my tires that night—"

All that contempt Melanie had been telegraphing got replaced by outrage, maybe even a little guilt.

Which was gratifying. "Maybe you could say that was the kind of mischief the police might be interested in talking to him about, but hey, I can't really prove he did it...even if I know he did."

Melanie folded her arms hard across her chest. "Are you going to the police?"

"Didn't I just say I wasn't?"

Melanie's eyebrow twitched. "Why are you bringing it up, then?"

"Because like I say..." She checked that Alpha Dog wasn't ambling over toward them in order to interrupt. "I wanted to apologize. I began to think, yeah, Melanie and Trey are entitled to not like my

Aunt Adele's books. They are, after all, an acquired taste."

That was one way of describing stories of doms and submissives.

Melanie narrowed her eyes at Tootsie.

Yeah, she was trying to figure Tootsie out.

"I realized that those opinions of yours can only come from a good place, right?"

More wariness. But silence.

Tootsie went on. "As adults, we have to make decisions all the time. What do we stand for? What do we champion, and after a lot of thought, we might even say to ourselves, listen, there are these other things we don't like all that well and we need to call them out for what they are."

As those last words fell from Tootsie's mouth, Melanie dropped the attitude. And her arms. Sitting back, like now she was in her element, she said, "You've got that right."

"See?" Tootsie clapped her hands, once, twice. "I knew you and I would find common ground even if we don't have that much ground in common, but hey, we can always try to find some."

Melanie narrowed her eyes at Tootsie again. Well, sure. She didn't know what Tootsie had just said and what was coming next.

"Seriously, Melanie. I really want to understand your position. I'd ask you why you don't like sex."

Melanie bristled.

Tootsie held up a staying hand. "What I meant was you have children. You have two kids, right? So, sex. Or am I wrong?"

Melanie looked away. "You're right. I have two children."

"Yes, and they're over there at the playground, I bet, because when you're here with your dog, you wouldn't leave your children home alone, you're that good a mother."

Except you also happen to be a mother who has a child she's ignoring.

"I must say," she babbled on, "I'm ashamed to say I don't remember what they look like."

Looking toward the playground, Melanie unbent a little further while raising a hand and pointing to a little boy who was climbing up a fake rock face, and a little girl who was on a slide.

"They're so cute," Tootsie gushed. It wasn't quite the truth because she couldn't see them all that well because they were both on the far end of the playground. But it wasn't a lie either. Because they looked like they *might* be cute. "I'm sure you're really proud of them."

"I am," said Melanie, self-satisfaction softening the glare in her eyes.

Tootsie gave Melanie's Alpha Dog a glance and then looked away as quickly as she could. He'd turned his massive head in her direction.

A chill snaked down her spine. Maybe she wasn't going to be able to extract the info she needed from

Melanie because given Alpha Dog's girth and weight, if he got ticked off enough at whatever she was saying to his owner, he could probably jump on her and crush her flat. Before he ate her up with, though Tootsie hadn't seen them, a set of giant, pointy teeth.

But then, good fortune. Out of the corner of her eye, she saw him look away.

Tootsie breathed in relief. "It's too bad you and Trey didn't decide to have any more kids because it's obvious you two know how to produce cuteness."

Melanie colored up a brick-red.

Tootsie laid a hand on Melanie's wrist. "Oh, I'm sorry. Did I say something I shouldn't have?"

Well, yeah. She always said something she shouldn't have...to people who were so not doing the right thing and too, too bad about that.

Melanie slipped her hand out from under Tootsie's. "No. You didn't."

Uh-huh. "Well, I'll just change the subject back to what we were talking about. Like I said I was just looking for you to explain to me if because of the sex in my Aunt Adele's books...you know the ones she's written as Candy La Plume...you want the library to have them in something like...I don't know...an X-rated section."

"All that is true." Melanie's attention got drawn away by a whole lot of yip-yipping. It was coming from the two dogs who had been partying down and now seemed to be trying to say sayonara to each other and it wasn't happening.

Melanie said, "Sex between a husband and wife is a beautiful thing. It's meant to produce children."

Tootsie's gaze was fixed on the doggie couple, who were joined at, if not the hip, joined. "It looks like there might be some children production going on over there. What do you think?"

Melanie's lip curled. "They're animals. They're doing what's natural. What's in your aunt's books isn't natural."

From what Tootsie could tell, though she hadn't done a lot of what was in Adele's books, it was completely natural. She wouldn't raise the point with Melanie. Who was on a roll.

"When people who call themselves authors write books filled with sex acts outside marriage? Trey and I don't approve. We believe things should be the way they used to be before the internet. Like *Leave it to Beaver* and *My Three Sons*, where the mother and father both had roles that they stuck to, and everyone was happy. We should bring back more TV shows like those."

She stood. "Now that we know the real identity of Candy La Plume, we're not stopping with just those books of hers. All those books she wrote as A.S. Silverstein about teaching history need to go, too."

Tootsie stood, too. She shoved her hands in her pockets, so Melanie wouldn't see that she'd made them into fists. "They need to go where?"

"Why, in the same X-rated section where her other books are now lodged in the library. As far from prying eyes as possible. Those books are just too dangerous to be anywhere where teachers or anyone else can find them. Your aunt is not the good person everyone thinks she is."

Tootsie looked at Melanie askance. *What was this?* "Why do you say that? Do you know her personally?"

Melanie flushed. "I just mean your aunt should retire. She was already old years ago. She should not be writing books at her age."

And then she shook her head as if in fond disbelief. "My sweet doggie apparently hasn't been listening when we talk to our children about sex. But she's an animal so of course she wouldn't be listening." She pointed toward the terrier and the shepherd who were now just standing there waiting for the moment of separation that surely would arrive soon. Like two sections of a rocket.

Melanie clapped her hands. "Monster! Come here, girl." And the terrier who'd been made love to by a brute, dis-attached and trotted over to Melanie.

Tootsie looked down at the little doggie face, and the tail that wagged back and forth like she was just so happy with life. Then, Tootsie looked over at Alpha Dog and said, "I thought that big black dog over there was yours."

Melanie raised one eyebrow. "Well, I guess you're wrong about a lot of things these days, Tootsie."

With that, Melanie bent, gathered the terrier in her arms, turned on her heel and called for her two little Mangolds to leave off doing what they were doing because they were all going.

Tootsie stared after them. She'd learned a lot this afternoon. She bent to pick up her purse from the bench and straightened to take a step toward the door to the dog run.

And was stopped in her tracks.

By Alpha Dog.

Who was staring up at her like he'd been waiting this whole time for her to give him her undivided attention.

Her heart jumped into her throat. "Nice doggie," she whispered.

He panted at her.

She put her hands behind her back. Because she did not want him to think she was trying to pet him. Which no doubt when she did, he'd bite her hand off.

He took two doggie steps toward her so that now they were body to body. He panted some more. His giant tongue came out and hung down a good six or seven inches.

Was there a relationship between long tongues in a dog and their equipment the way it was said that a man with big feet and big hands had...no, she was NOT going there.

She began to giggle. Well, yeah. Nerves.

He seemed to have expected some kind of show of humor because now he opened his mouth wide, so she could see that yes, he did have some really, really big, pointy teeth.

"All the better to eat you with," she muttered, and the giggling became more pronounced.

She heard quick steps and out of the corner of her eyes she spied a short man wearing a track suit coming toward her.

"Oreo, what do you think you're doing?"

Shock and awe...the dog was named after a *small*, chocolate cookie.

Oreo turned his head toward the new voice. But he didn't abandon his post smack up against Tootsie.

The man grabbed Oreo's collar. "I'm sorry," he said to Tootsie. "He won't hurt you. If someone came into my house to rob it, he'd probably lick them to death."

Which is what Oreo did now as Tootsie abandoned her hands behind her back pose and tried to pet Oreo's head...now that she knew she'd be retaining her appendage.

But the dog was fast. Before she could touch his sleek, black head, he had that tongue wrapped around her wrist.

She would not shudder. She would not take a tissue out of her purse to wipe his saliva off her skin. Until after.

To his owner, who was now doing his own serial petting of his animal, Tootsie said, "Nice to meet you and Oreo. But it's getting dark, and I have to get home. Bye."

She turned and ran and wasn't ashamed of herself because she did. Only when she got to her car, had slammed the door behind her, and her heart rate eased itself down from 150 beats a minute to a nice sedate 75, did she pump her fist in triumph.

She'd met the enemy, and the enemy was hers. Melanie knew that Tootsie knew of her other child. Her body language, when Tootsie raised the subject, told her so.

She also learned that Melanie was programmed. The words she used to describe why she didn't like Adele's books sounded like she'd read them somewhere and made them a part of who she was.

"And somehow, you don't just not like my aunt. Or her books. You have a history with her. It's beyond time for me to find it out."

CHAPTER SIXTEEN

After coming back from the park, the first thing Tootsie did was walk across the adjoining lawns to Adele's house. When her aunt opened the door, Tootsie blurted, "How does Melanie know you?"

Adele stepped aside so Tootsie could come in. "Hello to you too, *mamaleh*. Why not come in? We can sit down, and you can start again with a nice hello, how are you, Aunt Adele."

Tootsie snorted a laugh and bent to give Adele a quick kiss on her cheek. After, when they were sitting down on Adele's maroon couch, Tootsie did start at the beginning of her dog run conversation with Melanie.

Adele folded her legs at the ankles and her hands in her lap. "I don't know the answer to that question."

Tootsie swiveled on her tush to face Adele more completely. "Is it possible you've met, and you don't remember?"

In a cool voice, Adele said, "I hope you don't think my mind is going, because I assure you if I'd met that woman before, I would remember."

Oops. Tootsie wasn't questioning the effect of age on Adele's ability to think and remember, but, of course, Adele had taken it that way. She regrouped. "Of all the places you've been, and all the people you've met, isn't it possible that you could have forgotten having met her, since by this time, she's long out of your life?"

Adele tilted her head to one side. "That's possible. Perhaps we met and I said something she took to be rude?"

"I think I can say from the few times I've been around Melanie, the woman has a fragile ego. Maybe at another time in *her* life she was too insecure to speak up for herself. It's possible she let people walk all over her, maybe even her own family. If she's overcompensating now, it would explain why she's so obnoxious."

"I suppose." Adele nodded. "I certainly saw enough insecure girls in my history classes over the years."

Tootsie grabbed Adele's hand. "Aunt Adele! Is it possible that Melanie was one of your students?"

An arrested look came over Adele's face. "Let me think for a moment." She took her hand from

Tootsie's and stroked her chin. "I don't remember a girl named Melanie in any of my classes. I would remember that name."

Tootsie looked toward the dining room where all the pictures hung on the walls. "She still could have been one of your students."

"That is quite true." Adele tapped her lip. "I wonder… "Could she have changed her first name?"

Tootsie slumped against the stiff back of the couch. "That makes some sense. How would we find out because I'm pretty sure if we asked her, she wouldn't tell us."

There was a knock on the front door. It was Chris.

He said, "Steve and I want to know when you're coming home. There's a big crossover event with Chicago, Med, Fire, and PD tonight and we don't want to eat dinner late."

A lightbulb came on. Tootsie grabbed Chris's hand and pulled him inside the house. "I'm not worried about missing anything. Steve is recording all of them. I'll watch after. Right now, Aunt Adele and I need to talk to you about you helping us with something we don't know how to do, but you will."

His face brightened. "Okay."

So, Tootsie told him what they wanted. "We don't really know anything about her or even where she comes from. We think she might have been one of Aunt Adele's students. But maybe they have met at one of her talks she's given over the years?"

"Or even at a book signing?" Adele prompted.

Tootsie was pretty sure that wasn't it, considering how much Melanie hated Candy La Plume's books. She wouldn't say that, though.

Chris screwed up his face, thinking of the mystery of where Melanie had come into Adele's life. His face cleared. "She definitely could have been in one of your classes, Aunt Adele."

Tootsie said, "If Melanie was in one of Aunt Adele's classes, how would you be able to find her?"

Adele added, "All those graduating classes were quite large. Perhaps 600 or so children each year. Will that be a problem?"

"Aunt Adele." Chris gave her that look that only teens have long perfected...the *you know nothing* look. "I can find her. When do you need to know? Is now, okay?" He pointed back toward Tootsie's house where the laptop Tootsie and Steve had bought for him was probably already open on the desk in his room and waiting for Chris to come and bang on its keys. "Tonight?"

Tootsie did the chill-out' thing with her hands. "Don't you have homework? Because as much as we want your help, we also don't want you to get behind in your schoolwork."

He deep-sixed her worry with a look that said *Do you think I'm going to let homework stand in my way when you're asking me to do something that's a whole lot more interesting?*

Which is what worried Tootsie. She knew he wanted to go to either Harvard or Stanford because those two schools were number one and number two in universities with the best environment and ecology programs. That's what Chris wanted to do with his life. Sloughing off homework to help her find out if Adele and Melanie had crossed paths before would distract when he shouldn't be distracted. Which was what Tootsie told him. But it didn't work.

"Tootsie, you need to let me help. If it wasn't for you, I wouldn't have all the things I have now. If you want me to look for that lady, that's what I'll do. I'll just stay up later to do my homework."

He wasn't a tall kid. He was kind of stocky. He had heavy eyebrows, a square face, and hair that he'd let grow long. He leaned down now to her even shorter self and kissed her on the cheek. Then he did the same with Adele, after which he waved and backed out of the house.

Tootsie blinked away the tears that threatened to leak onto her cheeks. She noticed that Adele was struggling with the same situation.

"Well," Tootsie said louder than normal. As if the power of her voice could stop the leakage. And wonder of wonders, it did. "I guess you and I have a champion."

Adele sniffed and wiped her cheeks with the back of one hand, obviously not too proud to show she'd been warmed to tears by the boy. "He's such a good soul, a *gute neshama*." She pulled a tissue out from beneath her blouse's cuff and gave her nose a gentle blow. Then, all business, she said, "If anyone can find out what Melanie's name was, it will be him. I've watched him work on that computer of his and he's some wizard."

"Yes," Tootsie agreed. "Now it remains to be seen whether he can find out if she really did go to Teaneck High and take one of your classes. Won't it be interesting if it's true?"

The light was on in Chris's room, his door closed, when Tootsie strolled back in from Adele's a little while later. Steve was not in front of the TV as Chris reported he would be. Steve only watched the Chicago programs with her because she liked them. Well, amend that...she liked PD, not the other two. Hank Voight, with all his imperfections, was her hero.

"It's not real," Steve had told her early on in their relationship. "You want to watch a real cop show, watch *Forensic Files* and *Blood, Lies, and Alibis*."

"I'm not looking for real," she'd retorted. "I'm looking for escape. I've got plenty of real every day."

When she'd said that, he'd given her the side-eye because he didn't know her that well back then. Not like he knew her now and why he no longer suggested she watch a "real" cop show. When he watched *Chica-*

go PD with her, he kept his opinions to himself about the not-real goings-on in her favorite cop show.

After she came back home, and after *Chicago PD* was winding down, he'd come into the great room and sat down next to her until the credits rolled. She stood and stretched. "That was a good one. I'm glad Hailey finally saw the light of day. She needs to forget about Jay."

Taking the glasses off that he now needed in order to see—and excuse me, but those black frames made him look, if at all possible, sexier than he looked without them—he stood, too, and reached for the remote. "Yeah, the guy has a death wish going off like that to the South American jungles." He pointed the remote at the TV.

She'd begun to grin up at him because see, even he'd gotten sucked into the various PD storylines when she heard the promo for the eleven o'clock news just coming up.

"...local woman who you'd never think had it in her, is about to become more famous than she already is. Her publisher is getting ready to re-release all twenty very sexy romances this lady has written because women of every age are clearing the shelves of every one of this author's books. Stay tuned for this intriguing story."

Tootsie grabbed Steve's hand with the remote in it before his thumb could click off the TV. "Wait a minute. I hope they're not about to talk about Aunt Adele."

But they were. When it finally aired, halfway through the news program, the reporter made it seem like it was the biggest, greatest, least serious story ever. Ninety-year-old has a new life and a new career. Whoopty-doo.

"Oh no." Tootsie closed her eyes and slapped a hand to her forehead. "My aunt is going to hate this. It wasn't enough that Blaze did her thing. Now this?"

Hands on hips, his Black Windbreaker cop face on full display, Steve stared at their oversize screen. "Who gave the story to that reporter?"

Something Tootsie wanted to know, too. "If my aunt finds out about this before I can get over there to talk to her…" She hurried out into the foyer, pulled open her front door, and looked across to her aunt's house. There were no lights on. Closing the door, she turned back to Steve. She must be asleep. I better get over there first thing in the morning before she finds out."

"We'll need to be there before the sun comes up. She's an early riser."

Tootsie was aware. What she wasn't aware of as much was that use of pronouns of his. "Are you saying you want to go with me?"

He took a step back and looked down at her. The look said *what else would I do?* Since he didn't follow the look with words, her interpretation would have to stand.

Whether she'd been a good interpreter of that look or not, they were up and dressed before six, out of the house, tramping across their lawns, and knock, knock, knocking on Adele's front door, not worried that it was before dawn since all the lights in the house were on.

Adele opened the door right away. "You know?"

Tootsie had expected her aunt would be pale, eyes sad or worried. Or both. Instead, she had the cat got in the cream look on her very satisfied face.

Leaving Tootsie stunned.

"*Schmendriks* should always get what they deserve."

Tootsie looked up at Steve. Steve looked down at Tootsie. Tootsie looked up at Steve. They both looked at Adele.

Who gave a short bark of a laugh. "Why did you think I would be unhappy with that story? That Melanie… Even if she didn't see, she knows now that Adele Silverstein is no *nebbish*. I can hold my own. She wants to hide Candy's books from the world? Hurt me by saying my A.S. Silverstein books are *dreck*, though they are not? They want to make fun of me because I'm an old lady and I'm writing about sex? Let them. Keep talking, keep talking, I say. That TV story…it made me look good."

She reached out a hand. "Come, Tootsie, come *tatteleh*."

When Adele began calling Tootsie *mamaleh*, she'd started calling Steve *tatteleh*, meaning little papa, a real term of endearment.

Steve held up a hand. "Give me a moment. I want to walk around your house. See if there's anything that needs shoring up."

Adele reached way up and patted him on the cheek. "You do what makes you happy, *tattie*. Come in after." As Steve disappeared around the side, she took Tootsie's hand and drew her toward the kitchen. "I'm sure you didn't have breakfast. Let me make you an egg, and toast you a bagel."

While her aunt whipped up an omelet, Tootsie said, "Did you know your publisher was going to re-release all your books?"

"I guessed." Adele brought a plate to the table with the omelet and a toasted sesame seed bagel. She sat across from Tootsie, a serene look on her face.

At which point the light of day did more than peek above the horizon. Tootsie's brain peeked above its own horizon. "Tell me I'm wrong, Aunt Adele."

"Wrong about what, *mamaleh*?"

Tootsie grinned, now sure. "Such innocence. You did it, didn't you?"

Adele lifted her chin.

Tootsie gave her a slant-eyed look. "Your publisher didn't pitch that story. You did."

One side of Adele's mouth curled upward. "That publisher of mine? She's good at lunches with agents and book buyers. Not so good with publicity because talking to reporters she wants to tell them what to do and how to do it. Very bossy. Reporters don't like bossy."

There was the sound of the front door opening and steps in the foyer. Steve walked into the kitchen and Adele gave him one of her sweetest smiles. "You assured yourself that no one will break into my house? Good. Thank you, darling." She pointed to the table. "You sit. I'm making you some eggs. What do you want, onions, a little cheese? And the bagel, you want an everything, a sesame, or whole wheat? I have all three."

"Thanks, Aunt Adele." He unsnapped his jacket and hung it over the back of the chair. "No egg. I'll just take a bagel. Whole wheat is fine."

Adele bustled to the counter next to her stove. There was a brown paper bag there out of which she'd taken the sesame that Tootsie was currently finishing. "What do you want on it? I have cream cheese and also cream cheese with chives. Maybe you want a little Nova, maybe a little sable, or whitefish?"

After Steve placed his order...cream cheese and Nova...Tootsie cleared her throat. "I was just asking Aunt Adele how that reporter got the story about her books being re-published. What do you think I found out?"

Steve gave Tootsie a look, got up, ambled over to the coffee maker, poured himself a cup, and came back to the table to sit. "You found out that *she* pitched the reporter."

It never ceased to amaze Tootsie that Steve, who didn't always seem to be paying attention, was paying careful attention. And wasn't she proud that he was her lover, her *seriously smart* lover?

Her seriously smart lover added, "Because she knows when to take advantage of the situation."

Adele patted him on his shoulder. "Thank you, *tattie*."

To her aunt, Tootsie said, "All right, so that was bold. After Basil, you needed a win."

"Basil. That *shtarker*." Adele waved him away with a flick of her wrist.

"When were you going to tell me about the reporter?" Tootsie had the feeling these two people in her life, her lover and her relative, were somehow on the same page, while she wasn't even in the same book.

"Tootsie, *mamaleh*, I knew you would be upset because you would be afraid the same thing would happen that happened with Blaze. I knew it wouldn't. You are not the only one who knows reporters."

Tootsie thought her head might fall onto the table. "Aunt Adele." She clutched both hands together, as if that would help her to think more clearly. "Why didn't you tell me when I suggested Blaze interview you?"

Adele gave her an indulgent look. "Because I knew *of* Blaze only. Besides, you had strong feelings that you wanted to do something for me. I wanted to make you feel good."

Tootsie's eyebrows hiked upward. She'd been played.

She speared Steve with a look. He kept eating his bagel. And shrugged.

Tootsie leaned into her aunt. "You had a plan. You didn't tell me."

"I apologize, *mamaleh*. I should have told you. But I didn't know what was going to happen and I did not want to worry you."

"I thought it mattered to you that your two writing lives remain separate."

"I did want that. But I realized, when Basil called me to say he couldn't publish my books anymore, that there wasn't much more I could say to teachers about how to teach history to children. I could say much more about how tight you need to tie a submissive up and what kind of whip you need to subdue her. Or him." She winked.

Heat flooded Tootsie's face.

Steve ducked his head, but not before she saw the broad grin on his face.

Innocence rode Adele's face. The shine in her eyes gave her away. She'd known what kind of reaction she would get from them both. And was happy because she had.

But then her smile went away. "I was wrong to worry about keeping my two writing personalities separate. Am I proud of my work as Candy La Plume? Yes, I know. I always speak of Candy as if I, Adele Silverstein, am not Candy."

That was true. Tootsie had wondered about it but never asked.

"Now I realize how foolish I've been. I told you the story about that lady who found Candy's stories an inspiration and how *my* story helped her take control of her life. That's a wonderful thing. I'm proud of Candy and her work. I must stop speaking of her as if she's not me."

Tootsie marveled at Adele's self-awareness. How many people had it? How many people would rethink stories they told themselves because they figured out that those stories no longer defined them? Her aunt had.

Adele said, "Still, *mamaleh*, there are things, though I care about them and wish I could do something about them, I can't. That silly woman, Melanie, and her friends who think like her...their judgment of what's good and what's not when it comes to books is very, very misguided."

"That's one word to describe Melanie and her friends," Tootsie drawled.

"I want to show her she's wrong. But you know, Tootsie..." Adele bent a rueful smile on her. "At my age, I can't go after Melanie Mangold and her people. Yes, it was easy for me to call that reporter. I've known her a long time." Adele grinned. "She was one of my students."

She pointed toward the front of the house. "But I can't run from one bookstore to another gathering books for a banned book sale. I can't dress myself in a silly dress the way you did. It takes a lot of energy to take a fact-finding trip and come back home the same day."

She looked then at Steve. Then back at Tootsie.

"I'm a lucky woman that I have you to do these things for me. It's a good thing that I moved to Glen Allyn, and that I'm near my great-niece. It's you who have done what I can no longer do, and I love you for that."

Tear spillage ensued. What else? In a voice she had to work hard to make steady, Tootsie said, "Steve and I are right here, Aunt Adele. All you ever have to do is call on us and we'll be here."

Adele gave her a grateful smile. "I have a feeling I will have to."

CHAPTER SEVENTEEN

Later, when they were back at home, sitting at the kitchen table, Tootsie said, "She blows me away, how with it she is, how much she knows about things that some people half her age don't know."

"About some things, she knows more than you do."

Tootsie winced but then gave him a rueful grin. "That is sadly true."

She brewed some coffee. "But there at the end, she reminded us that she can't do what she used to do because she's got physical limitations."

"We'll help her with that."

Taking her man's warm and so capable hand in hers, she gave it a gentle squeeze. "Thank you. It's good to know that both you and I are here for her. After we talked about Melanie, when she put on that brave face of hers, for a moment I felt helpless. Because I haven't been able to solve the Melanie problem."

He took both her hands in his. "Tootsie, it's frustrating when you're in the middle of an investigation and you feel like you're looking at a lot of loose ends that don't want to tie together. But you don't let the aggravation stop you. You put your head down and keep going."

Didn't she know that? "You and I both know impatience should have been my middle name instead of Ruth. But I need to say I don't remember feeling so anxious when I was going after Elwood and Robert at the radio station. It didn't feel like I couldn't solve things with Neal and Chesty over the ridiculous parking garage. This time, though…it's harder. Because it's Adele."

"Yes, it's different." He started drawing figure eights on her palm. "This is personal and that's why, when you're a cop, you don't work a job that involves family members. Even friends. You're too close. You can't be objective."

She snatched her hand away from him. "What are you saying? I should drop what I'm doing and let someone else take on Melanie Mangold because I'm too close to the situation?"

"There's always me. I'd be happy to shoulder it all."

Provoked, indignant, she opened her mouth to blast him when he laid a finger across her lips.

"No, keep it inside, babe. That was hypothetical. I'm not saying you should stand down and let me take over. You keep doing your thing and I'll be with you on it. If I've got a client, the client will wait until we figure this Melanie thing out. Together. You and me."

She grabbed his finger and folded it under to make a fist with his other digits. And then raised that fist to her mouth to give it a kiss.

They let their eyes do the talking as they stared at each other. The messaging was total mush, which Tootsie, who'd never been into mush, now savored it as if there wasn't anything better in the world. Only when they heard steps pounding down from upstairs did they blink.

"Hey," Chris said, stomping into the kitchen. Not for the first time Tootsie wondered why teenage boys walked like elephants. "You know that job you gave me last night, to see if I could find out if that lady, Melanie Mangold, had another name back in the day? Well, guess what?"

Yeah, and that was another thing. Why did they also need to say 'guess what' instead of just saying what.

Without betraying that question that had no answer, she said, "Tell us."

He came over to the table and dropped his book bag, or said more truthfully, his book boulder, on the floor with a *thunk*. He threw himself onto the chair across from Tootsie and said, "Melanie Mangold was Melody Jones, and she grew up in Teaneck. Not only that, but in the last year that Aunt Adele taught history at Teaneck High, Melody was one of her students. She got kicked out of class. She even got kicked out of school. You want to know why?"

Tootsie couldn't blink fast enough. She sat so far forward on her seat, one wrong move and she'd fall to the floor. She was revved. She was flying high. Here it came. The answer.

"We most definitely want to know why."

He stood and drew a folded-up piece of paper out of the front right pocket of his jeans. He spread it out on the table and turned it so the words could be viewed right side up. He slid it across the table. "Check out these pictures."

Tootsie blinked down at the first picture, the face of an angry girl wearing extreme defiance on every feature of her face, plus a row of earrings along the cartilage of both ears, one or two rings in each eyebrow, and a nose ring. Her eyes were heavily made up and she wore dark, probably black lipstick. Her ink-black hair was a rat's nest.

There was another picture of her standing next to a locker, her arms folded across her skinny chest, which was covered by a loose, white undershirt. In days when having a tattoo was still not the thing it was today, Melody had tattoos all over her body. Both her arms were painted with lurid images from shoulder to wrist. She was wearing a short skirt in this picture. It showed tattoos on her thighs as well.

Tootsie glanced up at Chris. "So, now that we know what she looked like, you can tell us why she got kicked out not just from class but of school."

He pointed to the full-length picture of Melody standing next to the locker. "See where she's standing? That locker? Melody got kicked out of school because she set what was in that locker on fire." He hefted up his book bag. "That's what I found out. Is it good?" He slung said book bag over his shoulders. "I don't have time for breakfast. Gotta go. Tell me if you want me to do any more searching."

And he was out the door.

They heard his car, parked in front, start, and he was gone.

Tootsie looked up at Steve. "Well, that was an eye opener."

"It was."

You know I could tell that story to people."

"Blackmailing is a felony."

"Telling a story is not blackmail. Besides it was just an idea."

He gave her a dark look. "I know you, Toots. It wasn't just an idea."

"You're right. But think for a minute. Knowing we know might just get her to stop torturing my aunt. I mean, she comes off as the most righteous person that ever walked the streets of Glen Allyn. It turns out she was once a juvenile delinquent."

She punched a finger at the bottom of the page where Chris had made notes. "There's more. Here, it says she'd come to school drunk or high or both. Just imagine it. Melanie, aka Melody, will hate for people to know all this about her."

"True. Blackmail is still a felony."

She sighed. "Some laws are just too inconvenient."

"If you want, I'll call the attorney general and ask him to strike the ones you don't like off the books."

She gave him her usual love tap on the arm, making the point that he was being silly, and she was only joshing. "I need to find some other way of getting her to stop. It's too bad that everything I've tried so far has come to nada."

"Do us both a favor. While you're trying to think what comes next, don't mention blackmail to Chris. Considering how much he loves your aunt, I don't want him to think a little blackmail is the end that justifies the means. Like you do."

Even though her Black Windbreaker was no longer a cop, he never stopped being all about law and order. She raised her hand, palm out, like she was swearing to tell the truth in a court of law. "I won't broach the subject with him. I'll just thank him for finding out who Melanie Mangold really is."

Once Steve left, she waited only a little while before hiking over to Adele's to share what Chris had found.

Looking at the pictures he'd downloaded, Adele shook her head resignedly. "She was in my junior Modern European History class. That one had a defiant attitude. She walked in with it each morning, staring at me with those hard eyes. I tried to understand her, help her. But no matter how I talked to her, her answers were like her looks. Defiant. Angry. And yes, dishonest, too. Always."

Adele closed her eyes and shook her head. "The child didn't know how to be honest with me about what bothered her. Though I never met her mother, some of the other teachers had. They told me about how terrible Mrs. Jones was. She was both physically and emotionally abusive. Of course, Melody acted out in school. We all understood that and tried to reach her. But she would never let anyone in."

"Do you know why she set that locker fire?"

"I do know. In that class that year, there was another girl who was as different from Melody as two girls could be. Her name was Natalie. I don't remember her last name, but her parents came from Russia. They were new in the country. Every day, Natalie came to school ready and eager to learn. She dressed neatly, even a little old-fashioned—for those years. Probably new clothes were something her parents couldn't afford. Natalie did not speak English well. She struggled and Melody made fun of her."

Pensively, Adele rubbed one arm. "Melody was bullied at home, so she needed to bully someone else she regarded as weaker than she was."

"Poor Natalie," Tootsie sympathized.

"No need to feel sorry for Natalie. She got much better at English. She worked very hard to improve. It became harder and harder for Melody to make fun of her because eventually there was nothing to make fun of. Then, because she was a pleasant girl, Natalie made friends with many other girls."

"And that's when she burned what was in Natalie's locker? I assume it was Natalie's locker we're talking about."

"Yes, we're talking about Natalie's locker but that isn't when she did it. Natalie had won a prize as the most improved student at the high school, and that was when Melody must have decided though Natalie was a foreigner, even the world thought she was better than Melody, who was an American."

Tootsie would have no reason to feel sympathy for that girl. But she did. "And that's when she lit the fire, right?"

"In the middle of the day. She broke into Natalie's locker. As other kids stared, even laughed, she threw in a lighted match and the notebooks and papers on the top shelf of the locker started to burn. It was a lucky thing that one of the kids who was standing and watching ran to the office. One of the teachers brought a fire extinguisher and doused the flames. Melody was expelled immediately. She might have come back to school the following year. I don't know. That was the year I retired."

Tootsie said, "Somewhere along the way, Melody, who got kicked out of school for burning the contents of a locker, became Melanie who can do no wrong."

Adele's mouth was turned down in sadness. "I would like to know when that change happened."

Tootsie turned her coffee cup around and around. "What I still don't understand is why Melanie has decided to single you out with her righteousness?"

Adele looked mystified. "I've been thinking about that and so far, I cannot think of a reason. That was a long time ago. Perhaps it was something I thought was of no significance, but Melody did? Perhaps I could talk to her and find out."

"I don't think that's a very good idea. What do you think? She would tell you?"

"Why not?"

Yes, why not? Tootsie thought about that for a minute and then she said, "Okay. We haven't got anything else that's useful at the moment. Maybe if she tells us what it is, that maybe you said something you didn't mean, you can apologize, and Melanie will forgive and forget."

Adele brightened. "That is what I'll do, then."

"Not so fast, Aunt Adele. If you go to see Melanie, I'm going with you."

That had been a thing easier said than done. Though Tootsie called Melanie, and left several messages, Melanie never called back. Tootsie thought about playing one of her usual games…figuring out where Melanie would be and then accosting her there like, oh my, how did this happen that you and my aunt and I turned up in the same place at the same time? But her aunt was involved. She couldn't quite manage her usual trick.

"Maybe I need to go about this another way," she told Steve the next morning before he got ready to leave.

"Like what. I'm reminding you that blackmail—"

"Yes, yes, you broken record, you. It's a felony. I promise. No blackmail today."

He gave her a steely-eyed look. "Or any day."

She huffed a breath. "What a stickler you are." As she said it, she stood on her tiptoes and gave him a kiss. "I promised. No blackmail."

"Good. You know there's blackmail and this other trick of yours you're too good at and shouldn't be."

"Oh?" Tootsie still had her arms around his neck. She fluttered her eyes at him. Which he was not having.

"It's poking the bear. You've already poked the bear what…three, four times? How many more times are you going to be able to get away with it before the bear comes after you?"

Which even she had to admit, was a fair point. It had already happened. At the 7-11. Which meant she had to come up with alternative ways to help her aunt find out what grudge was so terrible that all these years later, Melanie was hell-bent on doing what she could to mess up Adele's life.

Tootsie decided a google search was the order of the day. This one was on Melody Jones' mother. After searching page after page, she finally found a reference to the woman's obituary. Karla Jones had died the year Melody would have turned eighteen. There was no information about the cause of death. Only that donations could be made to a hospital in Pennsylvania.

When she searched for that hospital—which turned out was more clinic than hospital—she realized that Melody's mother had had an addiction of some kind. Reading between the lines, she decided Karla Jones, dead at thirty-nine, might have died of an overdose. Something like that might have sent Melody into a tailspin.

It didn't explain why she'd turned out to be the woman she was today.

The following morning dawned gray and cold, a typical December day for New Jersey. She walked over to Adele's house to tell her about her search and finding Karla Jones, and that she was stymied and not sure where to turn next. Her aunt opened the door as Tootsie raised her hand to knock. Tootsie took a step back and stared.

"Aunt Adele. You look like you've been cleaning the attic. Your hair is every which way, your nose has dirt on it. You haven't been living here long enough to be doing that kind of cleaning."

"You're wrong about that, *mamaleh*." She held up a book with a white cover. "This morning I had a hunch and decided I needed to see if I could be right. And so yes, I went up into the attic where I had boxes of these things which maybe I'll unpack someday, or maybe I won't. I went through the box in which I thought I'd find it." She brandished the book. "This was what I was looking for."

She stepped aside. "Come in, come in. Let me show you what it is and how, once I saw the pictures, I remembered."

Tootsie followed her aunt into the kitchen. There, on the table, was a stack of other white-covered books, exactly like the one that Adele was holding. Walking over to the table, reaching down for one of the books, Tootsie knew even before she turned it face up, what she was looking at. "These are yearbooks, aren't they? They're yearbooks of different graduating classes from Teaneck High."

"Yes, they are." Adele placed the book she'd been holding on the table with its mates. She pushed the pile of other yearbooks aside. "This one here..." She patted the one she'd been holding. "This one is from the year *before* Melody would have graduated. It was a tradition back then to include photos of the rising seniors. In the year when Melody would have graduated, there would be no picture of her since she didn't graduate. But in the yearbook before? When she was a rising senior? I thought there was a chance I might see something."

She bent over the book and opened it some-where in the middle. "This is where I thought I would find a picture of Melody. These are casual pictures of kids that traditionally are included in every yearbook."

Tootsie looked over her aunt's shoulder. After turning page after page, Adele came to one with an array of pictures on it. "Here." She tapped a picture up in the far-right corner on the right facing page. "Here she is."

Tootsie squinted at the black and white picture of a group of kids, arms all over each other's shoul-ders. There were three boys and three girls. She'd be willing to bet none of these boys lettered in sports. The girls weren't cheerleaders. The boys weren't quite Goth. They were sloppy in their dress. The boys were wearing faded T-shirts with messages that Tootsie couldn't quite make out. The girls? They were Goth. They wore cropped tops, one shoulder hanging down, fishnet hose, knee-high boots, and skirts that barely covered their tushes. They all had long, straggly hair and heavily made-up eyes.

She laid a finger on the picture. "These girls all look the same. Which one is Melody?"

"She's the one looking as if she'd like to be any-where except where she is."

That seemed right to Tootsie. In the other couple of pictures that she'd seen of Melody her mouth was turned down. It was turned down in this picture. "It's interesting. In this picture it seems Melody is not a very happy camper. But everyone else is smiling.

Maybe she's not really part of this group? It just turned out that she was nearby when someone came along to snap this picture?"

"Oh no, she meant to be in this picture. That boy next to her. He was her boyfriend. Jason Allessi. I remember him though I never had him in any one of my classes. He was a troublemaker."

"Hmm. Like attracts like." She straightened. "So now we know that though she looks like she could have cared less who she was, she did have a group of friends."

"And a boyfriend. Jason."

"And a boyfriend," Tootsie parroted. "What does having a boyfriend have to do with anything?"

"It has everything to do with it, and it concerns the boy, too. He's part of the reason Melody disappeared."

Tootsie was beginning to see the light. "Okay."

Adele closed the cover of the yearbook and pushed it over next to the other yearbooks. She sat. "When I looked at Melody's picture, I remembered a rumor that went around and decided to make a phone call to one of my former colleagues, a teacher who retired soon after I did."

"What did she tell you?"

"What I expected she would...once she remembered."

An errant thought popped into Tootsie's mind. It seemed that Adele was a storyteller like Chris. She drew the thing out. For effect. Not that she'd mention it and stop the flow of this story. "What did your former colleague tell you?"

"She told me this boy, Jason, was known to be sexually active. He was sexually active with Melody. The result was what you'd expect. Melody got pregnant."

CHAPTER EIGHTEEN

One part of Tootsie said, yeah, that solves the mystery of where Melanie's older son came from. A girl steps onto the wild side and does the most defiant thing she can think of, a thing that will change her forever. Just to show she could. But no sixteen-year-old girl could understand how having a child would change her life. This was sad. "Does your colleague know what happened then?"

"She knew Melody had a little boy and that she did not give him up for adoption. She did not, however, stop drinking and drugging. Eventually, when the child was four years old, the state stepped in and took him away. That, it seemed, sent her into a tailspin. She OD'd. But she recovered and got better."

Like her mother, it seemed. But the outcome was not the same. Tootsie ruminated. "She must have loved the kid, after all. When she recovered, did she try to get the child back?"

"She must not have."

"I wonder why. I'd like to believe that if we knew how that trauma influenced her to become who she is now, we might be able to get her to leave you alone, Aunt Adele. If your colleague knows where Trey figures in, that would be helpful."

"I asked. She doesn't know."

They sat in silence until Tootsie said, "All these tantalizing bits…they're enough to tell us Melody had a whopping big reason to change. But what? Did the child figure in? Or not?"

Adele brightened. "If Melody thought there was some kind of shame…"

"I think shame would play a part."

They stared at each other, as if looking into another set of eyes would reveal more answer than each of them had separately.

"Well." Tootsie rose. "Steve's friend, Bert, might be able to do something with this secret baby thing."

Adele nodded her agreement as the two walked toward the front door. "I'd like to know where that secret baby is living."

Which Tootsie wanted to know, too. Which was what she said to Steve.

Who pointed out, "You know Bert's on it. He's taking time away for us from investigating cheating spouses, the bread-and-butter part of his business. I'll ask him if he has any contacts in the adoption community that can tell him how to find this so-called secret baby of Melanie's."

Knowing bits and pieces only...it was getting totally annoying.

When Fern came in...today she was wearing her black and white tiger tamer skirt...she observed that Tootsie needed to get out of the house and go somewhere to think.

If only she could. But Tootsie knew she was on information overload. Nothing seemed to want to come together.

She headed for her thinking place, anyway: Brookdale Park. Where, as she began to walk, her brain went into vacuum mode, and she wasn't talking physics or cleaning.

But then she stopped halfway around and sat on one of the convenient benches set at intervals around the park perimeter.

The wind came up as she planted her tush. She hunched into her puffy coat. Into its collar she said, "Let's look at this thing in some kind of order."

She tapped her foot against the dirt and dried grass in front of the bench. "First Melanie and Trey move to town and Melanie worms her way into the library. She says she wants to hide books she doesn't approve of but seems to be focused on one author more than others: Candy La Plume."

Two women Tootsie knew from when she headed the safety commission that was tasked with putting up a stop sign on the corner of Martling Avenue and

Lilypond Lane…where Chesty lived…passed by, giving her a smile and a wave.

Tootsie sealed up her lips. No good would come of anyone thinking she'd lost the plot, the book, the whole story.

She waited, then took a breath, and continued. "We try to shame Melanie at the library board meeting and Trey slashes my tires."

Or, as Steve had said, *allegedly* slashed her tires.

The result, that walk home in the dark. Tootsie nodded to herself against her puffy coat's zipper, "Yeah, that was Trey getting back at me for the scene with the dress at the library meeting."

She picked herself up and started walking again. "Then there's the troll. Was that Trey? Who had defaced Adele's walk? Was it Melanie? Or was it someone else? And where is the secret baby?"

By the time she got into her car and drove herself back home, she knew her thinking had gotten her nowhere.

Well, part of her thinking had. It was the part that had nothing to do with Melanie and it was, if possible, even more upsetting.

It had to do with the birthday party she didn't want. The party she had avoided thinking about this whole time she'd been worried about Adele. But the vacuum that was her brain filled with thoughts of who would be at her birthday party if she let Steve throw one. And what her birthday party would represent that she'd avoided thinking about.

Her sons. Sam and Josh. Especially Sam. They'd be at the party. And she'd have to deal with the strained relationship between Sam and her.

Not only that but she'd be forced to think about those thirty years. All the hellraising she would do now and in the future would never make up for when she could have been doing what she should have been doing and didn't.

Steve hadn't said a word lately about the birthday party. Was she surprised? No. He knew she was concentrating on how to get Melanie to drop whatever vendetta she had against Adele.

Was she going to tell him, yeah, go ahead? She had to tell him something, sooner than later. It was December. Her birthday was less than thirty days away.

"I've been thinking about Sam," she told Fern when she got back home a little after ten.

Fern looked up from her laptop. "You do know the more you think, the less you do, the more it eats you up."

Tootsie didn't mention the party and what she needed to tell Steve. She didn't want to be on the receiving end of any more of Fern's comments.

Who her inner voice said spoke truth when Tootsie didn't want to hear that truth.

The subject of the birthday party battled with the one that wouldn't let her figure out what Melanie's reason was for hating Adele. It lasted all day right up to when, shortly after five, Steve walked from the garage and into the kitchen.

As usual, he kissed her. But this one...whoa mama! This one was a winner. It involved him dropping his jacket onto the island, pulling her against his chest, winding his arms around her waist and pressing his lips, open-mouthed against hers.

In the space of no time, she went into Marvin Gaye territory. But when he stood back and grinned down at her, she knew they weren't going to get it on anytime soon.

Drat.

But she asked the reason for the kiss. And was told.

"We found the bastard who wrote those messages on your aunt's sidewalk."

She clapped her hands in appreciation. "Wow. Great news. What do you know and how did you find out?"

"First things first. How we found out. Your neighbor across the street has a Ring doorbell. He also happens to pay for a subscription, so the camera makes a recording of whatever motion triggers it. Just after three o'clock in the morning, on the day we found the chalking, the guy's camera recorded a car stopping and parking in front of Adele's house. A person in dark clothing got out of the car. Nothing happened for about five minutes. Then the camera recorded that same person getting back into the car."

Keys still in his hand, he turned to stow them in the tray next to the refrigerator.

Tootsie kept the grin to herself. Even with that move she'd so appreciated...and though he'd disappointed her because it was a move that went nowhere for the moment...her man still followed his routine. He put his keys where he'd find them in the morning. No wasting time searching all over for keys for Black Windbreaker.

She followed him into the foyer where he hung up his jacket. "Okay, so you're not saying whether it was a he or a she."

Steve closed the closet door and turned back toward the kitchen. "When your neighbor let me in and showed me the video, it was clear to me that it was a male."

Tootsie made a beeline for the coffee maker. "Boy, that's some camera that it can differentiate that much detail. Remind me not to step outside the front door in my nightgown."

"Nobody cares about your nightgown, babe. The ones you wear to bed lately look like something my grandmother would put on."

"That's only now when it's frigid cold outside. Plus, I haven't heard any complaints coming from you about my usual choice of bedwear," she shot back at him.

"That's because you don't wear any of it too long once we get into bed."

She made a shushing sound and pointed in the direction of the dining room...where Fern was working.

"As we were saying about that doorbell camera," she said in a loud voice. "I imagine all it could determine, other than the fact that the person was a male, was the kind of clothing he was wearing."

"Definitely a hoodie."

"So how do you know who it was?" You did say you know, right?"

"Kind of the same way you figured out Chesty was guilty of keying your car all those months ago."

She'd told Steve it was Chesty, not because of what he'd been wearing but because of the car he'd gotten into and in which he'd driven away, his Maserati. "Are you saying whoever wrote those messages had a unique car?"

She grabbed a mug from the cabinet and poured him some coffee.

"No, but he had a unique license plate."

She set the mug down on the granite counter with a loud clunk. "Every license plate is unique, but one plate is on the back of the car and one on the front. Not on the side. So, when he drove away, you wouldn't see the plate."

"That would be right. Except this guy decided he needed to head back in the direction he'd come from. He made a K turn."

Tootsie began to grin. "I assume this was...?"

"Yeah. Right in the middle of the street so the camera in that Ring picked up the numbers and letters on the front license plate as clear as if it had been the middle of the day, especially since the driver hadn't turned on his headlights yet."

"Now you're going to tell me you already know who that car belongs to because you've already spoken to your pals down at the station. So go ahead and lay it on me. Who did it belong to?"

"The kid's name is Logan Francisco."

Her eyebrows twitched. She laid a hand on her head. "Wait. How do I know that name?"

"Easy. He's the kid Chris tried to talk to at school about how to find the troll. He's the one who blew him off. That should tell you something."

It did. It rocked her. It was like doors flying wide open. "The computer nerd from school is the one who defaced my aunt's front walk?"

She began to smile. It widened in triumph. "I know you hate it when I do it, but can I now jump to a conclusion? The computer nerd, Logan Francisco, who has a way with chalk, is also my aunt's cyberbully."

"That's the right conclusion."

She leaned back against the counter, folded her arms across her chest, and stared hard at him. "Can I jump to another conclusion?"

Steve mimicked her posture, folding his arms across his chest, too. "You could."

"Logan Francisco is Melanie's son and he's working with his mother. Somehow, after all these years, they stayed in contact."

"Not proven. But probable."

Tootsie nodded, bobblehead style. "Probable is like when you do a Wordle and you get to the third line, and you have four letters, and you just know what the word is. But somebody who's looking over your shoulder says you should test out at least one more group of letters."

She nodded once more. With emphasis. "I've got this Wordle. Logan is Melanie's son. It would have to be some amazing coincidence that he's not Melanie's son when he decided to write nasty messages on Adele's sidewalk and go after her Candy La Plume books online when his mother is focusing on the same thing. I don't believe in coincidences."

Tootsie pushed away from the counter and began to pace around her island. "So, how did they both end up in Glen Allyn?" She came back around and stopped in front of the table. Steve swiveled around so he was facing her.

He pulled on her hand to get her to stop her circumnavigating and sit down. "Logan lives with foster parents. That car he was driving is in his name and yeah, he's not sixteen, he's seventeen years old. Bert says he's got the proof that Logan is Melanie's son."

"Now I have more questions than I had before. Like why doesn't Logan live with Melanie? Where do I find that out?"

He took one of her hands in his and began playing with her fingers.

She looked down at her hand and what he was doing. Suddenly, she wasn't concentrating so hard on Logan Francisco. She recalled how this conversation had started. With that kiss that was so much more than a kiss.

It took her way more effort than she thought it should have to pull herself back from the brink. Because no matter what else was going on in her life, her Black Windbreaker occupied the biggest space in her soul, heart, and spirit.

He raised her hand to his lips, placed a kiss on her knuckles, and lowered her hand back to the table. "The Glen Allyn cops will be paying Logan a visit sooner than later. But that doesn't mean you can't pay him a visit, too."

"Hmm." Wits once more working, she said, "I imagine the cops are going to bring charges against Logan. They'll arrest him, which would mean I won't be able to get near him to ask him anything."

"They will arrest him. If he's clean, and let's assume he is, the judge will release him on bail. He'll go home and you can visit."

Finished with her coffee, Tootsie carried her cup to the sink. "I'll have to tell my aunt what's going on. I think it will relieve her that we at least know Logan is the bully."

"You should do that." He stood and joined her at the sink. "Don't let her convince you to take her with you when you talk to Logan."

She raised one eyebrow. "No? She's pretty clever. She might be an asset."

"She might be. But you're cagier than she is. You need the kid to be focused on you. Not be distracted by the woman who he's been dinging."

Steve took her by the hand and began to back out of the kitchen. Tootsie knew where he was headed. Still, she somehow had the resolve to yell out, "Fern, Steve and I need to check on something upstairs."

Fern didn't respond right away. When she did, she said, "You do what you need to do." Then she snickered.

Tootsie was shocked at herself and her man, that they would indulge with Fern working away in the dining room. But there must have been a reason why Steve was so ready to rock in the middle of the day. She wouldn't question it. But she did say, "You have that much faith in me? You think I'm cagey?"

"I do. You could get a rock to talk, Toots. Go find him. Go do your thing." He reached the staircase to the upper floor and all the bedrooms. Still holding onto her hand, his boots did an about-face and he pulled her up the steps with him. "Wait until later to do it, okay?"

It was already four o'clock when she drove Viv to the garden apartments where Logan lived with his foster parents.

Tootsie still had the silly smile on her face that had been there since she and Steve went their separate ways. After being the furthest from separate for a seriously awesome hour. Or was it ninety minutes?

"Who's counting?" Tootsie asked herself as she pulled to a stop at the curb.

The lady of the house was home. Not that Tootsie could think of her as a lady in any sense once the woman opened the door. As Tootsie's mother, Francine, who judged everyone and hardly ever kindly, would say, she'd let herself go.

Logan's foster parent was short and round. It looked like she'd used the bright pink shirt she was wearing as a napkin. The jeans molding her outlandishly curved hips had rips...which Tootsie didn't think were part of how they'd been bought...and splotches of dirt on the knees and thighs.

Had she been gardening?

Not in December.

The woman gave Tootsie the once-over. She was holding a green plastic spatula. Changing her grip on the spatula, as if she was preparing to use it as a weapon, and with hostile speculation in her eyes, she said, "You here from Children and Family Services? Because I'm doing everything you people have already told me I need to. All the children in my care are doing just fine."

"No, I'm not. But I am looking for one of your kids: Logan. Is he around? He's been communicating with one of my relatives, an older woman."

That had the element of truth to it. Didn't chalking obscenities and threats on a sidewalk and hounding Adele online qualify as communication?

"She asked me to clarify what it is he needs from her. She's not able to do it herself. So, I'm here for her."

As long as Logan's foster mother didn't ask for details, Tootsie wouldn't have to make something else up.

The woman studied Tootsie's outfit, which happened to be the kind of thing Tootsie always wore in winter. A black turtleneck over a pair of black-patterned trousers and short boots.

Whether she decided Tootsie was whoever she thought she might have been or not, she said, "He's not here."

"Will he be back later?"

The woman raised up the spatula and scratched her head with the end. Tootsie flinched. How thrilled Tootsie was that this woman would never invite her to dinner.

"I don't watch him like I watch the others," the woman said. "Because they're younger, you know, I have to. Logan's different. These days the only thing he does is sleep here. I don't even have to feed him, and that's good with me." She added hastily, "But I would if he was ever home."

This was not getting Tootsie what she wanted. Trying again, she said, "Is there a place where you think I might be able to find him?"

She pointed the spatula in a vague direction somewhere down the street. "Yeah. You could find him at the FedEx office."

Tootsie blinked. "He works there?"

"Nah. He doesn't have a job at FedEx. But he works there."

"Okaay." That made no sense, but Tootsie was going with it, anyway.

Logan's foster mother continued. "I don't know how he does it, but the kid makes a crapload of money and I got to say it pisses me off after all I've done for him over the years because he doesn't give me a penny."

Still trying to compute why FedEx, Tootsie said, "What kind of work does he do?"

"Well, I don't know, do I? But I do know that he's always at FedEx when he's not at school."

She turned aside and sneezed. She did not do the socially acceptable thing and cover her mouth and nose. Then, wiping her nose with the back of the same hand that held the green spatula, the woman added, "You want to talk to him and it's not school hours? You gotta go to FedEx."

CHAPTER NINETEEN

S omebody else, somebody whose first name
began with the letter S, might have said wait;
get your thoughts together. Figure out how you're
going to approach the kid. Then go and pepper him
with any question you want to.

For Tootsie, that approach didn't work. Though,
Ruth was still her middle name, patience was riding
her anyway. Anyone who knew her knew that was
how it was. Including that guy whose first name began with the letter S. Then there was that thing called
kick the can down the road. Everyone knew what
happened with the can. It just kept on getting kicked.
After a while, everyone she knew who did can-kicking
got tired of it. And gave up.

She did not kick cans.

Besides which, Tootsie knew she did her best
work when she went with the flow, based on what her

target...and yes, now the kid was her target...said or did.

Which was why she did not pass go, although it would have been nice to collect those two hundred dollars, and she headed straight from the garden apartment where Logan lived, to the FedEx office where Logan's foster mother told her the boy hung out.

The FedEx office was the one where Fern did all their mailing business with and from which she sent Tootsie's occasional packages to Chicago and Singapore. It was on a busy street in Clifton, just down from a Trader Joe's and beyond a mall with a popular Italian restaurant where the food was great and always came hot. Tootsie had been to the Trader Joe's. She loved their sampling. She'd also been to the Italian restaurant.

By the time she pulled the FedEx's door open, it was dark outside. December...the darkest month of the year, but because of all the Christmas lights, it was also the brightest. That was kind of like the situation Tootsie found herself in now. She was what felt like perennially in the dark about why Melanie had singled out her aunt. But the light was about to shine, not just on Melanie and Trey, but now Logan.

The store was filled with people and their packages, the ones going to loved ones before December 25. Or in the case of Chanukah, before December 23 because yes, this year Chanukah was basically falling at the same time as Christmas.

She glanced around, looking for a kid. Too bad there was more than one present.

As she wasn't about to tell herself to come back another time—which would be can kicking—she went through the process of visual elimination. She ruled out the boys who were wandering around looking at the cute holiday merch that FedEx smartly displayed to encourage impulse buying. They were too young. The ones who were standing in line with a parent, yeah, no. Didn't need to be a college professor to recognize that none of them were Logan Francisco.

So, where in the FedEx was Logan Francisco?

She might not have noticed him, except as she was scanning all the store's corners, he picked that moment to stand up from whatever chair he'd been sitting in.

He was across the floor where there were three computer terminals and a whole bunch of printers, The store was all glass windows, so you could see in and see out. At the moment, this kid was staring out the glass toward Trader Joe's and its overflowing parking lot.

This kid was the right age. If she were profiling, his physical attributes looked to be the kind that a loner like Logan would be. A slight build. His back was curved like the top of a question mark. Probably from bending over a computer if what she knew about him was right. He was always online. He wore a dark gray sweatshirt. With a hood.

Well, would you look at that!

Even as she made her way across the floor and past the other customers loitering about, Steve's voice got on his soapbox in her ear: *you can't tell from looking at people who they are.* He'd said that about Elwood Robinson, who Tootsie had thought was just the mild-mannered business manager of WCLS, and look how wrong she'd been about him.

He'd said it about Glen Allyn's mayor, Neal Morgan, whom she'd always regarded as a wimp and a wuss. But it worked out that he was Chesty Kowalczyk's willing accomplice and wedded to the idea that there wasn't a municipal budget anywhere in New Jersey that couldn't support a little bogus bidding on building projects.

He hadn't said it about Sage Rust. Tootsie hadn't trusted the tech billionaire from the start, neither his looks nor the duplicitous words that fell out of his mouth.

So, why, she asked herself as she closed the distance to where the kid was standing and staring out the window, had she convinced herself that this kid was Logan?

Intuition…and she was going with it.

"Logan?"

He wheeled around.

Okay, right. As usual. "Your mother told me I'd find you here."

She purposely left off the word, foster. And got the reaction she was looking for. "She has no idea this is where I..."

Yeah, he stopped. Because he realized. A little late. But realized.

He worked his mouth. "What do you want?"

If Melanie had been standing next to him, no way could she have denied he was her son. Logan had his mother's features, the soft, undefined cheeks and round chin. He wore his hair parted on one side, no bangs, though. But it was the same mousy-brown color. His eyes were mirrors of hers, and currently regarded her with hostility and suspicion.

She didn't get any closer. But she said, "I was hoping we could talk."

His frozen expression gave nothing away. Well, except for his eyes which kept shooting those bolts of hostility at her.

Because yeah, he had it in the back of his mind that he'd chalked a sidewalk and gotten caught. According to Steve, who had somehow found out after their lovely afternoon idyll, the cops had already been to see him. Was she a cop, too? Or from some state agency?

He checked her out, like that would tell him something. "What do you want to talk about?"

She eyed a bar stool type chair pushed up against the wall next to where they were standing. Pointing to it she said, "Do you mind if I sit?"

He didn't bother to look that way. "I don't care."

She pulled the stool away from the wall and a little bit closer to the kid. Hiking herself up, she laughed, though there was nothing funny to laugh at here. "I'm so short, getting into chairs like this is always a problem. One of these days I'm going to miss and fall backwards onto the floor."

The expression on his face told Tootsie he didn't appreciate her attempt at a hardy-har-har.

No worries. She didn't need him to think it was funny. She needed him to not leave.

"So, Logan...you don't mind if I call you Logan, do you?"

He shrugged.

Taking that as acceptance Tootsie continued, "In case you were wondering who I am, and I know you are, it was my aunt's sidewalk you chalked."

He stiffened. His face, up until now emotionless, showed the first evidence of fear.

She held up a hand. "I'm not here to yell at you. About the cops... Whatever you work out with them is none of my business."

He glanced toward the terminal he'd probably been sitting in front of. There was a small, black-covered notebook next to the mouse. His hand twitched. Like he was reaching for it...and then once he had it, he'd make a beeline out of the FedEx.

"I want to understand you. That's why I want us to talk."

His gaze veered to the door to the store and then back to her. "You think I'm dumb?"

She put both hands on her knees and leaned forward. "That's the last thing I think. I bet you're smarter than most people." She pointed to his terminal. "You'd laugh if you saw me sitting in front of a computer. I can barely send an email."

Well, that wasn't true. But telling a little fib here and there to get the kid to open up was, in her mind, totally allowed.

"My son, Chris, told me you can do magic on that thing." She pointed to the computer terminal where he'd been sitting.

He got an arrested look on his face. "Chris Hart? He's your son?"

Thoughts chased themselves across his face, which told Tootsie he remembered Chris asking him for help.

"He's kind of my son." She paused. "Like some other people we know kind of have a son."

When he started to back away, because oh yes, he knew what she meant, she held up a hand. "I'm getting off the subject. I want to tell you, from what Chris said and what I know, I am just in awe of your talent. You have my complete admiration."

One thing Tootsie knew; everyone, no matter who they were, wanted to know that whatever it was they did with their lives, they'd done it well. This kid, who in every way she could see, was a loner and lonely, would be no different.

Of course, he didn't fall all over himself to thank her for the compliment. He hardly reacted at all. He was probably still thinking about that oblique reference to sons who weren't sons and mothers who weren't mothers.

So, she went on. "I know a little about you. And I guess now that you've been caught chalking those messages on my Aunt Adele's sidewalk...you know how you got caught, don't you?"

How you got caught... his face pinkened and he looked down at his feet. He knew about the Ring doorbell. He nodded.

"So, maybe we can start with you telling me why you did it. I ask because what you wrote scared her and she's an old lady."

Tootsie could almost hear Adele's screech.

Going on, she said, "I worry about that. You know, old people are not like the rest of us. They don't just slough things off like it's nothing. I don't want my aunt at her age...she's ninety...to worry. If you can tell me it was just a prank, then I can tell her it's all done. Nothing to worry about."

He folded his arms across his mostly concave chest and stared her down.

Okay, so far defiant silence was going to be the name of the game. She'd had lots of practice with this attitude.

"You know, I live with a guy who used to be a cop."

He straightened again and dropped his hands to his sides. The haunted look came back, and he shot his gaze toward the FedEx entrance/exit door again.

She held up a hand. "What I mean is he knows how people who are seventeen years old, and not adults, can get clear of trouble without anything serious happening to them where the law is concerned. You know, after what they've done. If they at least explain why and are sorry."

He brought his attention back to her. "That's not what the judge said."

"The judge isn't there for explanations." Well, that wasn't entirely true. But Logan didn't need to know that, now. "My friend, though he's an ex-cop, he still knows all the cops in Glen Allyn. After I leave here, I'm going home. Maybe I could tell him what I hope you'll tell me. Why you did it and how sorry you are. You never know how much that could help your case."

He glanced first up at the ceiling. Then toward all that glass and Trader Joe's in the near distance. Then, he focused back on her. "So, if I tell you why I wrote on the sidewalk, you'll tell your friend and then things will be okay?"

She made a cross over her chest...not exactly the most Jewy thing she could do, but he'd get why she'd done it...and said, "I'll tell him and then he'll tell the cops."

What she didn't say was that things would be okay. She'd never been above telling a fib, but telling an outright lie? Nope. Well, mostly nope.

A look of longing crossed his features. He took a deep breath and let it out slowly. And wasn't that relief if she ever saw it. Which was the first moment she felt sympathy for the kid. He was seventeen. And she'd begun to think, watching this kid's hostile and fearful reaction to her, a full adult…his mother…had been using him as her pawn. He couldn't be held to blame for that. At least in her mind. Which was what she would tell Steve later.

He shuffled from one foot to the other. "I didn't really want to do it. But this lady I know told me about how your aunt writes smut, and no one should write smut."

Tootsie still cringed when she heard that ugly word. It was so derogatory, so dismissive. Leveled, it seemed, at only one kind of subject matter and only at the people who wrote it: women. Sexism, as opposed to sex was not the subject she was about to school Logan on. Someday, she hoped, someone would. In the meantime, she had other things in mind.

Which was why she asked, "Do you know what smut means?"

He looked down at his feet, shrugged, and shook his head.

Okay, answer: He didn't know.

"I told you I met your foster mom."

His head came up. The hostility was back. "So?"

"Nothing really." She wagged her hands back and forth to show him the nothingness of what she'd just said. "She did not strike me as the kind of person who gets along with lots of people."

His lip curled up. "Ya think? She's always yelling. Or telling me I'm useless."

Tootsie tried to control the steam building between her ears. No one ever needed to be told they were useless. But they especially didn't need to be told they were useless when they were young...before their brains were fully formed. At a young age, things said by adults set kids on a path that was hard to come back from.

"You're not useless, Logan," she said in a soft voice. "I'm trying to tell you that." Not that she thought he would believe her. She was a stranger. And the damage had long since been done, if not by this particular foster mother, maybe by others. "But here's what I do believe. When someone says you need to do something, and you ask yourself if you should do it... well, you're a smart guy. You know that you can say no to that person if you want."

She waited a beat. Then she added, "Like whoever told you to write those messages on my aunt's walk. I bet you thought you shouldn't."

She didn't know any such thing. She hoped he knew he shouldn't have.

He began to shrug and then shook his head again. "She told me it wasn't any big deal."

Tootsie so wanted to take his hand. To offer him some support, even the little she could. She forced herself to remember her aunt and what this kid had done to upset her, and she decided she did not have to take his hand. "Who is she, Logan?"

Chin to chest, he mumbled something.

"I'm sorry," Tootsie prompted. "You said—"

His head shot up. "I like her. She's nice to me."

A zing of contempt curled through Tootsie's head. Melanie was one terrible human being. She was using this kid, being so-called nice to him. Nice, as in pretend to smile and wheedle and tell him he was doing something good when Melanie just needed him to help with her vendetta. And knew Logan wanted to please her. Because she was his mother and he wanted her to want him.

"So, let's see if you can tell me something. My grandmother, who was a very smart lady once told me something I never forgot."

One of Logan's eyebrows twitched.

"One day when I was at her house, I told her all my friends were cutting school to go to a concert in the city. I wanted to go, and I really thought I would. I wanted her approval because I always figured if I got her approval, I was good to go. Literally."

He stared into her eyes. As if he was trying to figure out if she was playing him. "Did you get it? Did you go?"

"Nope." She gave him a pointed look. "You know why?"

He gave her a lip curl again. "Yeah, because that's what adults do. Tell you what you shouldn't do."

"Many adults do. But not my grandmother. She told me if I wanted to go, I should. But she also told me to think about what I would do if all my friends jumped off the George Washington Bridge. Would I do that, too?"

He frowned. "That would be stupid."

"That's right. It would be. So, I guess what I'm asking you is if someone, even if that person you say is nice, told you to do something you knew you shouldn't, would you do it anyway, even if maybe you thought it was stupid?"

He opened his mouth to respond and then closed it. Then he pressed his lips together and looked away.

Yup. The kid knew. Which proved he was as smart as she'd thought he was. Oh, not smart in knowing what he knew about how to operate in stealth mode on the web. Because yes, he was that. But he was smart, as in oh, yeah. He realized he'd been manipulated.

Which was why now it was time to get down to it. "I know who wanted you to chalk my aunt's walk."

He stared at her hard. "How do you know?" he blurted.

As gently as she could, she said, "Because the lady who asked you to do it has used that same word you just used when she talks about my aunt's books. Smut."

His eyes opened so wide, Tootsie could see the whites. He was petrified. This woman, who hadn't even bothered to introduce herself to him, knew details about his life that he didn't think anyone could have known. Tootsie knew he was wondering what else she knew.

She hopped down off the stool and closed the remaining distance between them. She didn't think about doing it before she did it. She took his hand. She felt it grow stiff with resistance.

She didn't let go. "Logan, I know who this lady is to you, and I know why you want to make her happy. If I were you, I'd want to, too."

Squeezing his hand for emphasis…and so he couldn't run…she added, "I know she's your mother."

Tears made an appearance in his eyes and Tootsie began to have second thoughts about what she was doing. It would have been one thing if he'd been defiant. Or cursed at her. But no. He was acting like the fragile boy he was. In some ways he reminded her of Chris, who also put on a tough guy front but was fragile as a newly hatched chick. Now, she was almost as bad as Melanie. She was using this boy for her own reasons.

Tootsie reminded herself why. To right a wrong. To protect her aunt. But if while righting a wrong, she did something that was wrong, how bad was that?

Which was why, then and there, before another thought could jump into the part of her brain where rational thought lived, she decided she was going to make sure this boy got something out of his life besides duplicity from a woman who should have loved him.

Who should have never given him up.

"Logan, I'm sorry for everything you've had to put up with. I can't change any of it. But I can point out one thing for sure. When I said I'm in awe of what you can do on this computer where you've been working, I meant it. I bet there are a lot of people who think you're smart. Your teachers probably. People you've met online. I want you to hold onto that."

He looked at her longingly. He bit his lip. "I know I'm smart. I don't even study in school, and I get all A's. But I don't care about any of that. I want to know why my mother gave me up."

She did not know the answer to that one. Because she couldn't even imagine it. She took both of his hands. They were cold, sweaty. She squeezed hard. "Did you ever think about asking her?"

He tried to pull his hands from hers.

She refused to let go. "I think if you did ask her, she wouldn't be able to tell you. I know of someone who knew your mother when she was young, and you were little. She couldn't even take care of herself, let alone you. Maybe it was better for you that she gave you up back then."

When he didn't say anything, Tootsie went on. "I know this isn't what you want to hear but, like we both know, you're a smart person and you can figure out what this would have meant. Your mother did drugs, she got drunk. She got kicked out of school. You haven't gotten kicked out of school, have you?"

He shook his head.

"Do you get drunk?"

He shook his head again.

"Do you do drugs?"

He shook his head. Vehemently.

She breathed a sigh of relief because knowing how lonely and miserable he was, his foster mother treating him with contempt, his biological mother leaving him to strangers, and now using him for her own odious purposes, he could have done any of those things.

Because he didn't, it proved he was a whole lot more emotionally together than Melanie, when she was Melody, had been.

"There, see? You just proved my point. And, by the way—are you sure you weren't there when my grandmother asked me if I thought it was a good idea to jump off the George Washington Bridge?"

He gave her a little twitch of the lips, a reluctant smile if she ever saw one.

At last, she let go of his hands. Stepping back, she said, "Here's what we're going to do. First thing is I'm going to tell Steve…that's the ex-cop…that you're really sorry you wrote those things on my aunt's sidewalk. You're fine with that, right?"

He had not looked away, not once after she'd taken his hands. He'd made sure he was engaging her, his light brown eyes to her dark ones, as if they were connected, safety-net-wise. "Yeah."

It didn't bother her that he didn't use the word, sorry when he answered her. She didn't need the exact word. All the other words said sorry for him.

"Then, when you have to go to court to talk to the judge and you tell him how sorry you are for what you did, I'll be there with you. Plus, I'm hiring a really good attorney to be there with us. The lawyer will smooth the way for you. What happens to you won't be so bad as you've been thinking it would be."

And wasn't this when he became her best friend forever? The longing in his eyes said so. "Do you think the judge will listen to the lawyer?"

"Yes, I think the judge will listen. I bet you'll end up having to do something like community service and you know what, Logan? Community service might be fun. You might meet some nice people."

Which she was going to have to make sure, once she hired that attorney, that if Logan got off with community service, it would be something that could expand his understanding and acceptance of the world he lived in, especially because as he stared back at her, he appeared to be thinking everything was going to be okay.

"So, I'm just curious, Logan."

He raised an eyebrow. "What?"

"Do you know why your mother doesn't like my aunt, other than the fact that she doesn't like smut?"

He shrugged but then said, "I think your aunt didn't do something for my mother that she was supposed to do, and my mother thought that was terrible."

CHAPTER TWENTY

The word, terrible, covered a lot of territory. No matter how Tootsie tried to get him to narrow it down, he wouldn't. Not because he wasn't willing. Her promise to stand by him when he had to go before a magistrate, which as it worked out had been scheduled for just a couple of days before Christmas, had won him over.

He couldn't narrow it down because he didn't know.

Frustrated, Tootsie relayed her conversation to Fern who, though she'd normally have gone home at this point in the day, was still hanging around.

"I wanted to know what you'd wrung from the boy."

Tootsie threw her purse down on the kitchen table where Fern waited for her. "I wanted a commitment from Logan that he would stop bullying Adele online."

"That should make you happy. It's what started everything. So, the problem is solved." She made a face. "Except now we know that the boy's mother still wants to control what people can check out from the Glen Allyn Public Library. You have to stop her."

They were still sitting there, thinking, when the door from the garage opened and Steve came in. He shed his coat and this time, hung it on a hook in the short hallway between the garage and the kitchen, instead of the front closet. That meant he planned to go out again.

"Catch me up." As if he knew he needed to be caught up. Well yeah. Because he knew Tootsie was going balls to the wall as usual.

Fern stood. "You two can talk. Now that I heard what I stayed to hear, I'm going home." Turning back to Tootsie, she said, "I know you'll come up with something. You always do."

Once Tootsie explained the whole situation to Steve, including how she'd told Logan she'd find and pay for an attorney for him, and then go with him to his hearing...which Steve rolled his eyes at because he pointed out that she just kept adopting teenage boys...he said, "I know what you can do."

"Don't keep me in suspense. Tell me."

"Why don't you hold a banned book fair?"

It was so majestic in its simplicity it all but took her breath away. She jumped up and threw her arms around him. He barely had a moment to get his arms around her so that she wasn't hanging onto him like a monkey on a display in the zoo.

She crowed, "You're only the most brilliant person I know."

He gave her one of his eyes-only smiles. "How about a reward? Am I worth one?"

By now, he had his arms firmly around her hips and she was free to play with the short hairs at the back of his neck. "Well, now that I think of it, you are more than entitled to a reward. How and where do you think we should make sure you get one?"

Still holding her in his arms, he nudged her toward the steps that led to their bedroom. "I think we both know the answer to that question."

She levered herself up, so they were face to face, even as he kept walking toward the steps. Giving him one of those kisses that left nothing to the imagination about what it was that she knew they both intended, she didn't bother to respond verbally.

Later, when the three of them were sitting down for dinner...Chris had been a prince by not showing up until after Tootsie had finished giving her Black Windbreaker his so-called reward...they talked about what a banned book fair would look like.

"We'd have to have tables," Chris said, as he shoveled food into his mouth faster than a bullet train. Tonight, dinner was a tuna noodle casserole, but not one of the ones that came out of a box that

could be found in the freezer section in the super-
market. It was a Steve special.

"I agree with that." Tootsie was doing her own
shoveling. Her appetite was almost as good as Chris's.
Naturally. After all the rewarding she'd done. "We
can get as many tables as we want from Tarnower
Rentals. Each table should feature a different theme.
Like one table should display a dozen or so books
that have been historically banned, or even hidden the
way Melanie wants them to be and the reason why."

Steve added, "Others could be the usual culprits
these days. The ones that are LGBTQ. Or what some
people don't want to face up to about historic rac-
ism."

Tootsie swallowed a bite. "There could be a table
with books that some people would say are just too
upsetting."

Chris nodded. "Like *The Diary of Anne Frank*."

Tootsie swallowed her last bite. "Just too upsetting? Just think how upsetting Anne and her family
thought it was."

"Yeah," Chris had all but licked his plate clean.
"How about *The Bluest Eye* by Toni Morrison? I really
liked that book and I'm glad I read it because I
learned something I didn't know about what it means
to hate yourself for how you were born. I think we
should include that one."

"How about these?" Tootsie reeled off a series of
titles that people like Melanie wanted banned from

library shelves for all kinds of reasons. Steve added one or two as he took the plates to the sink.

Chris put up a finger. "You know what else is banned? ACOTAR."

Steve and Tootsie looked at each other. She imagined the look on her face was identical to the one on Steve's. Utter confusion. "What book is that? Aco…?"

Chris gave her the *how can you be so dense* look that teens rocked best. "It's an acronym for A *Court of Thorns and Roses*. That's Sarah J Maas' book that gets banned. All the girls I know would hate if they hadn't been able to get their hands on that."

Tootsie suppressed her smile at the look of disgust that passed over Chris's face. "What's the problem with ACOTAR?"

"Sex," Chris retorted. "Just like in Aunt Adele's books. And it's not real, like it's a fantasy. Everyone knows that." He paused. "Can we have a table just for Aunt Adele's books? I'm pissed at Logan and his mother. I want to get right in their face, and rub it in."

Which was exactly what Tootsie wanted. She walked into the dining room/office and pulled a piece of paper out of the center drawer of her sideboard. Coming back to the kitchen, she said, "Let's write all our ideas down and then talk about which ones will work and which ones won't. Then let's figure out who's going to do what to make it happen."

Their list was compact. Someone needed to get a permit. This time, they'd hold the event on the town square. They'd need the space for all the tables they intended to set up on the green. Steve volunteered for that.

Someone would have to purchase the books they intended to give away. Since Tootsie had already done it once, she volunteered for that duty again. "They know me at all those bookstores. Some of the people who work there might even want to help us out that day."

Chris volunteered to work with the people at Tarnowers and help set up the tables on the town square. And when she came in the next morning, Fern said she'd create all the flyers. Best of all, she'd call her niece, Fernie and her now fiancé Des to tack them up in as many coffee shops and bookstores as they could get to.

"Don't forget the libraries," Chris added. "Somebody needs to put flyers up in libraries."

Steve's twins, Carla and Stephanie…the ones Tootsie had thought would never get over Tootsie taking their long-dead mother's place in Steve's affections and had gotten over it…volunteered to put together a complete list of historically banned books and Chris said he'd make the trek around to get them posted, along with the flyer Fern created, in town libraries everywhere.

But Tootsie's biggest concern was how to get the word out to the wider public. Which she thought was key. For that she had an awful feeling she'd have to go back to Blaze Brotherton, despite the hatchet job she'd done on Adele because it seemed Adele's reporter friend had gone out on maternity leave.

Tootsie had Blaze's business card. With both station line and cell phone numbers, she had no prob reaching her.

"Tootsie Goldberg! How nice to hear your voice!" Yeah, the whole insincerity with its exclamation point all over it. Like Blaze was so happy to hear from Tootsie. Despite having screwed over her aunt in that interview weeks before.

"Yes, nice to hear yours, too, Blaze. Though I hear you every night when I watch the news." She paused. On purpose. For emphasis. "Except I stopped watching the news on your station a couple of weeks ago."

Tootsie could almost hear Blaze swallow her remorse.

Good. Tootsie wanted her to feel bad.

"Look, I know you have a producer, and the producer chose what parts of the interview not to air. You don't have to apologize."

There. She gave Blaze an out. But she wanted her thinking she should apologize.

She went on. "But there's more story to that story and you might want to convince your producer that you should cover it. Because you guys like stories with happy endings, right?"

"You know we do. I mean with all the negative stories we have to air, we like to throw in pieces that keep our viewers engaged. A story with a happy ending always makes them sit up and smile. Why don't you tell me what it is."

Well, okay then. "A whole bunch of us in Glen Allyn are holding a banned book fair. We want to alert people to what's going on in our town's public library."

It sounded to Tootsie like Blaze had pressed her phone against some part of her where she could muffle what she was saying to someone else. After a few seconds she was back. "So, this has to do with that woman…what's her name?"

"Melanie Mangold. Yes, you're right." She stopped before continuing, "She's the one you never interviewed for the Candy La Plume story you did."

There was more hard swallowing. Didn't it feel good to know that Blaze had a conscience? "You know, I think you're right, Tootsie. We need to do this story and I'm just so excited that the banned book fair you guys are holding is going to be the happy ending you want it to be and will get that lady to take her silly ideas and go away."

Tootsie breathed a sigh of relief. Blaze's reaction was exactly what they needed. She had put her chances of success at about sixty-five percent. But look at that! She'd exceeded her own expectations.

"The question is how are you going to convince your producer that you should do the story?"

"Don't you worry about my producer. The other day in front of everyone he had to fall all over himself with the 'you do great work, Blaze' thing. I got an award for a profile I did on an award-winning teacher who was retiring. Hey! There's my hook with the guy and how I can convince him to let me do the story."

"You mean you'll compare that award-winning teacher with another one, meaning my aunt, and this time add how she reinvented herself after she retired?"

"Exactly!" Another exclamation point in Blaze's excited voice. "You let me know time and place and my cameraman and I will be there. I'm going to tell my editor we're doing this story."

That was more than Tootsie could have hoped for. She wanted the cameraman to be taking shot after shot of the table displaying all the banned books, most of them brilliant, some of them major award-winners. She wanted her aunt to talk about what happens when books are banned, burned, or as Melanie and Trey did down in Flemington, drowned.

What she was pretty sure Blaze was hoping...though she did the big mea culpa guilt at the hit job she'd done on Adele...was that Melanie and her tribe showed up so Blaze could get a story that was not so much about a happy ending but instead about a conflict.

"Are you sure, *mamaleh*?"

"I can't be sure. But book banning is a big conflict around the country these days so letting people know it can happen here is something to highlight."

Adele brightened. "Here's what I can do. I'll let my supporters know that they can come to support all the books those terrible people want to hide. Including mine. I'll ask my publisher to send copies of my books and I will sign them. I'll let my supporters know they can purchase them and that all the proceeds will go to some charity. How does that sound?"

"How about the American Library Association," suggested Tootsie, getting into the spirit.

"Yes, and I could even tell my readers to bring the books they've already purchased, and I'll sign them, too." She rubbed her hands together. "Melanie will hate that, won't she?"

It amazed Tootsie how few days it took to get the details of the fair together. Genene made sure Steve had a permit with no questions asked. Yes, it could be on the green in front of town hall. Stephanie, with Carla's help, came through with her list of banned books. Fern made the posters. Tootsie made a trip to all the Barnes & Noble stores she could drive to, bought copies of each book on Stephanie's list, and found a wire crate to put them in.

As they loaded the books she'd bought into the crate, Tootsie said, "This is a great visual. Great books behind bars, so to speak. The crate should have its own table."

Fernie and Des reported in that they'd distributed flyers in all kinds of places beyond the Starbucks, Panera restaurants, and cafes. "We put them up in supermarkets. Even in all the Barnes & Noble stores around."

Tootsie was amazed. "Everyone let you?"

Fern nodded enthusiastically. "They told us they'd put the flyers up right in the front of their stores."

With all the excitement, with all the pieces finally in place, the day of the fair dawned cold and sunny. No rain. Or snow. It seemed even Mother Nature approved of their initiative.

The crowds came early. Tootsie and Steve stood off to the side near the table with the crate and watched. Of everyone who milled around between the tables, probably the most enthusiastic were Candy La Plume's readers. Two women, who Tootsie took to be a mom and daughter, came up to where she and Steve were standing. They were both loaded down with books.

The obvious mom, broad grin in place, said, "Candy told us that you two are responsible for this fair. I want to tell you how much we appreciate that you did it. Is there anyone better than Candy?"

The younger woman added, "We just can't get enough of her books. Some of these people that think it's all about kink and doms and subs, well yeah, that's in there. But the women in these books?" She juggled the pile of her books to raise one arm and pump her fist. "They rock. Whatever, they come out on top."

The two women looked at each other and snickered. The daughter got serious. "My mom and I like that. There aren't enough books out there where women win."

Maybe not in those exact words, but that was what Adele had said. From the story Adele had told her about the woman who'd read *Dangerous Love* and changed the trajectory of her life after reading it, and then hearing from these two women, Tootsie now knew why her aunt's books were so loved.

As the women were walking away, Steve left the position he'd held to—by her side—to walk across the green to the side where they had not put up any tables. Gazing after him, Tootsie followed his progress. What was he looking at? But she didn't have time to think about it as more than one person, residents of Glen Allyn, kept coming up to her to thank her for doing what needed to be done.

Among them was the man who had been so vocal at the meeting when Tootsie had dressed as…well, books. "I wish I'd thought of doing something like this." He gazed around at the tables. "I'm glad you did."

As he faded back into the crowd, Tootsie found herself more amazed than she'd expected to be. Despite the cold temperature the crowd was bordering on huge. She could all but taste the excitement. The line for Adele's table curved halfway around the square. Women *and* men...wanting to either have a book they already owned, or a book they were buying autographed by the author. Chris stood next to Adele, both guard and assistant, handing each book to her to be signed as reader after reader came up to the table, with smiles on their faces that were surprisingly similar in their adoration.

The local Barnes & Noble had provided a terminal for people to pay for books and three very enthusiastic book sellers who told Tootsie, "We understand the money made here today is going to the American Library Association. We're thrilled to be taking part. Thanks for including us."

Okay, so the word of the day was thanks. Could that have made Tootsie any happier? The only thing that could be better is if Blaze Brotherton came through and actually did the story she said she would. That would be a definite happy ending.

Fern came bustling up. She was wearing her menopause blue puffy three-quarter length jacket, an ankle-length yellow tulle skirt, and white sneakers. "Steve says come quick."

Now what? She looked past the crowds of people gathered around the exhibits and past the line of admirers waiting to have their books signed by her aunt. "I don't see where he is."

Fern pointed to the gazebo in the center of the green. "There. Melanie finally showed up and she brought people with her. And not for nothing, Blaze is there, too."

Tootsie didn't think any veins in her head had popped, but it felt like they might have. One more time, Blaze Brotherton, the woman she'd thought was big on being a person of her word, was showing that her word meant nothing.

Hurrying across the grass, she wasn't sure what she was going to say when she got to the gazebo. But she knew she would have to come up with something because yes, there they were, Melanie and friends, meaning Melanie, that precious husband of hers, and a gaggle of about ten others. Acting true to form, Trey was playing the bully protector of his wife. Even from a distance, Tootsie could sense the aggression pouring off his body. Interesting that he was staring at Steve, who had his Black Windbreaker face on. Standing a little apart from Steve were a group of four Glen Allyn cops. They weren't doing anything, looked like they were just there on the green, passing the time of day. Tootsie knew otherwise.

They were there to make sure nothing happened that wasn't supposed to.

And then there was Blaze with a mic stuck in Melanie's face, Melanie who had that ersatz, eager-to-explain face on and was talking a mile a minute.

Tootsie drew closer. She was within feet of the gaggle when Steve slanted his attention toward her. He nodded. It wasn't much of one. Since it was meant only for her, she saw it and knew. With that little motion, he was saying *do your thing. If you need me, I'm here.*

Doing her thing, to start with, was not going to be her ripping that microphone from Blaze's hand. Or pointing her cameraman's camera in another direction. It wasn't going to be waving her hand in the air to get Melanie's attention.

Nope. She was headed for Trey. Maybe it was to show him that she had never been intimidated by him? Or maybe it was because of all the main characters in this outrageous play, he was the only one not engaged in talking with someone else, not even the hangers on, cute little badges on their chests, badges that were too small for Tootsie to read.

She was within feet of him before he realized she was heading his way. His jaw hardened, his eyes narrowed, his face flushed.

"So, Trey, what's up with you and your minions?"

There...start off with a little insult. Always a good place to begin.

Before he could jump in Tootsie said, "I met your stepson."

Of all the things Trey might have expected her to say, of all the things Tootsie expected *she'd* say, this was it? Tootsie amazed herself that she didn't always know what words were going to fall out of her mouth anytime it opened for business.

Trey said, "I'm not talking about him."

"Well, I'm sure you don't want to, but he's part of this little drive you've got going to embarrass a ninety-year-old woman whom thousands of people love and while you're at it, use your misguided efforts to clear the shelves in the Glen Allyn library. No one asked you to, you know."

She held up a hand to stop what she could tell he was about to say. "No, please don't offer me any explanations. I've heard them from your wife. They were loathsome the first time I heard them. They'll be loathsome now. If you and your wife want to have a library where you have a say in what books get shelved and what books don't, I say go ahead and build one. But don't come into our *public* library and try to force your private judgments on us."

She wasn't finished.

"That boy, who is your wife's son, and is living within a stone's throw of you and her, you're so selfish you don't want to have anything to do with him? He's going to tell the magistrate when he's up before him why he did what he did. I think when the judge finds out that, even though you didn't personally send all those bullying messages to my aunt, he's going to know how you and his mother used her son to get your message across. Just think. That won't sound like you're much of a good guy, will it? Who knows? Maybe you'll get hauled up before the judge as well.

286

Either that or you'll be charged with child endangerment."

Of course, Tootsie didn't know if the Mangolds could be charged with any of that. But it sounded good. More to the point, she didn't understand why he wasn't trying to stop her tirade, either by talking over her or doing something physical. Why wasn't he?

Oh yeah. As Trey shifted, she saw why. Her Black Windbreaker was standing right behind her, hands on his hips, the cop look on his face. *Ta da!*

Feeling even more empowered than before, she folded her arms and gave Trey her *I mean business* look. "What have you got to say to all that?"

His lips edged up, a sign of his contempt. "What you think is going to happen makes no difference to me. That kid, he's not my kid. Whatever he did, I never told him to do it. Neither did Melanie."

Tootsie's mouth dropped open as she realized just how low this man could stoop. Throwing the kid under the bus.

He continued, "The kid found us. We didn't go looking for him. Besides he's got a place to hang out. He doesn't need our house."

So, Trey knew that Logan was using the FedEx office as his home base. "Maybe you could have invited him to live with you and then he wouldn't have to hang out in strange places?"

"No way. My wife walked away from the kid a long time ago. No way is he coming into our lives. I won't allow it. Neither will Melanie."

"Did she know he was trolling my aunt? Did she know he was going to vandalize my aunt's sidewalk with nasty messages? Like I say, if she knew maybe she's the one that needs to be charged with vandalism. You could deny it forever, but Logan is her son. And a minor."

What he might have said to that, she didn't know because apparently that was his cue to back away. He turned neatly on a heel. He didn't go stand next to his wife who was just winding up her interview with the turncoat Blaze. He left the square altogether.

Gaze following Trey's receding figure, she didn't bother to look Steve's way. But to him she said, "I think that worked out."

"Mostly because you came on like a wrecking crew."

"Excuse me, Tootsie."

Blaze and her cameraman were standing behind her, Blaze had an expectant look on her face. Just like that, irrationality came over Tootsie again. "Now you want to get our side of the story? Or maybe you want to go over where my aunt is signing all those hundreds of books for people who love her writing and do a hit job on her?"

Yup, just as the last words fell out of her mouth, just as she heard that small sound of dismay coming from Steve, the thinking part of her brain came back online. But hello. Rewinding wasn't possible.

The way Blaze's eyes rounded, the way her bottom lip dropped open told Tootsie she'd made a big mistake. Hurrying to say what she could to fix as much of that as she could before total disaster, she said, "How about if you forget I said any of that. How about if you chalk it up to a moment of insanity. How about I apologize. Profusely."

Blaze's lips twitched. She blinked. "You know, I think I had about fifteen seconds there where I lost all my audio." She turned to her cameraman. "Did you notice that, Paul?"

After a moment he nodded slow and steady. "I think you're right, Blaze. The same thing happened to me."

Tootsie held her breath. She needed to be sure. "So that audio you lost. Was it before or after you said excuse me, Tootsie."

"Oh, it was definitely after. Because I wanted to talk to you as the organizer of this banned book fair. They're all the thing now, these fairs, because book banners are crawling out from under the rocks where they've been lurking and making things, oh I don't know, but shall we say miserable for other people?"

Tootsie narrowed her eyes at Blaze. Was she saying what Tootsie thought she was saying? "So, how do you want me to frame what I say?"

Blaze smoothed out her hair, straightened the studio-issued cold weather coat with logo on the breast pocket she was wearing, and gave some kind of eyes-only message to her cameraman. Who seemed to know what she wanted. "I wouldn't want to tell you what to say but after you and I talked on the phone the other day, I did a little research on the history of book banning. I was shocked to know it's been going on for a long time and it's come back again big time."

To which Tootsie did not say *ya think?* Blaze was being earnest. Tootsie needed to leave the sarcasm aside. Not everyone was a student of history...although maybe that's why it kept repeating itself.

Instead, she said, "It's scary."

"So right." Blaze nodded vigorously. "I know why you were upset just now when you saw me interviewing Melanie. But truth is, her own words will expose what she's trying to accomplish. Your words will tell the opposite. So will your aunt's."

She fumbled for something that was in her pocket and drew out a folded-up piece of paper, which she opened. "I want to read this to you. It was written by Helen Keller, whose books were burned by the Nazis for her politics. She was addressing university students who were taking part in book burnings. She said, "History has taught you nothing if you think you can kill ideas.""

Tootsie's insides warmed like honey on a summer day. Wasn't she proud that Chris knew about the part of Helen Keller's life that Blaze was citing?

Look at that. Two people who otherwise might not have learned something historical, learned something historical. Look how it meant something today.

Blaze looked at her cameraman. "That's what tyrants do. Burn books, ban books. But in this country, we don't do that."

The cameraman nodded and raised his camera to his shoulder. "I'm ready when you are, Blaze."

Blaze gave Tootsie a militant smile. "My story is going to run on the eleven o'clock news. Will you be watching?"

CHAPTER TWENTY-ONE

Tootsie and Steve decided the late news was a perfect time to have a party. They invited Adele and Chris to join in.

Chris came home from the banned book fair doing an excellent imitation of a jumping bean.

"That was chill," he exclaimed, when describing his role as Adele's assistant at her book signing. "I mean I bet I handed Aunt Adele three million books. Her hand must have been ready to fall off after signing all of them."

Tootsie knew what Chris had meant. She wouldn't punch a pinhole in his balloon about the three million. But she had given her aunt an ice pack to lay on her wrist when they'd come home tired and elated from an afternoon when a whole lot of books that had been historically banned and ones that re-

cently had come up with that distinction were celebrated for the stories they told.

Adele was sitting on the sofa in the great room,
the TV volume low while she and Steve talked
about...well whatever they were talking about that
Tootsie couldn't hear. She and Chris were cutting up
some lemon bars Steve had made and put in the
freezer for just such a time as this.

The four of them were munching on the last of
the bars when Blaze's story finally came on.

Everyone said *shh*, as she began her story. As
she'd told Tootsie she would, she led with the quote
from Helen Keller from one hundred years ago and
then segued into today on the green.

"Glen Allyn resident, Melanie Mangold, will tell
you there are reasons why she wants books like those
written by Candy La Plume, AKA Adele Silverstein,
moved from the shelves where they had been prominently featured in the Glen Allyn Library."

"They weren't prominently featured," Adele
piped up. "They were on the shelves where they belong."

Everyone else said, "*Shh.*"

Blaze was talking about where in the library the
Candy La Plume's books had been moved to, as per
Melanie's insistence as a newly installed member of
the Glen Allyn Public Library Board.

The shot cut to Melanie. "No child should have
to be scarred by such explicitly sexual content," she
was saying in her deceptively soft voice. "If no one

else will do it, I felt it was up to me to take on the powers that be to make sure everyone's children will be protected from such filth."

The camera then scanned the crowd of people at the fair that afternoon. Blaze, in voice-over said, "But people who were in attendance at today's banned book fair in Glen Allyn were not in agreement with Mrs. Mangold."

In the next shot, Blaze held her mic up to a young mom with two kids who looked to be in the eight to ten-year-old age range. "I agree there are some books children shouldn't read but not because I think they might be scarred. I think they probably wouldn't understand the content. And by the way," she added, looking down at her kids, "parents should know what books their kids have picked up in the library. If they've let them wander around without supervision?" She shrugged. "Well, they're not being very good parents, are they?"

Tootsie and Steve looked at each other. And high-fived.

But Blaze wasn't finished because in the next shot it was clear that the line waiting for Adele to sign books was long and enthusiastic.

"What would you say to people who want to keep you from reading Candy La Plume's books, and books like what this author writes from being displayed where they belong in a public library?"

The lady who Blaze picked to speak to had a long ponytail and a pink headband perched on her head. She was holding a pile of Candy La Plume books that were as high as her chin. "I'd say *who made you the new sheriff in town?*"

Her friend standing next to her, holding an equally tall pile of books to be signed, laughed as did all the women around her.

But the best was last...Blaze's interview with Adele. The camera focused on the books on the table that Adele was signing.

"That's my hand there," Chris called out.

But then Blaze came back in the shot and said, "Adele Silverstein, who has written a number of award-winning books as A.S. Silverstein on how to teach history to teenagers as well as romances under her pen name, Candy La Plume, says people like Melanie Mangold should find another hobby."

"That lady doesn't like my books?" In the shot, Adele gave a dramatic shrug. "I'm not forcing anyone to read them. But because she doesn't want to read them, that doesn't mean there aren't others who want to. Just look around." She pointed to the crowd of smiling women and men. The camera followed where she was pointing and then came back to her face. "No adult should be told what they can read on their own time and their own terms. Least of all by Mrs. Mangold."

The camera refocused on Blaze. "For those who only know Helen Keller for the trials she had to overcome, looking back to the time she lived and how she spoke out against book banning and what happens after that... book burning...would do well to remember she could be very much a voice for reason today. Back to you in the studio."

Everyone jumped up from the couch and clapped, even Adele. Chris hugged Adele. Then he hugged Tootsie. But in case it might not be thought manly, he bumped shoulders with Steve. After which, Steve pulled him into a bear hug.

"I don't think I should call Blaze now," Tootsie said. "In case she's asleep."

"Call her tomorrow," suggested Steve.

At which point the party wound down. Chris went up to bed, and Steve walked Adele home. When he came back, Tootsie was washing the dishes. He came up behind her and kissed the back of her neck.

"You did good, babe. After today, no way is Melanie going to be able to keep on doing her damage. I'm betting it won't take long before your aunt's books are back on the shelves where they belong."

"I bet that jerk of a publisher who told my aunt he couldn't be associated with her, after the story broke that she's Candy La Plume, is going to be on the phone with her first thing tomorrow morning begging her to come back into his fold."

"Maybe he won't call tomorrow. It's Sunday. I'm thinking it'll be Monday morning. Like you said. First thing."

He reached over her and turned off the water. "Leave the rest. I'll get it in the morning."

She turned to face him, surprised. "What? You? You never leave dishes in the sink."

"I do when I want to have some celebration sex with my lady, and I'm not interested in waiting."

She gave him a slow grin. "You want to celebrate, do you?"

"Yes. The defeat of the evil Melanie Mangold."

She rolled her eyes but by that time she already had her arms around his neck. "Defeat? Evil? That sounds like some high drama thing I'd say."

"I do live with you. You must be wearing off on me."

She took him by the hand and led him toward the stairs. Of course, as they left the kitchen, he turned off the light. "Let's celebrate."

They did. Until the doorbell rang. At three o'clock in the morning.

Their neighbor across the street was an insomniac and thank God. Because otherwise the house, even with its brick siding, surrounded as it was with bushes, could have gone up in flames.

Not Tootsie's house. Adele's.

Steve raced across the lawn in the pants he'd thrown on to answer the door. He hadn't bothered to go back upstairs for a shirt. Or shoes. Tootsie rushing out behind him, a coat over her nightgown, brought him his boots and a shirt. It was why she was there to witness the three squad cars and two fire trucks come screaming to a stop in front of the house. The cops were sprinting toward where Steve and the neighbor had their eyes on an object from which a curl of smoke and a sharp, burned smell rose in the air. But whatever fire there'd been, wasn't a fire any longer.

The fire engine beams were swiveling around, casting bright red and blue the length of the street. Lights came on in all the houses. Three firemen stood in the bushes next to Adele's front door. Adele stood in the doorway.

One of the firemen was talking. Tootsie came up as he was saying, "...quick thinking. If he hadn't seen? If hadn't heard this thing smash against the wall and walk outside to investigate, seen the flames, hadn't call us? I don't know that we wouldn't be setting up now to put out a fire."

One of the men turned as he heard her steps. And that's when she saw what they'd been staring at because someone was shining a flashlight on it. The thing was small, a color that was neither black nor gray. It looked like some kind of waxed cardboard. Half was charred, the other half not. The thing was wrapped in duct tape and what looked like a small, charred stick stuck out of the top. The spot on the brick-sided house where the thing lay was black. The parts of the bush it lay in front of were blistered black, and acrid smoke lingered in the air.

Steve took the shirt from her hands and with spare movements threw it on. Buttoning it up, he said, "Leave the boots. Go to your aunt."

But she couldn't move to do what he told her to do in that sharp cop voice that he had never, not even in the beginning of their relationship, directed toward her. Her brain refused for a moment to accept what she was looking at. And then it did. "This is a bomb, isn't it?" she whispered.

"Babe." He took her by the shoulder and turned her toward where Adele stood, just outside her door, wrapped in a dark-colored robe. "I don't want you here. I need you to move. Please."

As Tootsie's brain whooshed back online, she did what he told her to, though her knees felt like they might not hold her up as she stumbled toward her aunt, who was shivering, her face a mask, her gaze looking off into the distance, seeing nothing,

The import of what had just happened sinking in, Tootsie took her aunt's hand and led her away from the house she'd bought from Ben Hart…was that only a couple of months ago…across their lawns, to Tootsie's own house. "Let's wait inside for Steve to tell us what happened."

By the time the sky had turned a light gray in the east, Tootsie had made numerous cups of tea for Adele and that many for herself. Eventually, Chris had come down, roused from his sleep by the incessant strobing of the fire engine beacons on the walls of his room. Though he stepped outside to check the scene over, he was back in no more than a couple of minutes, told, no doubt, by someone official to walk away.

All three of them had eaten breakfast that for once Tootsie had made...scrambled eggs and a bagel...by the time Steve walked back in. As usual, his mere entrance had her looking up. Even in a shirt that had a collar up on one side, and splotches of dirt in various spots on his chest, even with black scruff on his chin and cheeks, the beauty of his lustrous black eyes, his expressive mouth and hard jaw stopped her dead in her tracks. Had she not had a firm grip on the wooden spoon she'd been holding in her left hand, she might have dropped it on the floor. And yes, she'd started to make soup.

As Steve had once pointed out, she made soup for company, when she was angry, or when she was upset. Today, she was upset. But seeing her man return from the site of danger...even if there was no immediate danger to him gave her a sense that somehow everything would be all right. Though neither Adele, Chris, nor she had thought it could be after what could have happened this morning if not for their neighbor.

She went to her Black Windbreaker. Putting her arms around him, she laid her cheek against his chest. "Hi." She closed her eyes for as much savoring as she could get in. Because she knew it wouldn't last.

It didn't.

She stepped back, as did he.

Batting at the splotches on his chest, she said, "What happened? What do you know?"

He took the spoon she was still holding and crossed the kitchen to put it down on the counter next to the stove. "First things first." He glanced across to the table where Adele had come to her feet, as had Chris. They were anticipating. And not happily.

Taking Tootsie by the hand, he led her to the table. "Everyone sit."

Which they did.

Then, grabbing a cup of coffee for himself, he sat too. "The Sheriff's office sent their guys to investigate. They're still there. They'll be there for a little while longer."

"Dayum!" Chris's eyes opened wide. "CSI is on the scene. Just like on TV."

Steve gave him a look that wasn't quite the cop look but close. In a mild voice he said, "Language, dude."

Yes, because though Tootsie knew Black Windbreaker was an expert when it came to what he called language, he was one of those old-fashioned types. He didn't use any of it in front of women and children. Well, he did in front of her.

"And it's not CSI. It's CSU. The Crime Scene Unit."

Chris's gaze fell to the table, chastened. His idol had called him to task. That downcast look said Chris was going to do better next time. He mumbled, "What did they find?"

"I'm not at liberty to say. They're still processing the scene and gathering evidence."

Adele, who had said very little, knocked her fist on the table. "Evidence, *shmevidence*. Don't give me that 'I'm not at liberty to say' nonsense. Somebody tried to burn my house down with me in it. You will tell me, Steven DiLorenzo, right now, what you know, or you and I will have words."

Tootsie laughed. It was the first full out laugh of the day and it felt good. "You know, Aunt Adele, for one woman to have two totally different speech patterns, like you do, is super amazing. When you were signing books at the fair as Candy La Plume or when you gave that TED talk, you spoke in nice, rounded tones, as if you'd spent four years at a finishing school. But when you're with family or when you want something and expect to get it from us or else...then you become the immigrant from a *shtetl* in the Russian empire, or at least the part where Jews could live. Otherwise known today as Ukraine and Belarus." She turned to Steve and patted him on his hand. "You better tell her. Or else." She softened the order with a grin.

A look of resignation softened the resolve on his face. "This is not the first time I've been told what to do, when my better sense tells me I shouldn't, by someone in this family." He gave Tootsie a pointed look. But then he started to talk.

"According to the CSU investigators, this won't be a hard case to crack."

Chris leaned forward as if that would make the difference between him hearing everything or not.

"Whoever put that device there, left a lighter. He also left his footprints. And I bet, if he drove up to the house, your neighbor across the street is going to have him and his car on his Ring video. If we're lucky, it will show the fire starting in the background."

"And then my wonderful neighbor stomping on it to put it out," Adele added.

"He could have gotten hurt badly," Steve mused. "If that bomb hadn't been defective. We were lucky all the way around."

Tootsie got up to stir the soup. This one was lentil. No ham. As she'd once told Steve when they first met, though she didn't keep a kosher house, she was kosher in her heart and ham was not kosher. As she lifted the lid to give it a sniff…and yes it smelled very good…she said, "Trey did it. He's the guilty party."

Back at the table, Steve raised one eyebrow. "You know this without a doubt? Or are you guessing? I think you're guessing. Because it will tie everything that's been happening with Candy La Plume's books up in a nice, neat bow."

"No, I don't know for sure. It just makes sense to me. Who else has anything against Aunt Adele, besides the Mangolds?"

"I agree with you, *mamaleh*," Adele announced. "I think the Glen Allyn police should arrest him."

Steve winked at Chris. "it's a good thing these two aren't in law enforcement. There'd be too much picking and choosing about how to interpret the law."

Adele gave him a sharp nod. "We would know exactly who to arrest."

"Not just arrest," Tootsie jumped in. "But who to send straight to the guillotine."

Everyone laughed. It lightened the atmosphere.

Even if lighthearted was the last thing she felt.

Everyone went back to bed. Except for her. She couldn't sleep. Everything in her wouldn't settle. Not her stomach, not her heart. It was as if the walls of the house were fragile. That they would fall. She needed to get out to where she could put her thoughts together, without them tangling up further.

She threw on her puffy coat, slipped on her boots, and stepped outside. It was only seven o'clock in the morning. Early, though it didn't seem so. Since she'd been tossed from sleep four hours before.

Her street was quiet, and in the early morning, colored lights winked on the trees and garlands dripped from the eaves of homes of families who celebrated Christmas. In juxtaposition, the yellow crime tape around Adele's house seemed forlorn, even feeble. A sliver of moon, an afterthought to the night, sat low in the gunmetal-gray sky, ready to sink below the horizon. But until it did, it stood as a reminder to Tootsie about what had just happened.

What might have happened.

She wound her arms about her waist, clutched her hands around her elbows and hunched up her shoulders as near to her exposed ears as she could. But for a neighbor being up in the middle of the night, she might have been standing here looking across her lawn to the blackened, charred remains of Adele's house, dozens of firemen, trucks, ladders, and lakes of water everywhere.

And her aunt. Gone.

She took in a sharp breath and squeezed her eyes shut. "That's too much high drama," she breathed in a furious undertone. "Don't even go there."

If she could only stop the part of her brain that always managed to think the worst from thinking the worst. Maybe then, she could stop feeling like she wanted to throw up.

Not that she thought she'd learn anything. It was probably only curiosity she decided as she stared across to the spot where whatever inhumane brute decided it was alright to set fire to a house when he knew there was someone inside.

No matter what caution Steve told her she need-ed to hold to, she knew it was Trey who had done the unthinkable.

She had to turn away. She couldn't look any-more. The thought of such great loss made the tears come. For once, she didn't try to hold them back. She cried. Silently. And suddenly she wanted to run back to her house, run upstairs and hold Adele in a gentle hug.

But she was asleep. Tootsie wouldn't wake her just because she had a need to comfort herself. But when Adele woke again later in the morning, she would say those words to Adele that she rarely said to anyone.

She wiped the tears away with the back of her hand. Those words...she didn't even say them enough to her Black Windbreaker. Well, she did. Sometimes. But she'd grown up in a family that was long on guilt and criticism but not so long on voicing love.

It had been a little awkward since she'd been living with Steve. When he told her how he loved her, she'd said things like 'love you back' or 'love you too' and kissed him. Sometimes those kisses led elsewhere. She was good with the elsewhere. Not so much the words.

She blinked. She did love him. Without question. Without qualification. Her head and her heart both knew. So why the awkwardness when she said them? Was it in some way connected to her not wanting Steve to throw her a birthday party?

"No, you idiot," she muttered.

But yes. A door in her head slammed open. She didn't want Steve to throw her a birthday party because she couldn't face raw emotion. It was painful to think she was growing older and hadn't done everything she should have. Had failed.

"Which is totally ridiculous." This time she said it out loud. "It's not like you are one. Look at how you put the fair together. Even if it was Steve's idea. Besides which..." Her voice caught on an up tone. She took a step back and slapped a hand across her mouth.

"That's it," she whispered to herself, and she knew. Suddenly she couldn't stand here in the cold, in the quiet morning where the world was just coming to life again for the day.

Because her world had just become clear. For the first time she recognized something that she should have recognized a long time ago. With everyone in her life. Her son, Sam, who just needed to hear her say it. With Josh, with her mother. With her Aunt Adele. And Chris.

She raced toward her house like Trey was behind her.

She threw the door open, unsnapped her coat and threw it on the floor.

She rushed up the steps to the bedroom, and knew from this point on, she could never again call it *her* bedroom. She had to call it *their* bedroom.

She threw herself on his sleeping body. Well, she didn't really throw herself. That would have been too dramatic, even for her. But she did put her knee on her side of the bed, crawl across and wiggle her way into his suddenly willing arms.

He didn't open his eyes. That she saw before she closed hers to savor the naked heat of him.

"Mmm," he said, and then came fully awake. He sat up, drawing her with him. "What's the matter?"

His beautiful, but sleepy black eyes bored into hers.

She laughed.

He frowned.

"Nothing's the matter now. It's what's *been* the matter and I just couldn't wait to tell you." She pushed him down into their pillows.

She began to kiss him everywhere on his face. His arms came up to hold her. He smiled. "What's this about, babe?"

"I love you. Really, really love you. More than anything. More than the moon, more than the stars, more than the sun, more than Dutch baby pancakes."

His smile curved against her lips.

"Good thing. I wouldn't want to rate less than pancakes."

"I'm high drama enough and I'll never be different and I'm going to be high drama when I say I love you and give you my permission to throw me a birthday party. You can invite everyone I know. Everyone."

The kissing went on. And of course, it led elsewhere. As it seemed it always did with them. It was only after they'd calmed themselves down that he asked.

"Not that I'm objecting, but you want to tell me what brought all this on?"

She snuggled deeper into the covers and deeper into his arms and against his chest. "I had a moment of clarity. Partly about the birthday party."

He leaned away so he could look down at her. "I'm glad you're good with me making the party. I've already got ideas about what I'm going to serve. But I don't think it's the answer to my question. Explain a little better this time."

"You know how I told you that the reason I stopped being a hellraiser back when I was a kid was because I was afraid someone I loved would get hurt if I made waves like my grandmother did? That I was afraid someone would pay the price I should pay for standing up to the wrongdoers in this life?"

"I remember." He began to run his fingers through her curls.

"I just realized that wasn't it. Not at all. I was afraid *I* would get hurt."

He paused doing what he was doing before resuming again. "Hurt how? Afraid how? I've never known you to be afraid. Only that one time when you were in the ambulance after Chesty's goons ran you off the road."

She shook her head. "When I say I was afraid, I mean I was afraid to let myself be afraid. So, I closed myself down, so I wouldn't feel anything. That's what I mean about not getting hurt. If I thought too deeply about anything where I might lose, especially lose someone important to me, I wouldn't be able to go on."

She burrowed into him further, enveloped him tightly in her arms. "I couldn't go on if I lost you."

"Tootsie." He gathered her close. "Life is about love and it's about loss. I lost my wife. I grieved for Penny. I still grieve for her and sometimes It hurts me deeply. But not always and not often anymore. I'm breathing. I'm living. I have my daughters and my mother. I have my work. I have my life."

He ran a gentle hand over her shoulders. "I have you. I love you. I'm going to enjoy every moment I have with you. For as long as I have those moments."

She pressed her nose against his skin to absorb the scent of him, now as familiar to her as if he'd been in her life forever. "I closed myself off all those years against hurt because I knew. If I loved as hard as I'd loved my grandmother? If I lost anyone else as I'd lost her, it would destroy me."

She popped up out of bed, stood, and pulled him upright with her. Bending down on one knee at the edge of the bed, she took one of his hands in hers, smiled up into his eyes and said, "Will you marry me?"

CHAPTER TWENTY-TWO

He said yes. Well, she hadn't expected he'd say anything else, had she? He'd been the first one to say I love you; way back before those words hadn't crossed over and through her frontal lobe.

He'd been the one to say I'll come live with you three days a week. He'd been the one who, when she'd intimated that she wanted him to live with her all seven nights of the week, he'd said sure, no prob.

What had she expected when she finally opened herself up to honesty about what his presence in her life meant to her? She knew him like she knew no one else. It wasn't because she'd known him a long time. She hadn't. It wasn't because they shared similar backgrounds. They didn't. She was an Ashkenazi Jew whose grandparents had come from the Russian empire. He was an Italian Catholic whose grandparents came from a little hill town above Naples.

It wasn't because their lives had marched along perfectly aligned. She'd spent the better part of hers as a mother, wife, and marketing director at a radio station. He had been a cop. Even if he called himself an ex-cop, in his heart he would always be a cop.

None of that meant anything. It was because he was transparent. What he said was what you got. She never had to wonder what he meant when he said what he said. Or did what he did.

This morning, standing in the cold, looking at that obscene black stain on the brick side of her aunt's house, she'd finally realized it was time to stop living in fear of what might happen and learn to live fully in the moment. With love. No matter what that moment brought later.

That meant closing the chasm of misunderstanding with Sam. Whom she loved. She had to tell him she did.

She'd known Steve would say yes, he would marry her. Of course, she hadn't expected him to get all emotional, telling her how happy he was that everything between them was amazing, awesome, perfect…well, maybe not perfect. Had she expected him to get up out of bed and do a cartwheel?

Nope. That was her job. And though in her mind she was cartwheeling across the room and back, her body did what it ought, as only an almost 51-year-old one would. She got up off her knees, sat next to him on the bed, and kissed him.

Then she cried. Because yeah, happy tears were always allowed.

Later, at breakfast...and yes Tootsie called school and said Chris would be late and there was a good reason why...with Adele, Chris, and Fern all sitting down at the table, she and Steve made their announcement. There was a lot of celebration, more tears, lots of hugs, and toasts with coffee and one glass of milk as chasers for the Dutch baby pancakes Steve never made on Mondays but today was special.

The subject of the fire, that thank God and little fishes didn't happen, came up. While Tootsie filled Fern in on the details...and Fern's fan went full force...Steve made a phone call. He'd stepped out into the foyer because everyone was talking at once and not modulating any of their tones, as Tootsie's mother, Francine, was known to have said...more times than Tootsie cared to hear.

They all stopped talking when he came back into the kitchen.

Tootsie, who had been in the act of pouring another cup of coffee asked, "What did you find out?"

Steve sat back down at the table and served himself another pancake, now cold but still dee-lish. "I found out that some criminals aren't too smart."

He ate a bite. And swallowed.

Okay, so though now she had a commitment from him to marry her, she still wanted to give him a *gezuntah clopf* for stopping after laying that tantalizing hint on them without including what he meant.

The next thing she was going to have to work on, now that she was learning to live in the moment, was how to drop the high drama.

Um, maybe not?

She brought her lover…no, her fiancé…a cup of coffee and sat. "Whenever you're ready to tell us the rest, we'll still be here." She folded her arms on the table and leaned forward. "Though, by that time even Chris might have gray hair."

Her Black Windbreaker smiled as he usually did. With his eyes. "They've arrested Trey."

Tootsie clapped her hands. "See? I told you so."

Chris made a surprised sound. "You mean they were able to get his DNA off that bomb already? They don't even work that fast on TV."

Steve made neat cuts on his pancake, forked one of the pieces into his mouth and chewed. "They don't in real life either. No, the neighbor's Ring doorbell caught him. Trey didn't even bother to wear clothing that would hide his identity."

He jabbed another piece of pancake with his fork. Stuck the piece in his mouth. Chewed. Swallowed. Rinse and repeat. Then he said, "The video caught the reflection of the flames, him running back to his car, getting in, and driving off. It caught your neighbor stamping out the flames and running to your door, Adele, and then ours."

Tootsie grimaced. "Not for nothing, Trey Mangold should have left the arson to someone with a fully formed brain. And to put the kibosh on it, he should have also worn gloves."

"Oy, such a *schlemiel*." Adele's eyebrows were in the raised position. "Even I know if you commit a crime, you should wear gloves."

"What we didn't know when we were doing our due diligence, when we made that trip down to Flemington was there was a reason why the Mangolds left town, and it wasn't because Trey needed to be closer to the city and work."

"No?"

"No. You remember that woman in the library told us the Mangolds weren't favorites in town?"

"I remember."

"Besides Melanie poking her nose in places it didn't belong, the fight Trey had with one of the fathers who said Trey gave his own kid too much playing time and that incident when they poured water all over Candy La Plume's books."

"Hah," Fern muttered, her fan still going strong.

"What we didn't learn the day we took our trip was that someone stole into the garage of one of the fathers who complained and destroyed an expensive bike. The cops found fingerprints on the bike that weren't the owner's."

Steve pushed his plate away, finished. "There were no matching prints in the system. But one of the cops whose kid played on the team Trey coached made it his business to prove it was Trey. One day, he saw Trey mowing his front lawn. He had a water bottle in his hand. When he was finished mowing, he threw the bottle away in his garbage can that was out front because town garbage pickup was the following morning."

As everyone at the table hung on his words, he got that look on his face that said anyone doing something wrong better rethink what they were doing. "The cop snagged it. Same prints that were on the bike. They took Trey in, fingerprinted him. But then the case got tossed. The cop hadn't had a search warrant, and the lawyers were all over it because he hadn't. Case dismissed."

Steve rose and took his plate to the sink. "The Mangolds left town because that was one step too far and they were blackballed. Trey got stuck with a label he couldn't unstick."

Fern had hung on every word Steve had spoken. "So instead of being pains down there in Flemington, they became Glen Allyn pains. You would think Trey would learn. Or Melanie would have stopped embarrassing herself doing something that most everyone doesn't appreciate."

"Except…" Adele put one finger up. "She didn't start in right away. According to Serena…you remember her, everyone…she's the shy librarian…Melanie didn't start her shenanigans until after I moved in."

Tootsie piped up. "Which feeds into what Logan told us. That she's got something against you, Aunt Adele. You did something that changed her life for the worse."

"This is the thing I don't understand. I barely remember the girl. I..."

When Adele didn't finish, Tootsie said, "What were you going to say?"

With sudden vigor, Adele grabbed Chris's hand. "Go over to my house and take one of those pictures off the wall and then bring it back to me." She told him which one.

Chris jumped up to do what Adele asked him to do. Minutes later, he was back with the picture Adele had requested in his hand.

After dusting it off, she took the picture in both hands and stared down at it. "This was one of my world history classes. All the children in it were very smart young people. Many of them went onto universities and then when they graduated made wonderful careers, some of them in law, some of them in business, some of them in the world of academia where according to what I've heard, some are now tenured professors."

She ran her finger across the picture, pausing now and then. There were dozens of faces in the picture, including Melody's. Adele tapped the picture. "Here she is. Seeing her face, now I remember. Despite the rebellious appearance, she could be a sweet, shy girl. She didn't participate in class discussions. But her homework was always neat, complete, and correct. She aced all her tests. She was a good student. Until the day after the incident with the fire she disappeared from class and never came back."

"Did you ask the school to try to find her?"

"Yes, I did. I was worried. I even called the house myself. Before the mother hung up the phone on me, she said that Melody had gone to live with an aunt in Florida. Since Melody was sixteen at the time, social services checked in on the house and the mother was able to prove that Melody had indeed gone down south to live with an aunt and that was that."

Fern stood and shut off her fan, giving Tootsie a good look at her skirt. It was psychedelic stripes, with black, green, and white squiggles that curled their way around her hips and shot down to her ankles. Tootsie looked away before her eyes could develop macular degeneration.

Placing her fan on the table, Fern said, "But Adele, that doesn't tell us why she has it in for you."

It didn't. Tootsie nabbed the picture. "I think I'll go see if I can find Melanie."

"Tootsie…" There was more than a little warning in Steve's voice.

"I'll be careful."

Fern grabbed her fan again and turned it on. "Famous last words."

After a long lecture from Steve, and many words where Tootsie framed her intentions, she somehow was headed out in the direction she knew she needed to go on this very happy day. Her Black Windbreaker trailed behind her in his big, black truck. Next to her, on Viv's passenger seat, was the picture from Adele's wall.

She saw the moving truck the moment she made the turn onto the street where the Mangolds lived. Or, if the moving truck was any indication, where they weren't going to live much longer. "That was fast," Tootsie muttered to herself. "Are they making a tactical retreat?"

The front door to the Mangold's house was wide open. Two men came through just as she parked Viv in front of the house. They loaded a small desk onto the truck. Tootsie sat in her car and watched the action.

She glanced in her rearview mirror. Yes, there he was, her fiancé...and didn't that set up a bunch of giggles...was parked right behind her.

But no giggling now. Not as she was getting out of her car and headed up the walk to Melanie's house. But because manners were still manners, though the door was open, she still rang the doorbell. And because Melanie was, if not mannerly, like Pavlov's dog...when the doorbell sounded, she responded.

But she stopped cold when she saw that it was Tootsie. "You," she sneered in that deceptively quiet voice of hers. "Haven't you caused enough trouble?"

Tootsie pursed her lips. "Maybe you should look in the mirror. And while you're at it, why not grab your husband so he can look in the mirror with you."

"My husband is not here," she said through stiff lips. "You know where he is. That's your fault."

Tootsie thought raising her eyebrows wasn't enough of a reaction. "As I remember it, it was your husband, not me, who tried to burn down my aunt's house."

Maybe because she was not the kind of person who waited around to find out, and maybe because deep inside where that voice she never listened to occasionally had something smart to say, she decided it was time to stop with accusations and held up the picture of her aunt's world history class, the one she'd brought with her, the one with Melody in it. "Remember when this picture was taken, Melody?"

"My name is—" Melanie caught herself. But it had already been too late.

"Well, at least you know your real name."

But Melody/Melanie recovered quickly enough. She yanked the hem of her white turtleneck down, and now that Tootsie had seen that other picture of Melody/Melanie, she knew why she was wearing long sleeves.

Melody said, "That was a long time ago and another life. I'm not that girl anymore."

Tootsie turned the picture around, ostensibly to study it. Then turning it back, she pointed to where she stood in the front row. "You can say it, but this is still going to be you."

Melanie pushed hair that had fallen onto her face back behind her ear. "What do you care?"

"Whatever it was you did after this picture was taken, how far you had to go to have a baby, you're right. I don't care," Tootsie snapped. "What I want to know is how did you change from this girl to the woman you are today, and what have you got against my aunt?"

She turned the picture back around again so Melanie could look at it. "While we're at it, I'd love to know what kind of person lets her husband, who isn't the father of her child, tell her that boy can't live with you?"

Tootsie had unintentionally raised her voice. When she thought of Logan, living with that hag of a foster mother...and whoever knew how many other foster mothers...it made her burn inside. "He wanted you to notice him. He wanted you to want him. You used that desire of his for your own purposes and never intended to welcome him into your life."

There for a moment, it looked like grief shadowed Melanie's face. But it came and went so fast, that Tootsie wasn't sure she'd seen it. "You have no idea how bad my life was before I met Trey."

Tootsie sneered, "Let me get my violin."

She heard the clearing of a throat. She hadn't realized Steve had gotten out of his truck and walked up behind her. She turned and glared at him. The glare said 'don't hold me back. I know what I'm doing.'

The eyebrow he sent up his forehead told Tootsie he wasn't so sure about that.

Tootsie was. To Melanie she said, "You could have always made of your life what you wanted to."

Melanie had turned the red of the bricks on Adele's house, the bricks against which Trey had set his incendiary device. "No, I couldn't," she said, all but spitting the words. "I was weak. He was strong. He said he would save me. I wanted to be saved."

Melanie began to shake. Her features hardened into hate. Tootsie's neurotransmitters had been up and ready when she'd walked toward Melanie's front door. Now, they were at the shield-clashing stage. *Keep going, lady. We need to know. Tell us.*

Into Melanie's curiously fiery silence she added, "So, you let yourself be saved by a bully. And an arsonist. How is that saving you?"

Melanie sneered. "You just don't know because you got raised by someone who loves you."

On most days, Tootsie would say no, Francine had never loved her. But deep inside, she knew her mother did love her. Even if she didn't show it, the way Tootsie wanted her to show it. Like her Grandma Hannah had shown her.

In no way did Melanie even have a fraction of that love.

Yeah, and here it was again. Love was everything, wasn't it? When you didn't have it, its lack could do things to you. Unpleasant things. Terrible things. Which now that Tootsie understood, had happened to Melanie. Softly she said, "I'm sorry, Melanie. You deserved better."

Angry tears stood out in Melanie's eyes. "Don't you dare feel sorry for me. Go feel sorry for your aunt. She's a loser. I hate her."

"You hate her?" Tootsie cocked her head to the side. "Why? Tell me. What did she ever do to you?"

Tears began rolling down Melanie's face. "I asked her, and she said no."

Tootsie frowned. "What did she say no to?"

Melanie looked away. She didn't answer Tootsie. The way her Aunt Adele's nemesis kept silent, Tootsie wondered if that was all she'd get, if that meant Melanie wouldn't answer.

But then Melanie sighed and looked down to her feet. "She told me I couldn't live with her."

Tootsie shook her head. As if to clear it. Because she couldn't believe she'd heard what she heard. "What would ever tempt you to think that a stranger, your teacher, would want you to live with her?"

"She told me I was a smart girl every day I came to school. She was proud of me for the good work I was doing." Melanie had not picked up her head. She'd begun to twist her fingers together. Like a nervous child.

"She encouraged me to do better, to stop drinking. I did. I stopped going to parties where the kids were smoking weed and snorting and whatever. I stopped doing all of it myself." She sighed and picked her head up.

The tears had dried up. There was a blank look in her eyes. "My mother...she wasn't... She wasn't...

Melanie caught herself. I wanted a mother. I was stupid. I thought my teacher, who was kind to me would see she could be a better mother than mine and it would be okay if I came and lived with her."

She clutched her arms around herself and shivered. "She said no."

Tootsie had no idea what to say.

The blank look on Melanie's face disappeared. It was replaced by a burning anger. "I knew she had her own family, but she could have made room for me. She didn't. So, I thought to myself, why try? And I stopped trying. I did what I did whether it was smart or not. I burnt that locker up. I slept with any boy who wanted me. I drank, I snorted. I got pregnant and I went to my mother's aunt in Florida to have the baby. They wanted me to give it up, but I was tired of people telling me what to do and decided I would do what I wanted to do. So, I kept him. Logan."

"That was a good thing you did, Melanie," Tootsie said.

"Yeah," Melanie sneered. "Until I got back to doing everything I'd been doing before because nothing I tried, no job I took, no place I picked to live, worked. Then, the state took Logan away from me."

"That's when you almost died, right?" She couldn't help it. Tootsie was feeling sorry for Melanie. Who would have thought she ever would?

Melanie tossed her hair back. "That's when I met Trey. He was a mess, too. We drank together, got high together, lived in a homeless shelter together.

Until his father found us and said he'd pay us a lot of money to get better, to shape up. So, we did."

The father who owned the trucking company. Tootsie remembered Steve telling her about the man. "That's why you're living in this big house and why Trey goes to New York every day to his father's company. You got better."

Melanie lifted her chin. "All that is true. Trey gave me everything I need."

Except permission to bring the first child she'd birthed into the house where she lived with the children she'd had with Trey. That made him...cruel.

"Do you think there's any way I would ever do anything to lose what he's given me?"

Whatever sympathy Tootsie had felt for Melanie sloughed away. "Not the way you describe it." Which Tootsie had nothing but contempt for. "So, for him you kept Logan out of your life. But then Logan appeared, wanting a life with you. How did that happen?"

"I didn't know he was here. I'd lost track of him." Melanie had begun to whine. Tootsie's neurotransmitters began to grumble. "But then he heard I was going to be on the library board, and he reached out to me. What was I to do?"

"Maybe let him live with you?" She held up a hand to stop Melanie from saying what Tootsie knew was coming next. "Don't say it. You wouldn't because of Trey. But that didn't stop you from using the boy anyway."

Tootsie shook her head. "What I don't understand is how does a grown woman not recognize that she needed to stop hating that teacher, the woman she'd hated as a kid because she had no real reason to hate her. Yes, she could have been disappointed. But hate? No."

Melanie's jaw set. "Hate never goes away."

The two men who'd been loading the truck asked to get by. Melanie let them. Then, staring at Tootsie, she gave her the rictus of a smile and slammed the door shut.

Tootsie stood for a moment and then whirled around and threw herself into Steve's arms. "How can she?" she whispered. "I don't understand."

Steve ran a comforting hand up and down her back. "Don't think about it. She's an angry person. She'll always be angry. Don't try to understand. You'll never be able to. They're moving. Be glad they are."

It was the last time they saw either of the Mangolds. Tootsie decided not to tell her Aunt Adele why Melanie had harbored so much hate for her. What would it gain, she reasoned, other than to make her feel regret she could do nothing about? So, Tootsie made up a story that, of course, Adele didn't buy. But Adele didn't ask her for an explanation, either. So, they left it where it was and moved on to happier things.

Like the birthday party Steve was planning for her. And their wedding. On the same day.

It was January. They decided it was best to have the party indoors. Instead of the immediate world Tootsie had told Steve she wanted him to invite— she'd been kidding—they invited their nearest and dearest: Aunt Adele, their two mothers, Francine and Aurelia, Steve's daughters, Carla and Stephanie, Fern, Fernie, and Des, who had helped Tootsie defeat Sage Rust. Katie and Brian and their kids, her ex, Arlo and his wife, Raquel, and some of Tootsie's radio station buddies. Of course, there were her three sons: Sam, Josh, and Chris...Chris, who she and Steve decided they were going to adopt.

So, no one would feel left out, she decided that all three would walk her down the aisle, which wasn't really an aisle. It was a rose petal-strewn pathway Fern made that began in the foyer, next to Tootsie's curio cabinet with its Limoges boxes and silly Meissen monkeys, to the great room, where all the guests sat and oohed and aahed at their group entrance.

She wore a beautiful pink suit and a sparkling white jewel neckline blouse beneath it. She wore her highest heels, though in the end she took them off and went barefoot.

"I don't want it to look like, when we're standing under the *chuppah*, you're marrying a midget," she complained to Steve before she did.

He'd kissed her and said, "No worries. You're my midget."

The food was spectacular. In the end, though Steve grumbled about it, they did hire a caterer.

Tootsie said, "I don't want you to be in the kitchen putting the finishing touches on some sauce or another when the rabbi says "Behold, thou are consecrated to me, and it's the rabbi who says the word, me. I don't want to be married to the rabbi."

Steve did make the cake though. Like she'd said weeks and weeks ago when she'd told him it needed to be chocolate, it was chocolate. Just the way she wanted it.

"I love you," she whispered against his mouth, right after he broke the glass, and everyone was shouting Mazel Tov!

"I love you," he whispered back.

They separated and smiled at each other. Then they smiled some more.

She felt an arm come around her. She turned. It was her eldest, Sam. Tears came into her eyes. He was so handsome. He was so reserved. She loved him. He didn't know how much because she'd let silly differences come between them.

No more.

Sam didn't know it yet, but he was her next project.

If you loved reading this book, and have not read the first two books of the Tootsie Goldberg Mysteries, check out Book One, WHEN SHE GETS HOT, Book Two, WHEN SHE GETS SMART, and Book Three, WHEN SHE GETS BUSY.

And if you liked WHEN SHE GETS RILED, it would be awesome if you could leave an honest review at your favorite online bookseller. It would help new readers discover Tootsie, which would make me very happy.

Do you want to know the meaning of the Yiddish words Tootsie uses? She doesn't speak the language, but she does know quite a few words. If you want to know the meaning of those words, you can. Tootsie and I (well, *I*, not really Tootsie…she's fictional) have created a lexicon of the Yiddish words that you'll find in her stories. Claim your copy (https://dl.bookfunnel.com/fn6j2bbsmg) of the *Tootsie Goldberg Yiddish Lexicon* when you sign up for my newsletter. In it you'll find the latest news from me, funny bits, recipes, pictures of my garden, and news about releases. Enjoy!

Author's Note

Now, a little clarification. This is the fourth book in the Tootsie Goldberg Mysteries and shame on me that I haven't explained that there is no Glen Allyn, NJ. There is a Glen Ridge which is a small, lovely, upscale-ish enclave in suburban Essex County. Because I knew there were going to be so many shenanigans going on in my fictional town that Tootsie calls home, I decided not to tarnish Glen Ridge's perfectly good reputation. But I did like the sound of the name. So, I gave it a slight alteration. All the other town names in Tootsie's stories are real.

The Barnes & Noble in Woodland Park is real. However, no stool is needed because the shelves aren't that high. Neither does the romance section have a U-shaped alcove. But it should. There's no dog run at Brookdale Park, though it does have an expansive oval I've walked many times. The majestic trees are real.

I write funny. But book banning: what's funny about that? The thing is book banners seem to be in their element these days. They are infuriatingly smug, think of themselves as the arbiters of what to read and who should be permitted to read it. I wanted Tootsie to go after them. The book banner Tootsie defeats in WHEN SHE GETS RILED represents the whole wretched tribe.

If one of these book banning busybodies would somehow pick up WHEN SHE GETS RILED, and reading it realize it's wrong to tell someone else what they can or can't read, then I've done a good job.

I'm not holding my breath.

Acknowledgements

Some people I know think Tootsie is me. I want to respectfully disagree. I would never get up on a chair wearing a skirt. I'd wear trousers instead.

Tootsie and I have been called know-it-alls on occasion. That said, she and I recognize that we don't know everything about everything. That's why, as I began to write WHEN SHE GETS RILED, I sought out advice from some real experts, For any scene that took place in a library...or the Elks Lodge when Tootsie first confronts Melanie Mangold, I relied on Janette Pardo, Adult Reference Librarian at the Wayne Public Library in Wayne, NJ for an explanation of how different kinds of libraries run and their relationship to the communities in which they're located. Janette's fascinating telling of library business helped me picture the two libraries that are featured in the story: the fictitious Glen Allyn Public Library, and the very real Flemington, NJ Free Public Library. (In the interest of full disclosure, I never entered the Flemington Library. But Uncle Google showed me just enough that I could easily picture it.)

I relied on the divine Captain John Devine of the Paramus, NJ Police Department, to keep Black Windbreaker, Tootsie's lover and all around tall silent one (well, he does speak when he has to and every word he says is brilliant), true to all matters of the law, even when it came to Tootsie's law-breaking ways. John clued me in on the cop shows *real* cops like to watch on TV. Hint: they're not shows Tootsie likes to watch.

I'm grateful to my grandson, Sam Allenson, who himself is something of a silent one (but when he speaks, people listen) for help understanding something about the dark web, VPNs and how a troll could make someone's life miserable. (And no, I want to make clear to his parents that Sam doesn't know this stuff because he's a troll. So, cut him some slack…okay?)

Much thanks go to my esteemed editor, Gemma Brocato, who made the words and sentences that I wrote sound better than I could ever have imagined them. Paula Gardner made sure my sentences had nouns. And verbs. Thanks, Paula, for keeping me on the straight and narrow. Lisa Verge Higgins made this book look pretty. She taught me the elements of book formatting. The lessons didn't stick. Thanks for trying, Lisa.

I am forever grateful to my critique partners, Jennifer Wilck, Lisa Verge Higgins, and Nancy Herkness, who have, for all the wonderful years we've been together, kept me from going completely off the rails and/or from jumping off a bridge. Their advice, delivered gently but honestly, has made all my books so much better than they would have been otherwise.

May we continue to critique together for many years to come.

To my children and grandchildren, whose names populate all my books, including the aforementioned Sam...I know you might be horrified that my characters have your names. But see...I really want to make you a part of everything. Sam has an entire story about a character with his name in the next book, WHEN SHE GETS TICKED (out in spring 2024).

To my husband, Andy, my life partner and now my business partner, because no profit and loss statement wants me anywhere near it, thanks babe! You smile when I try to add and subtract in my head, or even on paper, and come up with a total wrong answer. You only laugh a little when you find my bottle of vitamins in the sink. Or when the head on the vacuum cleaner falls off and I tell you I don't know how to put it back on. This authoring thing would be very hard without you.

Finally, to you and all my readers...hearing from you, reading your emails and meeting you at book signings and hearing the wonderful things you say about my stories has kept me from sinking into the black hole of impostor syndrome. Thank you for telling me Tootsie makes you laugh. In this world we live in, giving people even one moment of pleasure makes me feel like I've done something worthwhile. Thank you.

About The Author

Hi again. It's me, Miriam. I write about women who are the heroes of their own stories. They stand up to the challenge and win. I write about Jewish women because I know Jewish women, since I am one.

When I'm not working on a book—which is almost never—I'm in the kitchen baking something. Ask me about my chocolate pound cake. Or I could be gardening on the "huge" 8'x5' deck of my apartment. I grow herbs. And jalapenos. Chances are I could be adding one more character to my 500+ Pez collection (no, I do NOT eat the Pez candy.). I like black licorice but not chocolate, polenta more than pizza, and baseball any day over football. Just sayin'.

I'm a happy resident of the Garden State, New Jersey and live with my fabulous husband, Andy, and near five of our seven grandchildren for whom I'm happy to do overnights and will serve dessert on request before dinner (parents…mind your own business).

How about you? Is reading your escape? Do you like a little romance, a little mystery, and a lot of laughs? Let me know at **miram@miriamallenson.com**.